TWISTED

ALSO BY HANNAH JAYNE

Truly, Madly, Deadly

See Jane Run

The Dare

The Escape

TWISTED

HANNAH JAYNE

Copyright © 2016 by Hannah Jayne
Cover and internal design © 2016 by Sourcebooks, Inc.
Cover design by Elsie Lyons
Cover image © Ardon/Arcangel

Published by Sourcebooks Fire, an imprint of Sourcebooks, Inc.
P.O. Box 4410, Naperville, Illinois 60567-4410
(630) 961-3900
Fax: (630) 961-2168
www.sourcebooks.com

Library of Congress Cataloging-in-Publication data is on file with the publisher.

Printed and bound in the United States of America.
VP 10 9 8 7 6 5 4 3 2 1

For my new husband, Graham Haworth,
for seeing my search history and marrying me anyway.

ONE

TEN YEARS AGO

The two men leering down at seven-year-old Beth Anne Reimer were huge. If anyone had asked her, she would have said they were at least seven feet tall, but no one was asking her anything. The men were simply shifting by her, giving her a wide berth while looking down with sad eyes and clicking their tongues or saying stupid, meaningless things like, "It's a damn shame."

The man on the left had a huge mustache that seemed to ooze from his nose. It was so black it was almost blue and dotted with crumbs of something fine. *Bread or doughnuts,* Beth Anne thought as he leaned closer, his hot breath sweet. He moved his big, meat-hook hands closer to her throat, and an electric shot of terror pulsed through her. She stepped backward, stumbling over her own feet, and didn't let out a breath until she felt her narrow shoulder blades grind into the garage door behind her.

"This belonged to Melanie Harris," the mustached guy said, tugging on the thick, gold ring that Beth Anne wore on a chain around her neck. She looked down at his fingers touching the ring, *her* ring, rubbing callously over the bright-blue stone that Beth Anne meticulously polished with her own small fingertips whenever she got scared or anxious.

"My dad gave it to me." Her voice was a small, pitiful squeak, and she wasn't sure if the mustached man didn't hear her or didn't care. He tugged on Beth Anne's chain until it burned against her skin and the lobster clasp was between his fingers. He unclasped her necklace and slid it off before she could find her voice again to stop him.

The mustached man held the chain and the ring up to his partner—a clean-cut guy with not even the slightest hint of facial hair and ears that stuck out of his head like satellites. The clean-cut guy held up a plastic Ziploc, and Beth Anne watched her necklace drop inside, coiling like a snake at the bottom of the bag.

"Evidence," the mustached man said.

Neither man said anything to Beth Anne as they zipped the bag, the ring's stone catching the light with a glorious zing of blue before they both turned away and left her standing on the driveway, the cement scratchy on her bare feet as they slammed her father in the back of the squad car.

• • •

PRESENT DAY

"Miss?"

Bex Andrews surged forward, eyes pulled open wider than she ever thought they could be, heart hammering like a fire bell.

"I'm so sorry," the soothing voice continued. "I didn't mean to startle you. We're going to be landing in a few minutes, and I need you to put your tray table up."

"Oh." Bex looked at her hands, her knuckles white as she gripped the tray table in front of her, then back to the flight attendant. She felt the familiar heat of embarrassment singe across her cheeks. "Sure. I'm sorry."

The flight attendant straightened. "Thank you." Her smile was as bright as a Crest commercial and her hair swirled behind her as she continued up the aisle, reminding the other passengers that they were landing soon.

Bex's heart didn't stop its relentless thump.

"Excuse me," she said, leaning forward in her seat.

The flight attendant turned. "Mmm-hmm?"

"Do I have time to use the restroom?"

"Quickly."

Bex made her way down the narrow aisle, wobbling with the rocking of the plane. She glanced away as people looked up at her, letting out her breath only when she escaped into the tiny lavatory and slid the little lever to *Occupied*. Under the glaring, yellow light, Beth Anne Reimer hardly recognized herself.

Her once white-blond, shoulder-length hair was blunt cut to her ears, the curls gone so that her new sandy-brown hair and pixie cut framed her face, hugging her cheekbones and falling against her darkened eyebrows. Her long bangs hung into her hazel eyes, and several coats of mascara made her short lashes stand out. She was wearing an outfit that made her look like every other teenager in the free world: tight jeans faded at the knees and fraying at the ankles, flip-flops, and a white zip-up hoodie with a surfer print. Instinctively, she pulled the hood over her head, and the fabric shaded her face and instantly darkened her cheekbones. Her bright eyes were suddenly small and menacing. She pushed the hood back.

She was a new person, at the other side of her home state and about to start a new life. No way was she going to fade into her hoodie and let people think she was a serial killer just because her father was.

Not anymore.

That was Beth Anne Reimer.

And she was Bex Andrews now.

TWO

Bex stared out the car's passenger-side window as the scenery zoomed by. She had never been to Kill Devil Hills, though she had seen postcards and TV shows set here, but what was whizzing by her—nondescript strip malls, Target shopping centers, and fast-food places—made her feel like the puddle-jumper flight from Raleigh, North Carolina, had landed her right back there. If it hadn't been for the woman in the driver's seat who was chatting happily about something Bex couldn't focus on, she would have wondered if this whole moving-across-the-state thing was just a big hoax.

"Does that sound good to you?"

The woman driving the Honda SUV smiled at Bex, her light-blue eyes sparkling even in the dim hint of twilight.

Bex felt her mouth drop open. "I'm sorry, what?"

Denise tucked a strand of deep-brown hair behind her ear. "I'm sorry, Bex. That's such a cool name, by the way. I'm probably just talking your ear off. We're just really happy to have you here. I know it can't be easy for you…"

The familiar lump started to form in the back of her throat and

Bex shifted in the car seat, working the seat belt strap between her fingers. Her grandmother's face flashed in her mind, and the familiar smells of the house where Bex had lived since she was seven years old filled her nostrils—her grandmother's powdery, lavender smell; the sweet, cloying scent of night jasmine when it wafted through her bedroom curtains; the earthy smell of hot grass as she tromped barefoot through it.

But that was a world away in another life. Her grandmother had passed seven months ago and Bex's home had been sold. She'd been shifted into a "temporary care situation," which basically meant she was stuck in a cross between an orphanage and juvenile hall until a foster home willing to take her opened up.

And when one did, it was across the state in the Outer Banks with Denise and Michael Pierson, a couple in their early forties who only knew that Bex had lived with her grandmother.

They didn't know the truth.

They didn't know that Bex's own mother had disappeared when Bex was only five years old and still called Beth Anne Reimer. They didn't know that Beth Anne was doted on by a father who lavished her with costume jewelry and funky purses.

They didn't know that all the gifts Beth Anne's father gave her had once belonged to women in the Research Triangle area of North Carolina. Women who Beth Anne's father—dubbed the Wife Collector in the press—had murdered.

Allegedly. The word gnawed at Bex's periphery.

It was Beth Anne herself, a shy, moon-eyed seven-year-old, who had pointed a chubby finger at her own father when the police came to her house. Yes, she knew the pretty blond woman from the photograph, she had said to the police officer. The girl had been with them for two days before getting into the car with Beth Anne's daddy. No, she didn't know where they had gone. All she knew was that the blond lady never came back to the house, never came back for the nubby scarf she had wound around Beth Anne's neck, so Beth Anne had kept it for herself.

It was just a few days later that Beth Anne's daddy was locked in that police cruiser and scuttled down to the courthouse. The newspapers and local news station splashed headlines everywhere and that single word—*allegedly*—seemed to grow smaller, to fade into the enormous text around it.

Jackson Reimer, *Alleged* Wife Collector Murderer, Held in Local Jail

Whenever one of the coifed and pinched news anchors said her daddy's name, that word was always attached: "Jackson Reimer *allegedly* murdered these women in a fit of rage…"

The memory still nagged her—her father, a murderer, and she barely a second grader, thrust in front of the media as "The Devil's Own Daughter" who did a noble thing by turning him in. Back then, she didn't have any idea what that meant. Back then, she wasn't able to decide if what she saw and what she was *told* she saw were the same thing. Back then, she didn't know her words would be used against the one person who had always taken care of her: her father. But he had never been tried, never been convicted, because he had disappeared. Then the news anchors started to drop the *alleged* all together.

Denise flipped on her blinker, the *click-click-click* bringing Bex back to the here and now. "Are you hungry?" Denise asked.

Bex shifted, pushing the memory—the broken look in her father's eyes, the sound of his shackles scraping on the cement as they led him away—as far out of her present mind as she dared. "A little bit."

"Well, Michael's at home. He's a master chef—at least he thinks he is. Really, he's lousy in front of anything but an open flame, and even that's iffy. He's doing burgers. I hope that's okay?"

Bex nodded. Her head was an absolute mess, the events of the last twenty-four hours humming in her brain like the whir of the plane's engine. Since Tuesday, everything had been new. The first time she had dyed her hair. The first time she had cut it more than an inch. The first time she had been on a plane. The first time she ever had real hope that she could put her past behind her and never again be the Wife Collector's daughter.

She swallowed hard when Denise aimed her car between the two huge, brick fences of the Kill Devil Hills beachfront neighborhood. Brush grass and trees lined the sidewalks, yawning into the night and softening the edges of the comfortable, cookie-cutter homes on either side of the street. Denise reached out and gingerly patted Bex's knee. "Home, sweet home, hon. You ready?"

Bex didn't know how to answer.

• • •

Denise was right. Michael wasn't much of a cook, but he piled Bex's burger with three kinds of cheese to make up for the half-charred puck of ground beef and talked relentlessly about the university where he worked as a professor of anthropology, and Bex kind of liked him. He was funny and animated, and by the time Bex's burger was reduced to crumbs, she and Denise were holding their stomachs and wiping tears from their eyes.

When Bex's eyes flicked to the clock on the stove—it was nearly nine by then—she realized that the last two hours of her new life had been just that: brand-new. She couldn't remember the last time she had eaten a terrible burger, laughed so hard it hurt, and not ached inside, missing her grandmother. She couldn't remember the last time she was this carefree, this happy.

"Can I help with the dishes?" Bex asked, standing.

Michael looked taken aback, his eyes going to Denise and then back to Bex. "Didn't anyone tell you?"

Heat burned the tops of Bex's ears and her chest tightened. "Tell me what?"

"You're a teenager. You're supposed to hate us, refuse to do anything, then stomp up the stairs screaming, 'You're ruining my life!'" He broke into a grin so wide it made his brown eyes crinkle at the corners. Denise swatted at him.

"Michael, leave her alone. It's only her first night. She'll have plenty of time to scorn your terrible dad jokes and be that teenager later. Come on, Bex. I know you must be exhausted. Let's get you settled into your room, and we can deal with chores and school and all that boring stuff in the morning. Okay?"

Bex followed Denise up the stairs, hugging her purse to her chest. Michael had already dropped her luggage into a room right off the hall, and when Denise opened the door, Bex sucked in a sharp breath.

"This is for me?"

Denise nodded silently.

The bedroom was enormous—at least twice the size of the one at her grandmother's house and a dozen times bigger than the four walls she shared with three other girls at the interim home. The walls were painted a soft green that matched the chevron stripes on the bedspread that matched the curtains fluttering lazily in the evening breeze. From where she stood, Bex could see that her room had its own bathroom, and the cool green continued there in fluffy towels and a funky pattern on the shower curtain.

"I hope it's okay."

Bex turned to Denise, who stood in the doorway, nervously wringing her hands.

"Are you kidding? It's amazing. I didn't expect—well, I didn't know what to expect. I mean…"

Denise batted at the air. "It's your home now, Bex. We just want you to be comfortable, to know that you belong here. We're so happy to have you." She avoided Bex's eyes as she started opening drawers and showing off the enormous, empty closet. "You're— you're our daughter." She looked up, her eyes soft, almost pleading. "We want you to be happy."

Bex nodded, too choked up to answer.

"And if you hate the color, you can blame Michael." Denise's grin was big but shy. She paused in the doorway for an extra second, her teeth working her plump lower lip. "If you can't sleep or if you just want to hang out, Michael and I will be up for a while watching TV. And eating ice cream. Kind of a nighttime ritual." Denise turned and shot another smile, her blue eyes bright. She was tall and naturally slim, and even with her shy grin, she had an easy confidence and grace that Bex instantly admired. She looked at home in her skin.

When Denise left, she shut the door behind her. Bex flopped on the bed, loving the smooshing sound of the pillow-top mattress and the soft, ultra-plush comforter. She could be happy here. She rolled over and spied a framed picture of Denise and Michael on one of her bookshelves. They were smiling, arms entwined, standing in front of a fenced-off waterfall somewhere.

They looked like parents. They looked like burger-making, ice-cream-eating parents who maybe had a Volvo sedan in a very neat garage and a shaggy dog and…a teenaged daughter. With her new hair color, Bex even looked a little like Michael, whose brownish hair was salted with gray, like they really could be father and daughter. But the second the elation of maybe actually belonging to a family swelled, it was hacked down by crippling guilt.

You have a father, the little voice in the back of her head hissed. *You sent him to prison for the rest of his life, remember?*

"I didn't," she said, teeth gritted, voice a low growl. "He ran."

You gave him no choice…

Bex blinked away the tears that swelled below her lashes. "He abandoned me just as much as I abandoned him," she muttered to herself. That was something the social worker had told her—that in deciding to run, Bex's father had already decided to abandon her. Bex mumbled the phrase every now and again when the guilt bubbled or she missed her father or she wanted to remember what normal was.

"Normal is ice cream," she said, tugging a sweatshirt over her head. "Normal is me having ice cream with Michael and Denise." She paused, then tried out the words. "My parents."

THREE

Michael and Denise were standing at the kitchen counter when Bex got downstairs, a supermarket stock of Ben & Jerry's pints set out on the counter in front of them. A gooey can of chocolate sauce, whipped cream, chopped nuts, and a half-eaten jar of electric-red maraschino cherries were also set out.

"I told Bex about our ice cream nightcaps," Denise said, handing Bex a bowl.

Bex blinked. "You said you guys had a little ice cream at night. You didn't say you were sundae masters."

Michael grinned at that and drowned his two scoops of chocolate ice cream in whipped cream. "We do all right."

After Bex finished creating her sundae—a stomach-stretching monstrosity of nearly every flavor on the counter—she followed Michael and Denise to the living room and took a spot on the couch, tucking her long legs underneath her.

The TV was already on the local news channel. From where she sat, Bex had a clear view of the news ticker running across the bottom of the screen and the concerned-looking newscaster standing somewhere that looked beachy.

"Authorities are reporting that another girl was found early this morning, her body discarded among the trash bags behind this local eatery," the newscaster said. A picture of a grinning blond, head pushed back, blue eyes rich and dark, appeared on the screen. "There has been no official identification, but authorities are speculating that this latest body might be that of seventeen-year-old Erin Malone of—"

Denise clicked the TV off. "We don't need to see that before bed. Are you excited about your first day of school tomorrow, Bex? You're barely three weeks into the school year, so the 'new kid' thing shouldn't be that bad."

Bex tried to tear her eyes away from the now-black screen. The girl in the photograph… There was something about her that Bex recognized, even though she had never heard of the girl or the restaurant where she was found. Maybe this story had made national news?

Ice shot through her veins when the shard of a memory fell into place: the girl with the scarf. All those years ago in Raleigh… This girl, this Erin Malone, was a dead ringer for the girl with the scarf.

The girl her father had supposedly murdered.

Bex pushed her bowl away.

"Are you okay? Michael, get her a glass of water. Bex, are you okay?"

"Yes." She pushed the word over her teeth.

It couldn't have been her father. Her father was gone. He didn't…

Bex was instantly shot to another evening in another time. She was seven years old, and her father had just been released from police custody. She was waiting at home, but over the years, with television and film and time, her memory blurred into her being at the police station, to her hearing the officer say, "Don't leave town," to her seeing her father tip his hat just slightly, never a true yes or no.

She had been lying in her postage-stamp-sized bedroom then, half-asleep while the fan lazed overhead. She should have been able to hear him. She should have been able to sense what he was going to do. But she didn't stir that night. Not when he cleared out his closet, not when he pulled the front door closed, not when he drove away and left his baby daughter to wake up in an empty house the morning after.

She had waited for him until the sun set again. Until the moon came up, until pink fingers of morning light cut through the blinds that second morning. Crowds lined up on the street, yelling about a murderer. And when the police finally came back, they only found Beth Anne.

He had left, and the murders had stopped.

Bex's eyes flashed toward the screen again, toward Michael and Denise with their drawn faces looking worried in front of her. *Until now?*

She reeled. *No. There was no way.*

For the first few years after her father left, there was nothing. When she was ten, there were signs, though Bex could never be sure if they were from him or if she had made them up—mumbled wrong numbers or hang-ups in the middle of the night. Blank postcards with Beth Anne's name written in a scrawl she never recognized. There was nothing concrete that said that he was out there, that he was innocent and missing her and thinking of her—except that the killing stopped.

Girls went missing from Raleigh and the Research Triangle in those other years, sure. And girls were murdered. But they didn't have his signature. Their names were never splashed across newspaper pages in thick, black headlines or run along the bottom of the screen news tickers with phrases like,

Wife Collector Claims a New Bride.

Beth Anne tried to believe that meant that he was innocent, that the real killer had moved on. The police believed that meant he was guilty and that he had moved on. When she had the stomach for it, she checked the Internet, doing blanket searches for sensational murders with victims missing digits. When nothing came up, a stripe of relief shot down her back because her father was out there and women were still alive. But nobody wanted to hear that. Nobody wanted to believe that, because Jackson Reimer was allegedly the Wife Collector—and even if he wasn't anymore, Beth Anne Reimer would always be the Wife Collector's daughter.

Heat prickled the back of her neck, and Bex prayed that Michael and Denise couldn't see the sheen of sweat that popped out on her upper lip. Guilt or fear or doubt sped up her heartbeat, and she gripped the edges of the table before shaking her head quickly. "I'm sorry. I'm fine. I-I guess I'm just a little nervous to start school. You know, new place, new people, and all."

Michael set the water glass down in front of Bex. He tried to look cool, but Bex could see him and Denise exchange a glance.

Great. They already think I'm a nut job.

She downed the water in one gulp and tried to put the news clip—and her father—out of her mind. "I should probably just get to bed. Jet lag and all."

Bex stood and climbed the stairs, feeling Michael and Denise looking curiously after her, probably wondering how a quick jaunt across the state could cause jet lag. But Bex wasn't in the mood to argue. The image of the girl on the screen was burned into her mind—*because I've seen it before*, that little voice protested. *No.* Bex shook her head. *My father is gone and this is—what? A coincidence?*

Every molecule inside her went white-hot and willed her to run: run downstairs and flick the TV back on, listen to the news, to the solemn cadence of the anchorwoman's voice. Listen for the one detail that hadn't been mentioned…

Bex remembered another living room, the light from the TV flickering silver over her father's face as he watched the news at their house on Flame Court. In her mind, she heard the chime—bum, bum, BUMMM!—of the Raleigh Super Eight news.

Though the authorities are being understandably tight-lipped about the details surrounding the discovery of this most recent body, they are willing to say that preliminary reports suggest she is most likely another of the Wife Collector's victims. Like the three previous, this current victim is female, blond, in her late teens to early twenties, and missing her left-hand ring finger—what has become known as this particular killer's "signature."

Bex remembered the fear that had trilled through her, that narrow knife slice of nausea as she thought about this poor, young blond woman—cold, dumped at the edge of Raleigh's industrial district, and missing her finger.

"Daddy?" she had asked.

Her father had paused a beat before clicking off the television and turning to her. "Yes, Bethy?"

"That won't happen to me, right? The Wife Collector. You won't let him get me?"

Bex tried to think back—had thought back so many times to that moment when her childish voice called out and her father stared at her. How had he looked? Guilty? Pleased? Smug? Was there any tiny nuance in his expression, in his voice that Bex could pick up on and point to as the aha moment as evidence of her father's guilt or innocence?

Closing the door behind her, Bex slid to the floor, back up against her bed. Every calming technique the shrink in Raleigh had taught her washed over her. She couldn't remember if she was supposed to let out deep breaths or hold them, focus on the good times she had with her father or let it all go, lie down and relax, or go for a walk. In the end, all she could do was slip between the cool covers of this strange bed in this strange room and try her best to be who she was now: Bex Andrews, a girl who didn't have a father.

She tried to sleep, but everything inside her kept tingling and her ears rang with the whirr from the plane's exhaust system, so she didn't hear the plaintive buzz from her phone as it flashed a Raleigh area code on her screen before going black.

FOUR

Bex's caseworker in Raleigh had told her that she would love Kill Devil Hills, despite the evil-sounding name. She had gushed about it being a tiny beach town where just about everything, including the high school, was on the beach.

But Kill Devil Hills High wasn't *anywhere* near the beach.

The student lot wasn't full of convertibles, the girls weren't wearing bikini tops, and no one ran through the halls tossing footballs or beach balls or smelling like suntan lotion and sea air. It was just a regular high school.

Bex held her books tightly against her chest and surreptitiously tried to glance down at the school map. After two wrong turns and a near spin through the boys' bathroom, she pushed open the first door she saw, praying that she was at least in the vicinity of her homeroom.

Every head snapped to look at her when she stepped through the door, and every muscle in her body tightened. She was ready to run until the door slapped shut behind her.

"Bex Andrews?"

Bex blinked, scanning the room. The kids didn't look mean or menacing—just curious—and for that, Bex was relieved…almost.

"Bex Andrews?"

There were two empty seats in the front row, bookended on either side by girls with glossy ponytails and Kill Devil Hills High School cheerleading uniforms who had immediately lost interest in Bex and started checking their phones.

"Ms. Andrews? Are you Bex Andrews?"

The voice calling her name finally penetrated and Bex spun, her heart thumping against her chest. "Yes. Bex. Me."

The man at the front of the room smiled warmly and spread his arms. "I'm your homeroom teacher, Mr. Rhodes. You can call me Mr. Rhodes." He laughed at his own dumb joke. "Welcome to Kill Devil Hills High. Class, say hello."

Bex stood, hoping the standard-issue school linoleum would open up and swallow her whole while the class muttered a sad hello. Some students still looked at her, but the majority had moved on to other things. She smiled thinly. "Hey."

Mr. Rhodes, who was short and possibly nine months pregnant, given the strain of his shirt against his belly, rolled his eyes toward the students. "Don't mind them. Now, Bex, you can take one of the empty seats."

One of the cheerleaders glanced up from her phone. "That one," she said, pointing. "This one is Darla's. She's just out sick today."

Bex nodded and wondered if anyone would notice her dragging the empty desk to the back of the classroom or out into the hall, anywhere but smack in the front of the class.

"Actually, Bex, before you sit, why don't you tell us something about yourself." Mr. Rhodes smiled as if he hadn't just asked Bex to splay her soul open to a group of bored teenagers.

"Um," she said, feeling her skin burn from her calves to the top of her head. "There really isn't much to tell."

Except that my dad is a serial killer.

On the run.

He doesn't know where I am. He doesn't know that I'm Bex Andrews now because he hasn't contacted me in ten years.

"I guess I'm just pretty regular."

"Where did you transfer from?"

Bex didn't want to announce that she had been homeschooled since the third grade when kids started coughing things like "socio" or "psycho killer" into their hands whenever she passed. She didn't want this new class to know that she had never been invited to a birthday party. No one wanted to have anything to do with the serial killer's kid.

"I went to school in Raleigh, North Carolina," Bex said, her voice sounding weird and tinny in her own ears.

"And you came here why?" Mr. Rhodes coached her.

Bex's throat was dry but she tried to swallow anyway, coughing into her hand. "My dad got a new job," she lied.

"And he is…"

Bex wanted to run. Her entire body thrummed with the overwhelming desire to dart for the door and through the hall, out of the school and out of North Carolina. Where she would go, where she would end up, she had no idea. All she knew was that she didn't want to be here. She didn't want to be Bex Andrews, the foster kid. She didn't want to be anyone.

"He's a college professor."

She slid into her chair and busied herself, pretending to look in her backpack before Mr. Rhodes could continue the trial.

Bex made it through the entire homeroom period staring straight ahead. Every once in a while she could see a flicker out of the corner of her eye as the two cheerleaders gestured to each other around her, but she didn't dare look. Even if they didn't know anything about her, she was still the new kid—and if movies and television had taught her anything, it was that cheerleaders were to be avoided at all costs.

So when the homeroom bell rang and the two girls cornered Bex, she knew that her fate was sealed. Images of being shoved into lockers and covered in pig's blood at prom swam in her head as one of the girls tightened her already-perfect ponytail and the other studied her.

"I'm Laney," the dark-haired one said. "And this is Chelsea."

Chelsea, with a sun-gold ponytail and blue eyes that took up half her face, nodded.

Bex said a low hello to each of them while her stomach quivered. She waited for claws or teeth or a biting remark about her hair or her clothes.

"Do you know where you're going next? It's easy to get lost around here," Chelsea said, her ponytail bobbing. "KDH is a pretty big school. Was your old school very big?"

"'Big' isn't really the right word for it," Bex said, hiking her backpack over one shoulder. "And I have—uh—ethics with Mrs. Chadwick next."

"Oh, she's great. Basically you just sit and she reads the paper and asks stuff about what it's in it. It's a pretty cool class until she makes you do that stupid newspaper log. Ugh."

Chelsea rolled her eyes. "That was torture. I had black fingers for weeks."

Bex's eyebrows rose. "Black fingers?"

Laney nodded. "Yeah, you have to follow something that has been in the headlines for a month and cut out all the articles and write a bunch of crap about them."

"But she makes you use *real* newspapers. The paper kind." Chelsea looked absolutely mortified. "Chadwick's weirdly old-fashioned and slightly decrepit."

"Come on," Laney said. "I'm going in that direction. I can walk you over there."

Laney and Bex chatted the whole way, and by the time they entered the junior hall, Bex was breathing normally—laughing even.

"Okay, you're right there," Laney said, pointing to a door over Bex's shoulder. "I'm down there. Find me later. We'll have lunch."

Bex pressed open the classroom door without any of the trepidation she'd had before. There were only a few kids already in class, and the teacher—a youngish-looking woman with her dark hair clipped back in a low ponytail—was chatting with a kid in the front row. He was hinged forward, his shaggy, black hair dragging across his eyes as he shook his head against everything she said.

"No, no, no. It's art."

Mrs. Chadwick—possibly fifty years old and nowhere near Chelsea's description of "decrepit"—shook her head but was smiling. "It's illegal."

"Oh, jeez, this again? You'd think the guy would give it a rest already."

Bex spun, stunned, and found herself nearly nose to nose with the kind of guy who showed up in all those California high-school-on-the-beach movies. He had wide, brown eyes and brownish-blond hair that looked like it had been colored by the sun. When he smiled, the entire room brightened and Bex felt her temperature rise at least ten degrees. She was sure she was blushing; probably so much that her eyeballs were red. She took a fumbling step back. "Oh, I'm sorry."

"No, that's okay. I'm sorry. I didn't mean to scare you. You must be new, or I must really have been sleeping through this class. I'm Trevor."

"I'm new." Another ten degrees. "Not new. I mean, I'm new here but my name is Bex." She paused and bit her lower lip. "That was really smooth, wasn't it?"

"Nah, you did great. The name question is a hard one for a lot of people." He gestured toward two empty desks. "Here."

"Thanks." Bex sat next to Trevor, her eyes going over his head to where the student and the teacher were still engaged in heated debate. She jutted her chin in the student's direction. "So what's that all about?"

Trevor glanced, then shook his head with a low groan. "That's Zach. He thinks he's some big feature filmmaker because he's the camera guy for the school news channel. He's really just a huge pain in the ass. Argues about everything." Trevor held up his hands. "Wait, sorry. Not argue, debate. He likes to debate everything. Probably hoping for an all-out brawl so he can whip out his GoPro and win a Pulitzer or something."

"That's journalism."

"What?"

Bex's eyes were still on Zach, watching the passionate way he argued, his body poised as though he would hop over the desk to prove his point. "The Pulitzer is for journalism. Not filmmaking. Does he do this all the time?"

Trevor leaned back and kicked his legs forward, resting his feet on the desk in front of him.

"Yeah," he said with a yawn. "Better get comfortable."

When the bell finally rang and ethics was over, Zach followed Bex out of the class. She could feel his eyes on the back of her head, studying her, boring into her. She swallowed, wondering if he could read her mind and why, whenever she considered the idea of mind reading, she went directly to her most horrid memory—that night on the driveway when she learned what her father had done.

Zach followed her all the way to her locker.

Bex paused, turning. "Is there something I can help you with?" she asked. She was surprised at the composure in her voice since every inch of her body seemed to be quaking, ready to crumble, certain that Zach was going to pinpoint who she was and then turn around and tell the entire school, heck, the entire town—even Denise and Michael—that her bloodline included a man who the newspapers called "one of the most heinous and depraved serial killers ever."

Zach blinked at her. "I don't know. Do you know the combination to my locker?"

Bex stepped back. "What?"

"My locker." He brushed a hand past her shoulder. "It's right here."

"Oh," Bex said, her mouth suddenly dry. She forced out a small laugh while her bones turned to hot jelly. "I'm sorry. I thought that—"

Zach pulled open his locker, shoved in a book, then turned to her. "You thought that I was the geeky comic relief? The big nerd who falls for the cool girl?"

"Cool girl? What are you talking about?"

He reached into his locker and pulled out a small, fancy camera and held it up to his face. A red light flicked on. "Okay, new girl. Tell the world about yourself. What's your greatest dream, your deepest, darkest secret?"

Bex's eyes went wide. "What? What are you—"

"Everyone's going to find out sooner or later, Beth."

Beth?

FIVE

Bex's heart slammed against her rib cage. The red recording light on Zach's camera flooded her vision until everything she saw was coated in a haze of glowing red, bright as fresh blood. Her stomach turned and heat prickled her scalp.

"Wouldn't you rather share the whole dirty story here, in your own words, instead of having it run through the KDH mouth breathers' PA system?"

Images plowed into Bex's mind. She was eight years old and dressed in an itchy navy dress with a thick, lacy collar, her grandmother dragging her by the hand as they dodged a maze of reporters. The flashes from their cameras were blinding her, snapping like the jaws of hungry alligators, one after another after another. People shouted her name—strangers who knew things about her, about her family.

"Beth Anne! Do you know where your mother is?"

"Beth Anne, is it true your father gave you jewelry and presents from his victims?"

She could feel her grandmother's hand tighten on hers, her grandmother's jaw going hard.

"Shut up, you miscreants!" Gran had yelled. *"She's only a child!"*
Beth Anne had had to look up the word "miscreant."

"Come on, Beth," Zach prodded. "Inquiring minds want to know."

"Shut up," Bex said between gritted teeth. "Shut up, shut up, *shut up!*" Each one louder until she was yelling, hands fisted, fingernails digging into the soft flesh of her palm.

"Hey." Zach dropped the camera to his side, the little red light flicking off, but Bex couldn't stop herself. Every synapse was firing, her blood roaring through her ears.

"Shut up!"

She didn't know when she started crying.

She heard the body slamming against the locker first, Zach's shoulders hitting the slick metal, his head lolling back.

"Leave her alone, asshole. No one wants to be in your stupid movies!"

She could see Trevor, his outline blurred through her tears. He stood a whole head taller than Zach and leered down at him. His mouth was moving so she knew he was talking, but her head was filled with the same buzzing static that she had felt before. She saw Laney and Chelsea pushing through the halls, students parting for them without so much as a word, and it was like Bex was out of her body, suspended above the whole scene. She saw herself standing there, looking wooden and hollow as Trevor yelled at Zach and Chelsea threaded an arm through wooden Bex's, Laney stretching a protective arm across her shoulders.

They tugged at her and she was back in her body. Zach looked at her, eyes wide, slightly fearful, completely apologetic.

"I'm sorry. I didn't mean to freak you out, Beth."

"*Bex*," Trevor spat out, bits of saliva landing on the collar of Zach's polo shirt. "Her name is Bex."

She watched Zach, a tiny triangle of his pink tongue darting out and brushing over his bottom lip. "I'm sorry, Bex. I didn't mean anything. I was just joking around. I'm a documentary filmmaker."

Laney narrowed her eyes into sharp slits, stabbing Zach with a look. "You're a joke."

Bex wanted to stay angry but she saw the crushed look in Zach's eyes even as he tried to avoid hers. She felt the same hot stripe go up her neck—the one that she had felt so many times before when she was the joke, the stain, the kid that no one wanted to play with.

"It's okay," she said, but Zach had already turned around.

Trevor shot her a grin, and Laney nudged Bex's hip with hers. "Don't worry. You can tell us all your deepest, darkest secrets when you're ready."

Bex made it through her next class without incident, and when the lunch bell rang, Chelsea and Laney were waiting by her locker. Bex found herself glancing around for Trevor and then gave herself a mental head slap. Not even through the first day, and she was already crushing on someone.

Bex's cell phone chirped. She glanced down at the readout, the sounds of her new friends and her new school going weird and tinny when she saw the area code preceding the strange number: 919.

Raleigh.

In her mind, she heard the muffled sounds and clicks that preceded a collect call, the robotic voice that informed her that she was receiving a call from a speaker who held the phone too close and mumbled his name. She remembered the one and only time she had heard that robotic voice, the way she had frozen, her hand gripping the old-fashioned receiver her grandmother had on the kitchen phone. She had finally croaked out the words, "I accept the charges."

Fifteen minutes seemed to lapse between the clicks and beeps, and then she heard what she thought was her father's voice—gravelly, low, nearly unrecognizable. It sounded like the caller said her name but blood was pulsing in her ears, and she even though she strained, she couldn't make out the man's mumbles. He hung up and she stood in the kitchen, pressing the receiver to her ear and pretending that her daddy was talking to her, saying soothing things and that he'd be home soon. Instead, she let the dial tone drone in her ear until her gran hung up the phone.

"You okay, Bex?" Chelsea had her hand on Bex's shoulder, and Bex forced herself to pump her head in a positive nod.

"Yeah, sorry. It was just a weird number on my phone. Probably nothing."

Chelsea offered a warm smile and linked her arm through Bex's. "Okay, now I will tell you absolutely everything you need to know about living in Kill Devil Hills. Do you have three and a half minutes?"

"No," said the man who stepped into the hall in front of them. "She doesn't."

Bex's mouth dropped open, her throat going bone dry. The

man in front of her was smiling but it didn't reach his flat, emotionless brown eyes.

"You're Bex Andrews."

Bex wasn't sure if he was asking or telling, but she nodded anyway. "Uh-huh."

"I'm sorry we haven't met sooner. I'm Terrence Howard, your guidance counselor." He offered a hand that Bex stared at before limply shaking. "Care to step in my office?" The way he spoke wasn't unpleasant, but something about him set Bex on edge.

"I guess."

"Hey, we'll catch up with you later," Chelsea said.

Bex followed Mr. Howard into his office, a small room with the same utilitarian furniture that she suspected populated every other public school administrator's office in the world, and sat down in the visitor's chair across from him. As he settled himself, she glanced around the room, noting the same cache of "You Can Do It!" posters that had lined the cinderblock walls at what passed as the schoolroom at the juvenile facility where she had been held.

Then she glanced at the newspaper on his desk. The body found in the Dumpster was the topic of the main headline, accompanied by a full-color picture of the cordoned-off crime scene and insets of anguished onlookers. Bex knew she should look away but found herself skimming the headline, the article, trying to glean new information.

"It's horrible, isn't it?"

Bex's head snapped up. "Excuse me?"

Mr. Howard gestured toward the newspaper. "Terrible business. A young woman like that, taken in the prime of her life."

Bex nodded stiffly. "Yeah."

"Anyway, Bex." Mr. Howard smiled again, this one easier, seemingly more genuine. "That's an interesting name, Bex. It's not short for anything?"

He held her eye for an uncomfortably long moment, and Bex shook her head. "No."

She could see that her file was on the desk in front of him, the name *Andrews, Bex* typed in a twelve-point font.

"Well, I just wanted to make sure that you're settling in well here at KDH. Are there any questions I can answer? Anything I can help you with?"

Before she could answer, Mr. Howard prattled on. "I understand from your file that you've been homeschooled up until this point. Are you having trouble adjusting? I know it can be hard. Everything is all new to you here, I'll bet."

"I'm okay." She cleared her throat. "People seem to be nice so far."

"It seems that way, doesn't it?"

Bex had been set in front of enough psychologists in her life to know that Mr. Howard was mirroring her—using her own words and body language to theoretically make her feel more comfortable, but the way he said, "seems that way," struck her as weird and all Bex wanted to do was get out of his office.

"I appreciate your help, Mr. Howard, but I'd really like to get to class. I don't want to fall any more behind."

"Oh right, of course. Well"—he stood, gathering a sheaf of papers—"these are from your teachers. Some books you'll need to pick up, some additional reading material for catching up, and I've included some helpful material about the area, about making friends. You'll be sure to come and see me, should you need anything, right, Bex?"

"Yeah. Sure."

Bex shoved the papers in her backpack and made a mental note to avoid Mr. Howard at all costs.

• • •

The rest of the school week passed quickly and smoothly for Bex. For the first day or two people smiled at her and gave her the obligatory new-kid greeting when prompted by the teacher, but by midweek she was a regular kid. Not once did she feel the bitter burn of eyes on the back of her neck or hear the chafing whispers, "Stay away from her. She's bad." By Friday morning, Bex was actually looking forward to going to school. She knew where her classes were, had memorized her locker combination, and had been absorbed into Chelsea and Laney's circle of friends.

"Ugh!" Chelsea was growling at her cell phone as she and Bex merged into the crowd in the hall. "I've texted Darla seventy times, and she hasn't texted me back."

"Darla? Your friend from Rhodes's class? I thought you guys said she was sick. Maybe's she napping or something, or her parents took her phone."

Chelsea shot her a bemused look. "Darla's not really sick. She tends to take the occasional mental health day. Or, in this case, week. And her parents? Mom's a flight attendant and dad's a pilot."

"Sounds kind of romantic."

"Darla says it's more passive-aggressive than romantic since they work very hard not to ever be on the same schedule. Or in the same city." She went back to her call. "Answer your phone, bitch!" Chelsea rolled her eyes when Darla's nasal voice boomed out from the phone: *You've reached Darla's phone. Lucky you!*

"Hey, Dar, it's Chels. Again. If you don't call me back, I'm officially kicking you off the squad and busting you down to mascot. So, if you don't want to wear a giant devil's head that smells like ass for the rest of your high school existence, you'll call me."

Bex spun the combination on her locker. "Remind me to never get on your bad side."

Chelsea winked and pointed at Bex. "That'd be best. Anyway, tell your parents you have plans tonight."

"I do?"

"Party at Darla's house. She might not be answering the phone, but I know she'll answer the door. I'll shoot you the info. Bye!"

Bex was too stunned to wave. She hadn't been in school—hadn't even been Bex Andrews—for more than a few days, and already she had friends and a social life. She felt a slight tingle behind her ears. Could it really be this easy?

"See you later, Bex!" Laney passed her in the hall as Bex opened her locker.

"Bye!"

I can do this.

She pulled books from her locker and shoved them into her backpack, her hand hovering over the stack of papers from Mr. Howard. Bex had stashed them away on Monday and avoided them since. Just the thought of the man gave her the creeps, but she pawed the pages into her bag anyway, vowing to trash them at home. She slammed the metal locker door shut.

"Hey." Zach was crouching next to her locker, picking something up. "You dropped this."

He slid the postcard into Bex's hand without making eye contact and kept walking.

"Thanks!" A tiny niggling feeling in her gut hoped that Zach would turn around and smile at her to give some indication that he was okay, that he didn't somehow blame her for Trevor's reaction. He had studiously avoided Bex and her whole group all week, and for some reason, it bothered her.

"Next time," she muttered under her breath, glancing down at the postcard he'd handed her.

Bex had to blink several times to read the words. They couldn't be right. They blurred and swarmed and re-formed again.

Greetings from the Research Triangle!

There was a cartoon picture of the state of North Carolina, a red line forming the Research Triangle of Raleigh, Durham, and Chapel Hill. The same line could be drawn to mark the locations of most of the Wife Collector's victims.

Bex shook her head. It was a coincidence. A joint ad for UNC and Duke, maybe something from Mr. Howard's stack of brochures to familiarize herself with the area.

But the Research Triangle is almost 250 miles from here...

She flipped the card, hoping to see a preprinted message about applications for admissions or campus tours. She didn't expect the hastily scrawled message:

DADDY'S HOME.

SIX

The words throbbed in front of her eyes.

DADDY'S HOME.

They burned into her retinas, into her mind, and paralyzed her. All around Bex, lockers slammed and kids shuffled down the halls, the din of doors opening and closing and chatter and overhead announcements that the last bus was leaving all morphing into one crashing whoosh that swelled in her ears and slammed through her mind.

Daddy's home.

Somehow, Bex turned. Somehow, she scanned the hall and the few students left. No one acknowledged her. No one snickered behind their hands or tried to hide a sinister smile, responsible for this sick joke.

Daddy's home.

She tried to breathe but it was like she couldn't remember how. Her chest tightened, her head pounded, and her vision blurred.

Just a joke.

It had to be.

She was nine years old, and her grandmother had dropped her off at vacation bible school at Our Lady of Grace out in High Point. It was a glorious summer day, the kind that whitewashed everything and prickled your shoulders and hung on in memories as summer perfection. Her grandmother had plaited Beth Anne's hair into two long braids that hung down her back, nearly to her waist, the white blond almost blending into her pale cotton tank top. Sue Reynolds was holding her hand.

Sue Reynolds had the soft-edged accent of her Georgia home. It was her first summer in North Carolina, visiting her grandparents, and when they had dropped her off in their beaten-up Coup de Ville with the mismatched hubcaps, the other kids had stuck their tongues out at Sue, had turned their backs. Not Beth Anne.

Beth Anne sat silently next to Sue and held out half her sandwich. Sue took it without looking at her, the way misfits did, and chewed carefully, still quiet. When she and Beth Anne finished their last bites simultaneously—dumping the soggy crusts in the grass for the ducks— they smiled shyly. Sue found Beth Anne's hand.

"Do you like ponies?" she whispered.

Beth Anne was about to answer that she did, but a whistle cut through the humid-heavy air and distracted her. That first rock hit Beth Anne in the temple, shooting a starburst of pain through her head. She had to blink several times to get her vision to clear, and when it did, she saw the kids in front of the church, a half dozen of them with narrowed eyes and angry, wicked grins.

"Killer!" A redheaded boy standing on the bottom step of the church porch cupped his hands around his mouth and shouted: "Killer!"

Another boy, one step down from the first, selected another rock, his arm reeling back for the throw.

"She'll kill you!" a third kid yelled.

Sue looked at Beth Anne, eyes wide, and broke her hold to protect her head as a handful of pebbles rained down on them.

"Hey, new girl." A brunette Beth Anne had never seen before ran toward them. "Stay away from her. She's a psycho. Her daddy murders mommies and eats them!"

Another rock came sailing from the church, this one hitting Sue square in the chest. The girl looked at the dirty mark it left on her T-shirt and then at Beth Anne as if she was the one who put it there. And in a way, she was.

"Come on!" The brown-haired girl snatched Sue's wrist and pulled her up, tugging her into a run. "You can't play with her," the girl admonished. "No one can. She's bad like her daddy."

The taunts of the kids—*killer, murderer, psycho*—still rang in Bex's ears, still hung in her head. The postcard trembled between her fingers, the fading image she still held of her father sharpening in her mind. Pale complexion. Larger-than-life stature. Kind eyes.

She shoved the postcard deep in her backpack, smashing her books on top of it.

Bex Andrews didn't have a father.

It was only three o'clock, but the thick haze of gray fog made it look later and Bex shivered at the damp chill. School had let out less than ten minutes before, but the grounds were emptying at record speed as kids crossed the street en masse and a long line of SUVs and minivans snaked through the front lot, collecting kids and disappearing into traffic.

"Bexy!"

Bex whirled at the loud voice and waved at Laney who was hanging out the driver's side window of a VW Bug painted a hideous fluorescent green that shone through the fog. Bex could see a spray of silk daisies wobbling on the dashboard and something with a crystal hanging from the rearview mirror. Even though Bex barely knew her, the whole car seemed to scream "Laney." Chelsea was in the passenger's seat, staring at her cell phone, when Bex jogged over.

"Hey, you need a ride?" Laney asked.

"Oh." Bex was stunned, still certain that somehow the week had been a colossal joke that she was the unwitting butt of, that the postcard was simply the start of her old life chipping away at her new one.

"You don't even know where she lives," Chelsea said, snapping her gum.

Laney shrugged. "Need one?"

"No thanks." Bex waved at the air. "I'm actually not entirely sure where I live yet. I know it's that way." She pointed in the general direction Denise had come from that morning. "Anyway, D...my mom"—Bex had trouble pushing out the words—"insisted on driving me today. First week and all that."

"All right. See you later then!"

Laney stepped on the gas just in time for Bex to glance in the tiny backseat of the car. Monday's newspaper was on the seat, the picture of Erin Malone, the body from the Dumpster, smiling out at Bex. Her breath hitched, the words on the postcard already seared in the back of her mind.

Daddy's home.

Erin was a pretty blond, vibrant and happy from the looks of the newspaper picture, and she had been dumped in the trash like she wasn't worth anything at all. *Just like the rest of the Wife Collector's victims*, the little voice in Bex's head taunted. She gritted her teeth and tried to edge out the thought.

A train of cars followed Laney's out into the street, and Bex was left at the crescent-shaped mouth of the school driveway, waiting for Denise. She glanced at her phone and rocked on her heels. What if Denise had forgotten her? What if Denise had figured out who she was and wasn't coming for her at all? A strange heat burned through Bex and she pushed up the sleeves of her hoodie, even as the fog turned to a cold wet mist.

Another few moments passed, and then there was a cacophony of honking and a stressed-looking Denise screeching into the driveway. She frantically rolled down the passenger-side window and pushed open the car door.

"I'm so, so sorry," she said before Bex could reach the car. "We got absolutely swamped at the station. The news editor is out sick, and my editor's water broke and—"

"It's okay." Bex smiled, pulling the door open farther. "You're not really late. Everyone just takes off the second the bell rings, I guess."

The look on Denise's face softened and she grinned back. "I love that you haven't learned teenage angst yet."

Bex slid into the passenger seat, her temperature still rising, her heart still thundering in her chest. When her cell phone buzzed, it nearly sent her into a tizzy. Denise glanced at her, and Bex forced a nonchalant chuckle.

"Oh," she muttered, when her heart no longer threatened to launch itself from her mouth. "It's just Chelsea." She flicked her thumb over the message.

> Chng-o-plns. Bonfire 2night @ corollabeach.
> Still cant find that skank darla!!!!

· · ·

Bex dropped her backpack in her closet when she got home from school. She glanced at it sitting there in the half dark among her shoes and new cleats. Even though the stupid postcard was buried inside under her books, her gym clothes, and a few notes from Chelsea and Laney, it still seemed menacing. Taunting.

She was pulling the closet door shut when Denise knocked on the door frame. "Hey, Bex," she said. "Can I come in?"

"Yeah." Bex dropped into her desk chair while Denise took a spot on the bed. "You okay, hon? You seemed a little distracted on the drive home."

Bex bit her lip. "Oh, yeah. It's nothing. Just tired."

"You know you can talk to me or Michael about anything, right?"

"Oh, yeah. Of course. Thanks."

There was a slow pause. Then, "So, do you have any plans for tonight?"

"Well, Laney and Trevor and them are going to have a bonfire. Someplace called Corolla Beach?" She couldn't stop herself from shooting a glance toward the closet, toward the postcard. "But I don't think I'm going. I'm kind of tired."

"Oh no! You should totally go! Corolla Beach is beautiful!"

"It'll be dark," Bex said, laughing.

"The beach is beautiful at night. And high school bonfires are a tradition. But"—Denise held up her hands—"it's totally up to you."

"What's going on in here?" Michael poked his head through Bex's open door, eyes narrowed as he feigned a suspicious glare.

"I am just telling our daughter that bonfires at Corolla Beach are a high school tradition."

"Aw, we used to bonfire on the beach too! Bunch of guys, bunch of girls, bunch of blankets…" His voice trailed off and then he shook his head emphatically. "No. No bonfires on the beach. Bonfires, blankets, bad. You know what's fun? Hanging out with your parents and a gluten-free pizza. So fun. Right, Denise?"

"Don't worry, Michael. Bex wasn't going to go anyway."

"Well, I don't know," Bex said, starting to smile. "You've suddenly made beach bonfires sound very appealing."

Michael moved to protest, and Denise put a hand on his arm. "What if she promises to avoid blankets?"

• • •

The drive to Corolla Beach took nearly forty-five minutes and Bex, Laney, and Chelsea laughed the entire way. Trevor and his friends had left ahead of them, tasked with finding wood and building the bonfire. As Laney navigated the last few winding miles toward the beach, Chelsea turned down the radio and leaned over the backseat.

"Okay, Bex. We have to tell you something about Corolla Beach."

"Let me guess. It's not really a beach? Or, wait, it's a nude beach?" She waggled her eyebrows but sincerely hoped that wasn't the case.

"No." Laney laughed from the driver's seat. "And, Chelsea, way to make it sound so ominous. It's not that big of a deal."

Chelsea gaped. "It's totally a big deal. Someone *died* there."

Bex felt the smile drop from her lips, her blood running cold. "What are you talking about? What do you mean?"

"A girl drowned there when we were freshman."

Bex could finally breathe again—not that drowning made anything better, but it wasn't murder. It wasn't anything like what her father had done.

Allegedly. The voice, nearly a breathless whisper, was at the back of her mind again. She clenched her teeth against the unwanted intrusion. *Innocent men don't run,* Bex's mind ticked. She tried to push her father and his crimes—alleged or otherwise—out of her thoughts.

"That's awful," Bex said.

"Yeah. And someone tried to murder a young couple there last summer."

Bex bit her lip. "And we're going there, why?"

"Oh"—Chelsea spun back to sit forward in her seat—"that guy got caught. Or died. Or something. It's not like he's still out there lurrrrrking in the night, looking for his next kill." She pounced on Laney, who screamed and swerved the car, its headlights cutting yellow streaks over the dunes and beach grass.

"Chels!" Laney caught Bex's eye in the rearview mirror. "And by the way, she's totally lying."

"I am not," Chelsea whined, turning her attention back to Bex. "They say the guy who murdered the young couple had a hook for a hand."

Bex giggled, then heard the tires spin over the sand, trying to gain traction. The girls all jerked when it finally did, the car righting itself on the road with a clunk.

"Why are you trying to kill us?" Laney asked, trying to maintain her anger over her laughter.

But Chelsea wasn't listening.

She was leaning forward in her seat, hands flat on the dashboard. "Aim that way again," she said, pointing toward the area where they were nearly beached.

"Why?" Bex asked, picking up the towels and chips that had flopped off the seat when the car lurched.

"I thought I saw something."

Laney slowed the car but didn't stop. "What are you talking about? What did you see?"

Chelsea blew out a sharp sigh. "If I knew what it was, I wouldn't have asked you to light it up, now would I?"

Heat began to prick on Bex's ears. "You guys, this is a little too horror movie for me," she said with a nervous giggle. "Can we just get to the beach?"

Chelsea spun to face her. "You just want to get your freak on with Trevor. Like we haven't noticed him puppy dogging you all week. Turn around, Lane, just for two seconds."

"It's probably nothing," Laney said, turning anyway.

"Could be pirate treasure. Give me the booty!" Chelsea screamed in the worst pirate accent Bex had ever heard. "See? There!" She bounced on the seat as she pointed.

Laney and Bex leaned forward, squinting. "Oh my God, someone's out there."

Bex cocked her head. "Is it two people? Are they having sex?"

Laney stopped the car and slammed on the horn, the headlights fully illuminating a pair of bare feet in the sand. She honked two more times, and Bex's stomach started to fall as a memory nibbled at her periphery.

It was a pretrial hearing in one of those cavernous courtrooms that was supposed to be closed to the public. But it was packed nonetheless.

"Counselor," one of the attorneys—Beth Anne couldn't keep their names straight—raised his hand as he stood. She remembered thinking how strange it was that a grown man, a grown man in a suit even, still had to raise his hand when he wanted to speak. "I'd like to request that the defendant's daughter be excused before viewing the crime scene photographs. She's only a child—"

"No!" A stocky man from the prosecution's side of the room jumped up. "She should have to sit here and see what her father done! What he done to my little girl!"

The judge slammed his gavel hard and yelled something. The courtroom started to murmur and Beth Anne heard it again: "She's just a little girl! She had nothing to do with anything!"

Kasey, the advocate assigned to her by the court, wiggled through the crowd and held her hand out. Someone pushed Beth Anne forward, her hand finding Kasey's—but not soon enough. There was already a photo on the screen: the soles of two bare feet, blotched and purpling, peeking out from underneath a blood-speckled sheet. A little, yellow tented number was placed next to them, the words VIC: HAYLEY DAVISON, 19; EXH 1 *printed in black Sharpie across it.*

Chelsea and Laney kicked open their car doors, but Bex wanted to stop them. She wanted to scream at them to get back inside, to start the car and go to Corolla Beach, but she couldn't move. Everything fell into silent slow motion. The sand kicking up behind Chelsea's flip-flops. Laney's hair fanning out behind her as she beckoned for Bex.

Woodenly, Bex pushed the seat forward and slipped out of Laney's door. She heard nothing as she stepped onto the sand, still warm from the sun. Laney and Chelsea had turned back by then, their mouths open, their faces tortured. Chelsea was yelling at Bex, pointing at the phone in her hand. Bex didn't react, and Chelsea finally snatched it from her. Laney's face was red, mascara running down her cheeks with the tears.

Bex stopped, the bare feet mere inches from her own.

They belonged to a woman—no, a teenager—lying facedown in the sand. Her hair was spread in a graceful blond halo, the edges disappearing into a clump of sea grass. Her head was turned, lips blue and slightly parted, eyes open as though she were staring down the beach. Her right arm was laid gently at her side, fingers curling over her palm. Her left arm was arched over her head, her fingers half-buried in the sand. Bex didn't need to see them to know that the ring finger was missing, because that was his calling card.

The Wife Collector.

Her father.

Daddy's home.

SEVEN

No, Bex thought.

It couldn't be. Her father had been gone—on the run—for ten years now. The murders had stopped.

But what if he's started up again? the tiny voice in the back of her head asked.

"No." She shook her head. "No." She didn't realize that she had said it out loud until Laney turned to her. She was trembling.

"Darla," Laney murmured, her index finger shaking as she tried to point. "It's Darla."

Bex didn't know how long it took for the police to come. The three girls waited in Laney's car, the silence deafening until Chelsea said, "I've never seen a dead body before."

Neither had Bex, in person.

"Not a body," Laney said, her voice a breathy whisper. "Darla."

The police came in a flood of red and blue lights. No sirens, just lights that bled across the sand, lending the evening an even more morose and eerie feeling. When the police got out of their squad cars, it was like the clock started again—radios cackling, the steady hum of cars continuing to arrive, waves crashing in the near distance. Everything was happening.

"Bex!"

Bex snapped to the voice, and Trevor launched himself from the driver's seat of his car, cutting through the sea grass toward her. One of the officers stepped in front of him.

"We're going to need you to stay back, son."

"But they're my friends," Trevor said, his hands falling listlessly at his sides. "And that's my girlfriend."

Bex should have felt something—an exhilarated zing, a delicious anxiety, even a pop of irrational fear. She had eaten lunch with Trevor exactly five times and shared an ice cream cone and her history notes—and now he was calling her his *girlfriend*. She had always wanted to have a boyfriend, to be normal, one of the gang. Now that it had happened, all she could feel was numb. The bees were buzzing in her head, pricking hot spots down her spine.

This can't be happening. This can't be happening...

One of the cops—his name badge read Officer Kelty—shuffled the three girls away from Trevor and into the shadow of his black GMC.

"We're going to need to ask you ladies some questions." He jutted his chin toward Laney and Chelsea. "You two hang back right here for a second. I'm going to talk to..." He raised his eyebrows but Bex didn't say anything.

"Her name is Bex," Chelsea put in. "Bex Andrews."

That's not right, Bex thought. *That's not my name...*

As Officer Kelty gently steered her to a slightly more private area, she steeled herself, repeating that she was Bex Andrews and that what was happening now had nothing to do with her father. But still that little voice persisted.

"So, Bex, can you tell me why you and your friends were out here tonight?"

The temperature seemed to drop by ten degrees and a crisp wind sped across the dunes, picking up grains of sand and re-dispersing them. Bex zipped her hoodie up to her neck.

"Bonfire. We were going to have a bonfire."

Kelty nodded, his eyes never leaving the tiny notepad he wrote in. "And how was it that you came upon the body?"

Bex heard herself relating the story but her eyes were flitting over the police officer. He was young—twenty, twenty-five at best, and clean-shaven—and when he looked at her, he smiled, his eyes warm. He was nothing like the officers she had met before, the ones from her old life who took away her father. Those two stood out in her memory, hard and almost gray, with sinister smiles and gnarled, bony hands that reached for her to steal away everything that was important to her.

"I'm really sorry you had to see this," Officer Kelty was saying. "But if you remember anything else, even if it doesn't seem important, please call."

He handed Bex his card and then beckoned for Chelsea. Bex stared at his embossed name, at the gold, foil police star right next to it on the card. She had lied to a police officer. She said she was Bex Andrews.

I am Bex Andrews, she reminded herself. *I am.*

Behind her, Bex could hear the snapping of the crime scene photographer's camera. Each flash, each snap of the shutter sickened her more, and she felt the bitter salivation that starts before being sick. She pinched her eyes shut, trying to block out any memories.

"Bex!"

Her head snapped toward the voice. It was Trevor. Every other sound melted away, and all she could hear were his sneakers pounding the pavement as he came toward her. Was he going to accuse her now, call her a murderer, tell her it ran in her blood?

Sick. Twisted. A monster. A demon. The devil's spawn.

When she was Beth Anne Reimer, she had pretended the words didn't bother her because she could see the way they tore at her grandmother, pricking her skin and leaving tiny scars well after they'd gone.

"They're just angry, Beth Anne," Gran would tell her, her hand tightening around Beth Anne's. "They are blinded by their grief. 'Bless those who curse you.' They know not what they say."

But Beth Anne had seen the hatred in their eyes—so Bex steeled herself for the barrage from Trevor.

"Hold it, miss." Another officer stepped out from behind one of the parked cars, his hand splayed out, stop-sign fashion.

"This is a crime scene. You're going to have to come around this way, please."

It was then that Bex noticed the yellow "Crime Scene" tape strung around the perimeter. She was inside the tape and Trevor was outside. The barrier seemed to have sprung up out of nowhere, a physical reminder that she could only move so far away from her old life. Normalcy would always be just beyond her reach.

Trevor's eyes shot from Bex to the officer. "But she's my friend. I just want to make sure she's okay."

The officer cut his eyes to Bex, who nodded. "Yeah, I'm okay."

"I can take you home."

Bex looked over her shoulder. Chelsea was talking to Officer Kelty, and Laney was leaning up against her car, her arms wrapped around herself, eyes glossy and unfocused as tears slid down her cheeks.

"Thanks, Trevor, but I think I'm going to stay here and ride back with Laney and Chelsea. They were good friends of Darla's." Her voice rose at the end of the sentence. She was assuming since she didn't know much about Darla's relationship with either Chelsea or Laney, except for the fact that she sat between them in ethics.

"Yeah." Trevor cleared his throat. "They were best friends. Um, I guess I'll just talk to you later."

He hugged her over the "Crime Scene" tape, and Bex was stunned. No yelling. No accusations. No god-awful names.

Because you're Bex Andrews now, the tiny voice inside chided.

Bex watched Trevor get back in his car and turn it around, his headlights casting a glow over the whole horrible scene. They also caught the edge of a car pulled off the road half a football field away. Someone was out there. Someone was watching. Bex started when she saw the glint of a tiny, red light in the blanket of blackness.

Like the red light on a video camera when it was recording.

* * *

The sunlight streamed over Bex and she rolled over, loving the soft warmth on her face. It took her a full minute to remember what had happened the previous night, and when she did, her blood ran cold and goose bumps shot up on her flesh.

"Bex!" Denise called from downstairs. "Wake up, sleepyhead! We've got pancakes!"

"And I didn't cook them," Michael joined in. "So they're good!"

She kicked off the covers and trudged downstairs, the sweet scent of maple syrup meeting her halfway down.

"Hey, sweetheart. How was the bonfire?"

Suddenly the smell of syrup was overwhelming, the heat from the griddle suffocating. Bex shook her head, trying to swallow the lump in her throat. "It was awful," she managed, surprised at the tears that started to fall. "Awful."

"Oh, honey!" Denise gathered her up in a one-armed, one-spatula hug.

"Was it the boys? Did they do something?"

She could see Michael sitting rigid in his chair, his coffee mug in midair, knuckles white on the handle.

"No, no, nothing like that." Bex sniffled. "It was—" She turned, pointing to the news on the muted TV. "It was that."

"*Authorities aren't saying much about the body found last night off Corolla, except to say it is that of a young woman, probably in her late teens to early twenties. There has been no comment on whether this young woman has any connection to Erin Malone, found just over a week ago, and police won't confirm if this latest victim's death will also be classified as a homicide. What we do know is that the body*"

TWISTED

was found by three Kill Devil Hills area teens who, we understand, are not suspects."

The news anchor was in a little square at the corner of the screen while footage of the previous night rolled in front of Bex's eyes. She saw the clumps of sea grass, the fluttering, yellow "Crime Scene" tape, Officer Kelty, and the assembled police units.

"Oh my God, Bex, were you and the girls the ones who found her?" Denise stepped back but kept her arms around Bex.

"Yeah."

Michael pulled out a chair and gestured for her to sit. "Oh, honey. I can't imagine how hard that must have been for you." He reached out and squeezed her hand. "You must have been so scared. Why didn't you call us to come get you? Or at least wake us up when you came in?"

Bex wagged her head mutely, but everything inside her wanted to spill, to finally confide the secrets she had been carrying ever since she could remember. She wanted to tell Michael and Denise that the dead girl wasn't a woman but a teen like herself—a teen from her high school who her new friends knew. She wanted to tell them that she wasn't scared of the body; she wasn't scared about what had happened—she was scared about what it meant.

They continued to watch the news, Bex rapt but dismissing every word. She was sifting for a few in particular, the few that would confirm her wildest fear: a missing ring finger. The anchorwoman droned on, flashing back to cases in other years and in other states where teens had been found, adding a few details here and there: the

55

body was unclothed, no confirmed method of death but rumors of asphyxiation and possible sexual assault.

Finally, the channel moved to a story about a platoon of local vets coming home, and Bex let out the breath she didn't know she had been holding. There was no mention of a missing ring finger. It was the best she could hope for, she reasoned.

EIGHT

After breakfast, Bex went to her room and stretched out on her unmade bed, staring blankly at the ceiling and letting the hum of the bees in her head block out any rational thought. Denise and Michael took turns checking on her every hour or so. Stepping in and wringing her hands, Denise urged Bex to talk or eat. Michael popped his head in and cleared his throat, opening his mouth and shutting it again, then finally blurting out something innocuous like, "Can I get you anything?"

It hurt Bex to see them so worried about her. It was a strange, uncomfortable feeling and she had a hard time not remembering her grandmother, the way her hand tightened over Bex's, the papery feel of Gran's thin skin against her own fingers. She had only had her mother's mother, Gran. Her father's biological mother had left when her daddy was just six years old. After that, according to him, his dad had a series of wifely stand-ins. Flitty blonds and brunettes who burned toast, resented their new beau's boy, and eventually ran off when the next fleet of truckers hit town.

Bex had met Pa Reimer once and had no question why he ran women off. He had all the charm of a taxidermied snake and was only half as warm. There weren't any pictures of Grandma Reimer—not even one. Her daddy said that was because she didn't stay around long enough for "the film to develop," but Gran said he had burned them all. She had seen one though, and Grandma Reimer then—young, with a wide, openmouthed smile—looked like a teenager with crooked teeth and her blond hair in pigtails. She looked a little like the waitress from the Black Bear Diner. The one who had curled her phone number into Bex's daddy's palm. The one the media called Victim #4.

The image of Darla—a cute blond who, from her pictures, had the same easy smile and young-bride looks that her father seemed to favor—flashed in Bex's mind again, and she felt the bile itching the back of her throat. She ran to the bathroom and retched, her palms burning against the cool porcelain. When nothing came up, she flopped back onto her bed, the sweat growing cold on her forehead.

Bex must have dozed off because when she opened her eyes, graying twilight had replaced the sun, chilly air ruffling the curtains on her open windows. A Post-it note was stuck to her lampshade: *M went to pick up a pizza. I'm out in the yard.—D*

She plucked the note off the shade, stretched, wandered down the stairs, and pulled open the front door.

"Hey." Denise called from the kitchen. She dropped her shoes at the back door and closed the distance between them. "You're up."

Bex started. "I was about to go looking for you."

Denise wiped her brow, leaving a smudge of brown-black dirt on her cheek. "I was working out back. How do you feel about rock gardens? It's become increasingly obvious that plants aren't my thing. Everything is dead."

Bex swallowed and Denise looked pained, springing forward. "Oh, honey, I'm sorry. I shouldn't have said that."

Bex batted at the air. "No, it's okay." She went to close the door she was still holding open, then paused.

A tiny, gift-wrapped box sat on the doormat outside. She pointed. "What's that?"

Denise came to look over her shoulder. "No idea. Pick it up."

"Is this some kind of feel-better gift from you and Michael or something? Because I appreciate it but—"

Denise stepped around Bex and stooped, picking up the box herself. "No. Is that what we're supposed to do?" She looked worried. "I read online that we're supposed to create a place of openness and comfort for you, and possibly explain our feelings about death to create an open dialogue. Michael thought we should get you a kitten."

"No." Bex held up her hands. "I don't need any of those things. At least not a gift or a kitten. And you guys have already made me feel comfortable." She offered a small smile.

Michael drove up and parked in the driveway, appearing on the front walk with a pizza box raised over his head. He looked from Bex to Denise, slight confusion in his eyes.

"What's going on?"

"Nothing. There was just this"—Denise held up the box—"on

the front porch. Oh…" She plucked out a tiny, white envelope that had been tucked under the bow. "It says 'Bex.'"

Michael frowned. "Were we supposed—"

"No." Denise tried to hand Bex the box, but she just stared at it, at the curlicues on the wrapping paper, the ends of the ribbon spilling over the box.

"Here."

"I don't… Who's it from?" Bex wanted to know.

"There is a card," Michael told her. "You should read it. But can we move this little shindig inside? Pizza is getting cold."

Bex followed them into the kitchen, sliding her finger under the flap of the envelope. "There's nothing inside."

"No card?"

Bex shrugged, turning over the envelope as proof. "Nothing."

"Open the box," Michael urged.

Bex did as she was told, the wrapping paper uncovering a smooth, white jewelry box. She pulled open the top and her breath caught. Nestled on a cloud of cotton was a dainty silver necklace with a tiny open heart hanging from it.

"That's beautiful!" Denise murmured. "Honey, don't you think that's beautiful?"

Michael looked up from the pizza slice that was halfway to his mouth. He nodded and offered some pizza-garbled approximation of the word "beautiful."

"Put it on!" Denise clapped. "Here"—she turned Bex around—"I'll do it for you. Oh! It's so nice on you!"

Bex glanced at her reflection in the hall mirror, her fingers going to the silver heart charm. It had weight to it and hung perfectly, the silver standing out prettily against her new beachy sun-kissed skin.

"I wonder who gave it to me."

Denise dropped a pile of napkins on the table and handed Bex three plates. "Didn't you talk about a guy?"

Heat flushed Bex's cheeks.

"He's not, like, my boyfriend or anything really. He's just a guy."

She thought of the haunted look on Trevor's face as he came running toward her. He was calling *her* name. Not Chelsea's or Laney's—hers. He'd called her his girlfriend. She blushed again. "We hardly know each other. Why would he leave me a necklace? We haven't even gone on an actual date yet!"

Michael's eyebrows went up. "We're dating now?"

Denise gave him a playful slap on the arm. "She's seventeen, Michael. She can date."

He narrowed his eyes playfully but with a hint of seriousness. "We can talk about it."

Bex could only stomach one slice of pizza before bounding up to her room and checking herself out in the mirror. The necklace really was pretty, hanging at the perfect height and somehow making her look more sophisticated, more polished. She grabbed her cell phone and flopped on her belly on her bed, dialing. She had never called Trevor before—she hadn't called any boy before—and her stomach was a riotous mess. Her heart was pounding and her ears were hot; the single slice of pizza sat like a rock in the pit of stomach, and every muscle seemed to be vibrating.

She hit the Send button.

The phone rang, and Bex was sure she was going to vomit. By the third ring she thought her heart would bound out of her throat. She was starting to hang up when she heard Trevor's voice.

"Bex?"

Her voice was trapped in her throat.

"Be-e-x?" Trevor strung out her name. "Did you just butt dial me?" His voice was jovial, and that calmed Bex down the smallest bit.

"Hey… No. Hi… Hi, Trevor. It's me, Bex."

He laughed and the heat raced from her ears, prickling all over her body. *Is he laughing at me?*

"I kind of figured it was you by the caller ID. That's why I said your name."

She let out a long whoosh of air. "Oh, right. Yeah—that was dumb."

"So, what's up?"

Bex found the pendant and rubbed the little heart behind her fingers, loving the smooth feel of the polished silver. "I was just calling to thank you."

There was a short pause, then Trevor's puzzled voice. "For what?"

"The necklace! I got it. It's really beautiful. But why didn't you just ring the doorbell?"

"What? I didn't give you a necklace."

"The package you left on my doorstep. The silver necklace."

She could hear Trevor shift on his end of the phone. "Bex, I didn't leave you a package. I don't even know where you live."

The call dropped.

NINE

Denise slowed in front of the high school on Monday morning, Bex's eyes widening as she leaned forward, taking in the U-shaped drive that was now bumper-to-bumper cop cars. Her stomach fluttered but she sucked in a deep breath when Denise patted her shoulder.

"Are you going to be okay with this, hon?"

Bex licked her parched lips, not taking her eyes off the squad cars. "What do you think they want?"

Denise shrugged. "They might be asking questions, or maybe they're here to answer them. Look, Bex, I know you didn't know Darla, but if you want to stay home, I understand. All of this"— she waved her hands, and Bex wasn't sure if Denise meant the cop cars or the events of the last two days or life in general—"is a lot to take in."

Bex briefly considered going back home and tucking herself underneath her cheery mint-green comforter, then spending the day with Denise doing mom things—which were what, exactly? Bex didn't know. The offer was almost tempting but at home, tucked in the drawer of her nightstand, was the white box with the silver heart necklace set neatly inside. It had taunted her all night—*A kind offering? Some kind of joke?*—and Bex didn't want to be near it.

"No thanks, Denise." She steeled herself and forced a smile that, when she caught her reflection in the rearview mirror, looked more like a bared-teeth grimace. "I'll be okay."

The vibe on campus was somber. Everyone seemed to move in slow motion. Where there were usually groups of chattering, joking teens, there were red-eyed mourners walking aimlessly and clutching the straps of their backpacks. Bex saw Trevor walking in from the student lot and detoured directly into the girls' locker room, her heart thundering in her throat, her shoulders pressed against the cold brick wall. She didn't want to see him, didn't want to see the "Are you crazy?" look on his face after last night's phone call.

"I heard Laney and Chelsea *found* her," came a rough whisper from between the lockers.

White-hot heat started at the base of Bex's spine.

"They practically stepped on her," another female voice added. "They were with that new girl too. Beth or Rec or something."

Bex's heart thundered in her ears and she held her breath, straining to hear. *Were they going to accuse her?*

"I heard poor Darla had actually been missing for a week. No one even went looking for her."

Tears pricked at the base of Bex's lashes.

"It's so sad. And now there's some crazy psychopath on the loose."

Bex was breathing hard, teeth gritted, trying to block out the images that came at her full speed. They were newspaper headlines,

TWISTED

television snippets from another time, another world that wouldn't leave her alone no matter how far away she was.

"...Isabel Doctoro had been missing for more than fourteen days before her body was found..."

"...need to find this psychopath..."

"No one knew to look for her."

"Hello? Hell-ooh?"

Bex snapped out of her daymare and blinked at the two girls standing in front of her. They were both decked out in black-and-red Kill Devil Hills basketball sweats, with their long hair pulled back into slick ponytails topped with black-and-red hair bows. They were school spirit through and through, right up to their made-up lips, now tugged down into deep frowns.

"Were you listening to our conversation?"

"N-no," Bex stammered. "I-I just walked in."

The girl who hadn't spoken—the one with the glossy, black hair and blue eyes that took up half her face—stepped in front of her friend, scrutinizing Bex. "Hey, aren't you the new girl?"

Bex nodded, suddenly mute.

"You were with Chelsea and Laney when they found Darla."

Again, Bex's heart started to thud. Her stomach folded in on itself and she briefly glanced toward the bank of bathroom stalls to her left, wondering if she would make it there before vomiting.

"What was it like?" The dark-haired girl's lips quirked up just the tiniest bit, her expression a macabre mix of interest and sheer fascination.

Bex shook her head, unable to form the words as images

bombarded her—images that no child, no one at all, should have to see: graying faces, unseeing eyes; the photographs of bodies strewn across an overhead projector; beautiful girls, alive and vibrant on one side, their desperate, empty shells on the other, supposedly carved by her father's hand.

"He was a butcher…"

"An animal…"

"These young women were nothing but things to him, things to take and use and ruin and then discard like so much trash…"

She saw Darla's toes, half-buried in the sand.

The girls were still staring at Bex, the dark-haired one practically leering, leaning in to her. Bex stepped between them, silent, and pushed open the doors of the locker room, letting the warm, outside air wash over her cheeks.

She didn't realize she was crying.

• • •

No one had followed her, but Bex couldn't shake the image of Darla or of the girls pressing into her in the locker room, sucking her air, wanting Bex to tell them what she knew.

The thought made her stomach lurch.

When she saw Chelsea and Laney coming out of their classroom up ahead, she cut down the nearest hall. She didn't want to talk to them.

"Are you waiting to see someone?"

"What?" Bex blinked and noticed the woman in the hall.

She was standing in front of Bex, smiling lightly and holding a clipboard to her chest. She was dressed in a nondescript navy-blue pantsuit, her graying hair pulled back in a severe bun.

"Did you want to see one of the grief counselors? You don't have to sign in. It can be completely anonymous."

Bex glanced through the windows, her eyes scanning the library. It was slightly dim and seemed blessedly quiet, an easy escape from people asking her questions.

"Do I have to talk?"

"No." The woman shook her head. "You don't have to talk about the event."

Bex briefly wondered when they stopped calling it a murder and started calling it an "event."

"You can just take some quiet time in the library if you feel that's what you need."

Bex nodded, stepping inside. Another woman, this one slightly taller and without a clipboard, made a beeline for her.

"Hi, I'm Renee. Can I help you?"

Bex opened her mouth but her tongue felt weighted.

"Why don't you come over here and sit? We can chat awhile."

Renee led Bex to a tiny office and began chattering in calm, soothing tones as she poured Bex a glass of water and sat down across from her.

"How are you doing today?"

Bex was silent for a beat. "I didn't know her."

She knew that Renee was trying not to look judgmental or surprised, but her eyebrows rose.

"Are you talking about Darla?"

"I didn't know her. I..." Bex's fingers found the straps of her backpack, and she worked the thick, woven material back and forth. "I'm new here."

Renee sat back in her chair. "You didn't have to know her to be upset. It's okay to have a lot of feelings. The circumstances are tragic and rather terrifying."

"Circumstances?" Bex looked up.

"You know that Darla was murdered."

Her blond hair was fanned out on the sand, a few strands bouncing up on the wisp of ocean breeze.

"I know."

"We don't know exactly what happened to her yet, but someone out there does. Do you want to talk about that? Is the uncertainty bothering you?"

Bex blinked. "Are you a real doctor?"

Renee seemed slightly taken aback. "I assure you, I'm qualified to help. And yes, I'm a real doctor. I'm a psychiatrist, which means I have my MD."

Bex licked her lips, which suddenly seemed Sahara dry and cracked. "So you know about mental…diseases."

Renee seemed to reset her professional smile. "What can I help you with?"

"The person who"—again, Bex couldn't say the word—"hurt Darla. He…he had to be crazy, right? Sick?"

"Well, there are a lot of reasons people kill, and yes, mental disease can be one of them. Psychopaths do exist."

"Is that…" Bex shifted in her chair but kept her eyes on Renee's shoulder. "Is psychopath—psycho—"

"Psychopathy."

"I mean, you don't catch it. The psychopathy. Either you are or you aren't, right? It's just in you?"

Renee nodded carefully and Bex was spurred on.

"Is it hereditary? Can it be passed along?"

Renee cleared her throat. "Well, some psychiatric diseases are, in fact, inherited, but that doesn't mean that if someone did something while suffering a—we call them breaks, psychotic breaks—if someone did something during a psychotic break, that doesn't mean you would do the same thing, even if you inherited the same psychopathy."

Bex lost her breath. "Not me. I didn't do anything."

"I'm sorry. I didn't mean you... What's your name? I didn't mean you in particular. I meant the global"—she made air quotes—"you."

Bex could feel her temperature ratcheting up, could feel pressure at her temples. Her saliva soured in her mouth. "But it's possible."

"Theoretically. Are you worried about something, honey?"

Bex stood quickly and slung her backpack over one shoulder. "No, no, I'm fine, thanks."

Renee stood too. "We can continue to talk. Are there other questions you have?"

"No, I'm good."

Renee may have still been talking, but Bex didn't hear. Her blood was pulsing with Renee's answer, with the possibility that if her father was a psychopath, there was a chance that Bex was one too. She walked straight through the library, eyes focused directly ahead, not stopping when she saw Zach at the door to Renee's office, not thinking about the shocked look on his face.

TEN

"Hey, Bex!"

She had gotten through her morning classes without seeing Chelsea, Laney, or Trevor, doing her best to blend into the swarm of kids moving from class to class. Anytime anyone looked at her with the somber look of grief, Bex flinched, guilt welling up inside her.

She remembered Dr. Gold, the court-appointed shrink they made her see after her father disappeared and her gran took custody of her. Dr. Gold had watched Beth Anne for a long time, the two sitting in companionable silence while the woman fingered the tiny, silver bird that hung from a chain around her wrist. It had jeweled pink eyes, and Beth Anne couldn't help herself. She reached out to touch the tiny head of the bird, and the doctor smiled.

"It's a finch," the doctor said.

Beth Anne said nothing, playing the smooth body of the bird against her fingertips. "The eyes are tourmalines."

Beth Anne still wouldn't speak, not at first, but every session started the same: Dr. Gold unclasping the bracelet and re-clasping it on Beth Anne's arm without a word. Beth Anne would color, letting the silver bird glide over her paper.

Bex remembered the soothing sound of the doctor's voice as Beth Anne colored one day in her office—long strokes of purple bleeding into blue, bleeding into yellow, into pink—a rainbow. Dr. Gold prattled on about all sorts of things: her daughter was only two, but she was already a handful; her husband was forever thinking he could fix things that he couldn't. Week after week, Dr. Gold spoke and Beth Anne colored silently, learning to relax into the rise and fall of the doctor's kind voice. And then, one day, Dr. Gold laid her hand on Beth Anne's arm.

"It's not your fault, Beth Anne. None of it."

Beth Anne had a crayon in her fist—red, glaring, and angry, the heat from her hand making the wax weaken in her grip.

"They don't blame you."

She eyed the crayon and smelled the scent of the wax. It didn't smell red; it smelled like a crayon. All crayons smelled the same.

"He didn't do this because of you."

When Beth Anne held the point of the crayon against the paper, the point flattened.

"He gave you things because he loved you—not because you were a part of this."

A red tail arced from the plane of the crayon. Bright, bloodred.

"This wasn't about you."

Beth Anne put the crayon down carefully and turned, her eyes fixed on Dr. Gold's.

"Yes it was," she said.

Dr. Gold gave Beth Anne a humorless smile. "Why don't you tell me why you think this was your fault?"

Beth Anne's hand went over the crayons all lined up at the edge of her paper and selected a blue one, pressing it hard so the color was dark, dark.

"Beth Anne?"

Her name was Isabel Doctoro, and she had been sleeping in Beth Anne's father's room for three nights. She had a big, soft leather purse that she threw on the couch before she'd disappear with Beth Anne's dad, and once the bedroom door shut, Beth Anne would rifle through the bag, through Isabel's world. Inside, there was lipstick the color of cherries. A frosted-glass, finger-sized vial with a roller ball on the end that Beth Anne pressed against her skin, breathing in the oily, lavender-laced scent it left behind. A compact with a broken mirror. And a scrollwork bracelet with a hunk of real turquoise.

Beth Anne slipped on the bracelet and promptly forgot about it until that night at dinner. The three of them were eating pizza straight from the box when Isabel grabbed Beth Anne's arm with her clawlike fingernails.

"Where'd you get that bracelet?"

Beth Anne glanced at her wrist, feeling the heat burning on her cheeks.

"That's mine, isn't it? You took it from my purse!"

"Now, now," Beth Anne's father said, trying to calm Isabel.

"No, Jackson, that was in my purse. It's mine. She stole it from my purse!"

Through lowered lashes, Beth Anne watched her father's gaze rake over her. "Did you take that bracelet, Bethy?"

Beth Anne wagged her head from side to side, still studying her pizza slice.

"She's lying! She's lying! She's out-and-out lying, Jackson. You've got to punish her!"

Isabel snatched the bracelet from Beth Anne's wrist and pinched her cheeks with one hand, making Beth Anne's lips pucker. "Your daddy's gonna teach you that it's not right to steal." She slapped the bracelet on her own bony wrist, and Beth Anne thought the richness of the stone made Isabel's yellow-hued skin look that much more sallow.

"Go to your room, Bethy." Her daddy's voice was even, relaxed.

Isabel didn't spend the night that time. When Beth Anne woke up the following morning, Isabel was still gone, but the bracelet was sitting in the center of the kitchen table.

It took fourteen days for the police to find Isabel Doctoro's body.

"Bex!" Trevor was moving toward her at a dizzying speed. "I've been looking all over for you." He squeezed her arm, then pulled her into a hug.

Bex stiffened. The feeling of Trevor's warm, muscled body pressed up against hers was both intimate and weird.

"Hey"—he didn't let her go, his mouth a hairbreadth from her ear—"it's okay. I'm here." He squeezed her a little tighter and Bex felt herself melt into him, exhaustion crashing over her in white waves. She wasn't sure how long they stayed like that, if it was a minute or hours, but however long it was, it felt too short.

"I'm so sorry. Jeez…" He looked away and raked a hand through his hair. "I feel like I'm kind of responsible."

Heat ricocheted through Bex, exploding like gunfire in her ears. "W-what?"

"I don't know. I feel like…" Trevor looked down at his feet, the tops of his ears flushing a fierce red. "I feel like I should protect you. Like, I don't want you to have to experience anything bad."

Bex was frozen, rooted to her spot in the hall.

"I know that's stupid, but"—Trevor looked up at her, his eyes finding hers and pinning her there—"I really like you, Bex."

She blinked at the small smile that played on his lips, every synapse in her brain firing simultaneously, random triggers flailing: *He likes me! Run! It's a trick. It's a joke. I like him. Someone actually likes me! A boy, a boy likes me! He's lying. Everyone's lying.*

Something overrode the wild clatter in her brain and Bex's lips were moving, sound coming out. "I like you too, Trevor." Heat grazed the back of her neck, and her palms started to sweat in that millisecond between her answer and his response. Her stomach started to lurch, then flutter.

"So, we like each other then," Trevor said, a wide smile pushing up his red-apple cheeks.

The bell cut through Bex's response while Trevor's hand found hers, his fingers intertwining with hers.

There were grief counselors in all the afternoon classes. Bex saw Renee slip into the class across the hall from hers and shrunk back in her seat, hoping that the doctor wouldn't turn around and see her, wouldn't announce that she had talked to Bex about the heredity of mental illness.

At half past the hour, all the classes filed into the cafeteria ten minutes early for lunch. A long line of adults stood behind a podium, all with somber faces and wearing every shade of navy-blue pantsuit imaginable. Bex figured that black must have given off too dark a vibe so the official color of teen grief must be navy blue. She wasn't certain why skirts were off-limits and let her mind wander while the principal tapped a microphone and waited for the clattering of dishes and lunch bags and Starbucks cups to die down.

"If we can all just take a moment of silence," Principal Morse started.

Chelsea and Laney looked at each other and then at Bex, pulling her into a crushing embrace while they bowed their heads. Bex chanced a glance up and met Trevor's eyes. He was sitting across from her, staring. They both bowed their heads for one enveloping moment of pulsing silence, Bex staring at her kneecaps under the table and listening to the *thud-thud-thud* of her heart. She remembered a story that her only Raleigh friend, Mel, had told her about, something that Mel was reading in class. It was about a man who killed another man and was driven to admit it because he could still hear the dead man's heart beating—"The Tell-Tale Heart."

Bex hoped the heart she heard was her own.

When she looked up, she was met with Darla's pale-blue eyes staring down at her from a huge photograph projected on the cafeteria wall. The girl was smiling, head cocked, blond hair in corn-silk waves over one shoulder, but the smile didn't reach her eyes.

They were dull but accusing.

"Darla's dad took that picture. We were there. It was Corolla Beach last summer." Laney was whispering in Bex's ear, her chin jutting toward the picture of Darla. Bex was immediately pulled back to that North Carolina courtroom, to that twanged voice dripping with anger and hate: *"She should have to sit here and see what her daddy done. What he done to my little girl."*

"I have to go." Bex stood up and tried to extract herself from the table and the cafeteria as quickly and quietly as possible, keeping her eyes trained on the floor. But she knew they were all looking at her, wondering how she could so callously get up and walk out while the principal memorialized a dead girl.

A noose was tightening around her neck as Bex escaped the cafeteria and burst into the hall. It was hard to breathe, each thread of rope tightening against her throat. She pushed out into the commons, dropping to her knees and sucking in air, coughing, sputtering.

It wasn't him, she told herself. *There was absolutely no indication that Darla was killed by the Wife Collector.*

The jaunty image of the postcard emblazoned with the Research Triangle flashed in her mind.

Daddy's home.

Bex tried to shake out the image, the memories, the voices, but they crawled and picked at her like fire ants on her skin. She fished out her cell phone and with shaky fingers dialed a number she'd hoped never to have to dial again. It rang twice before a jaunty voice greeted her.

"Dr. Gold's office. This is Maria. How may I help you?"

Bex was silent for a minute, letting Maria's voice soak in.

"Hello?" Maria said again. "Dr. Gold's office?" Her voice rose at the end of the greeting.

"I'm sorry," Bex pushed out. "I'm sorry. I need to talk to Dr. Gold."

Maria paused on the other end of the line, and Bex could hear another line ringing in the office. "May I ask who's calling, please?"

Bex froze. *Beth Anne Reimer. Bex. Bex Andrews. That's who she was. That's who she was now.*

"Bex Andrews."

"Ms. Andrews, Dr. Gold isn't in at the moment. Were or are you a patient of hers? I can schedule you an appointment or take a message—"

Maria's pleasant, all-business voice was cut off when Bex hung up the phone.

• • •

Bex sat in the coffeehouse until the sky went from crystal blue to a low, muted gray, the sun beginning to set. She nursed a single cup of coffee, sipping slowly, refreshing it constantly so that each time the liquid burned her lips. The pain somehow satisfied her.

"Oh, oh thank God, there you are!" Denise rushed toward her and nearly toppled the chair, throwing her arms around Bex. She let Bex go, then looked her up and down, the relief in her face quickly dissolving to anger. "Bex, you scared the hell out of me and Michael."

Bex looked up at Denise and noticed Michael over her left shoulder. He put a hand on his wife's arm and muttered something in her ear. She shook him away. "No, Michael, she needs to know that she can't just run off." Denise looked down at Bex again. "Bex, the school called and said you missed your afternoon classes, and when I got to the school, no one knew where you were. You can't run off like that. You just can't."

Her voice wavered between anger and sadness, and Bex shrank back in her chair, unsure of what to do. "We must have called you thirty times. And your boyfriend said you ran out of the cafeteria at lunchtime. You didn't even tell him where you were going. Why, Bex?" Denise leaned on the table, palms pressed down, eyes blazing.

"Honey!" Michael pulled her back, and she crumpled in his arms. "We were incredibly worried about you, Bex."

"I'm sorry," Bex said. "I didn't—I didn't mean to frighten you."

Michael stroked his wife's hair as her shoulders rocked. "Come here." He stretched out an arm for Bex. When she dutifully went to him, he engulfed his wife and his daughter in one tremendous hug. "It's going to take some time for us all to get on the same page. Come on."

They filed out of the coffeehouse in a straight line, silently getting into Michael's car. Bex kept her eyes on her sneakers as he pulled out into traffic. Denise turned around in her seat. "I'm not mad. Well, actually I am. You can't walk out of school like that." She glanced at Michael's profile. "We understand that today was probably really hard for you, but you have to talk to us. You can't just act out, okay?"

Bex heard the words but couldn't process them. Didn't they know who she was, why this had happened?

No, because you're Bex Andrews now. Beth Anne stayed in Raleigh. The Wife Collector stayed in Raleigh. You're normal now. You have to be normal.

She cleared her throat and made the effort to look into

Denise's eyes. "I'm really sorry, you guys. I just—I kind of freaked out, I guess."

"We can dig that."

Both Bex and Denise shot Michael looks.

"What? I'm just trying to say that we understand. Man!"

Denise turned back to Bex. "We're not going to punish you this time, but skipping school is not okay and not letting us know where you are is definitely not okay. If you want to talk about this—about anything—we're here for you. Okay, Bex?"

Bex nodded.

"And if you don't think you can talk to us, there are always the grief counselors, or Michael or I can find you someone else for you to talk to."

Bex nodded again, the lump in her throat too big to allow her to speak.

Denise squeezed Bex's knee. "We love you, honey."

"I love you too." It was barely a whisper, but one of the truest things Bex had ever said.

ELEVEN

Bex slipped her cell phone out of her backpack when she got home. She had thirteen missed calls between Michael and Denise, plus missed calls from Trevor, Chelsea, and Laney. Then, there were the texts:

> Denise: Where are u?
>
> Trevor: U OK? U bolted.
>
> Chelsea: ????
>
> Laney: T tore out after U. TruLuv <3 <3 ;)
>
> Denise: Pls check in
>
> Trevor: W8D 4u

Bex deleted them all, her thumb hovering over the garbage-can icon when she got to the last text. There was no name attached to it, just a phone number: 919–555–0800.

Something dark and black hung on the edge of her periphery, weighing down her shoulders and slicing through her gut.

She remembered rolling the numbers on her Gran's old-fashioned rotary phone, her nine-year-old finger dipping into the hole over the number nine. She remembered swiping the wheel, the way it sounded as it clicked back into place. She poked her finger into the number-one slot, flicking the wheel a short half inch. Then back to nine again. She could see herself dialing the rest of the numbers, but she couldn't remember what they were. What she did remember was the fuzzy sound of the phone ringing against her ear, then the flat voice of the woman who answered: "North Carolina Central Court House. Holding department."

Bex glanced down at the number on her phone, at the little smiley "You have a new text!" bubble. She swiped it.

919–555–0800: Hello.

That was it.

Hello.

The numbers and the word blurred in front of her. The soft green of the chevron stripes on her comforter fell away, the mint-colored walls turning a deep, mossy green before they went gray as cinder blocks, like the walls of a cell. The message was innocuous. The number was terrifying. The area code, 919, was Raleigh.

Did he know? Does my father know who I am now? Where I am? He couldn't still be in Raleigh...

An involuntary and sudden lump formed in Bex's throat. Had her father been nearby her whole life but never bothered to contact her?

If he was in Raleigh, he couldn't have killed Darla...right?

Who...

Bex pinched her eyes closed, and in a moment of strength, she highlighted the number and hit Dial on her phone.

It rang.

Once, twice.

Her heart slammed against her ribs, the thuds as loud as Mel's story, as loud as "The Tell-Tale Heart."

Three, four.

Thud, thud.

Simultaneously, the chimes started on the phone and her heart stopped beating.

"Bex, hon, dinner's ready."

Denise was standing in the doorway, head cocked, wearing heavy shoes that had *thud-thud-thudded* up the stairs.

"You have reached a number that has been disconnected. If you think you have reached this number in error..."

Sick itched at the back of Bex's throat, and sweat stung as it dripped into her eyes.

"Oh, honey!" Denise was at her side, gathering her up and pressing a cool palm to Bex's forehead. "You look sick, and you're all warm and clammy. How do you feel?"

Denise pried the phone from Bex's hand and dropped it on the bed. Bex stared at the phone's lit-up face, her eyes drawn to the icon of the red telephone hanging up, text blaring out Call Dropped. Denise seemed to follow her gaze and picked up the phone. "I'm sorry. Cell service is so bad out here. Probably for the best." She slid the phone onto Bex's dresser. "You should just get some rest. I'll have Michael bring you up something to eat."

• • •

It was pitch-black in her room when Bex woke up. She was still dressed from school, her backpack on the floor where she had left it, her cell phone on the dresser where Denise had set it. There was a half-empty bowl of chicken noodle soup on the nightstand, and Bex's head was pounding like a like a bass drum. She pulled the ponytail holder from her hair and massaged the throbbing spot on her head, lost in the dark haze of just waking up. It took her a second to remember what had happened, for the day to come crashing back on her.

She grabbed her phone, nestled deep in bed, and texted her friends, thinking a blanket text would be the least painful.

Bex: Srry I bailed, guyz. Sick. Barf. Gross.

Chelsea texted back immediately.

Chelsea: Nice 1, barf breath. T'll B all over that!

Bex rolled her eyes but checked her phone, hoping that Trevor wouldn't respond with anything that referenced her barf breath. Chelsea pinged again.

Chelsea: Y u up?

Bex glanced at the clock.

Bex: 2am?! LOL Just woke up. U?

Chelsea: Cnt sleep

Bex: Y?

Chelsea: Thnkin. Darla. No1 missed her 4 a
week.

Bex: U did. U called everyday.

Chelsea: Didn't do anything tho. Her parents
didn't kno she was missing. Scary. Do u think
ur parents miss u?

Bex paused, about to respond, when another text from Chelsea broke through.

Chelsea: I mean ur real parents.

The breath caught in Bex's throat and she felt her lungs collapsing, constricting. *What did Chelsea know?* Her eyes were watering, and she could hear the sad wheezing as she clawed at her chest and tried to breathe.

The Wife Collector.

Her father.

Do U think ur parents miss you?

Her mother.

What did Chelsea know?

The scream was out of her mouth before she knew it.

"Bex, Bex!" Michael flicked on the light and Bex cringed from it, the brightness burning her retinas. He and Denise flew to her bedside, eyes wide, concerned.

"Relax! Relax, look at me." Denise kneeled in front of her, her hands on Bex's, squeezing. "Keep your eyes focused on me. Try to breathe slowly."

Bex felt as if she were breathing through a pinhole. The tears were streaming down her face and her lungs screamed, sending a searing heat up the back of her throat.

I'm going to die I'm going to die I'm going to die.

An image burned in front of her eyes—another headline, another victim:

Amanda Perkins: Wife Collector's 6th Victim?

Bex was seven when she learned the word "asphyxiated."

Hands on her throat. Her windpipe narrowing, closing. The searing heat, the struggle to breathe, to live.

This is what it feels like. This is what it felt like for Amanda Perkins.

Bex's lungs swelled with air and she sputtered, coughed. Denise and Michael were staring at her anxiously, Denise on her knees, still holding Bex's hands.

"What happened?" Bex squeaked, her throat feeling raw and dry.

"Michael, get Bex some water." Denise focused on Bex. "I think you may have had an asthma attack. Do you have asthma, Bex?"

Michael returned with the glass, and Bex sucked down every last drop before shaking her head. "No, not that I know of.

That's never happened to me before. I mean, not that I can remember."

"It wasn't listed in any of the medical reports, was it, hon?" Michael asked and Denise shook her head.

"I don't think so."

Nausea rolled through Bex's stomach. "You have my medical records?"

A smile quirked the edges of Denise's lips. "Of course we do, honey. Your caseworker sent them over before you arrived so we could enroll you in school. We needed your vaccination records and all that, because we wanted to be sure that you'd have everything you needed once you"—she paused and bit her bottom lip—"came home."

Bex was worried that her caseworker hadn't changed the names on her reports—*was* worried until she heard the pull in Denise's voice when she looked at Bex, eyes soft, and said, "home."

She was Bex Andrews and this was her home.

She was *just* Bex Andrews.

TWELVE

The fight to breathe had taken everything out of Bex and she slumped. Her cheeks were flushed, and little prickles of heat and sweat beaded at her hairline.

"You going to be okay, honey?" Denise asked.

Bex nodded. "I think I'm going to take a quick shower." She glanced at the clock. "Is that okay?"

"Of course it is. Just take it easy, and try to get some sleep."

Bex turned the water on lukewarm, half-certain that the droplets would sizzle on her fiery skin. Instead, she broke out in gooseflesh, her teeth chattering as she let the water pour over her head for what seemed like hours. When she stepped out of the shower, the house around her was uncomfortably still. She knew it had to be her imagination or the whoosh of her own blood pulsing in her ears, but she swore she could hear Denise's and Michael's breathing—a steady in-out, in-out—and it felt like the house breathed with them. The walls pulled closer, then pushed out slightly, the whole house a live entity that gave Bex the creeps.

"I'm safe, I'm safe, it's okay," Bex chanted as she slipped into a fresh pair of pajamas, hoping for sleepiness that wouldn't come.

She pushed her hair back and glanced out the sweeping bay window that overlooked the drive and the street out front. The sky had gone from an inky black to a wistful gray blue, almost promising but still shrouded in shadows. One of those shadows—a twitch from it, actually—caught Bex's eye. A car was parked across the street, one of those ancient sedans that made her think of old cop movies. It could have been the flick of the streetlight or a trick of the dark, but she thought she could see someone sitting in the driver's seat.

Bex squinted, expecting her imagination was conjuring monsters. The light didn't switch, but the shadow did.

Now she could make out hands resting on the top of the steering wheel and the darkened outline of a baseball cap and wide shoulders in the front seat. The driver was leaning forward, head tilted, looking in Bex's direction.

She dropped onto her hands and knees, heart thundering in her ears. She stayed like that for a quick beat before peeking up again, just enough to glance out and see that the man—she could tell now that the person was a man—was still looking at her window.

He's probably just a neighbor, Bex scolded herself. *And he probably thinks the Piersons are fostering a lunatic child!*

She waited for the soft purr of an engine coming to life, something to tell her that the man sitting in his car had been about to go to work on the graveyard shift when he thought he saw something in the neighbor's window. He would look again, assume it was nothing, then drive his car away, and Bex could be left with her hammering heart and her paranoia.

The engine didn't sound.

Bex wanted to shrug off the phantom car, but her subconscious kept replaying a scene.

It was from another time, another place.

The smell of pine and moist earth was overwhelming, and Beth Anne didn't like the way it tickled her lungs when she breathed deeply. She wouldn't say anything though. She hadn't seen her daddy in almost two weeks and he was here with her now, just him and her in the woods. They had driven for what seemed like ages, Beth Anne bouncing on the front seat of her daddy's pickup truck while they loudly sang along to the old songs Daddy liked to listen to. Crooners, he called them, "the ole' crooners."

She liked the way the word sounded on her tongue and she repeated it under her breath, wanting to remember everything about the afternoon when it was just her and him: They had stopped at a diner called the Black Bear that Beth Anne had never heard of and was sure no one would ever find. It was at the end of a long, cracked road but they had served her ice-cold sweet tea, and even though the waitress in her pink uniform was flirting with Daddy, she brought Beth Anne a single, perfectly round scoop of white vanilla ice cream when she hadn't even asked for it.

The waitress had slipped something to her daddy too, something she put in the palm of his hand and that made him smile in a weird way—not the kind of daddy smile that he flashed at Beth Anne.

Afterward her daddy sang louder in his deep, smoky voice, until he cranked that old behemoth truck to a stop so quickly it kicked up dust all the way to the windows.

"We're here, Bethy."

Beth Anne looked around, sliding her knees underneath her on the hot vinyl seat so she could get a look around. "What are we doing out here?"

"Come on out and see."

She pushed open the car door and the heat rushed at her. Humidity clung to the trees and their drooping pale-green leaves. It dampened her hair and the skin behind her ears and seemed to push in on her chest. It wasn't anything Beth Anne didn't know though. North Carolina could have heavy heat that clung through the dead of fall.

Her father came around the side of the truck, and Beth Anne's eyes went wide. He was carrying a shotgun.

"We're going to go hunting."

Beth Anne blinked. She didn't want to hunt. She didn't want to kill anything, ever, not even the ugly black spiders that crawled through the kudzu or poked through the crack in her bedroom window. But she wouldn't say anything.

Her daddy took her by the hand and suddenly stopped, pulling her quickly down beside him. She loved being close to him, shoulder to shoulder and sharing something mysterious.

"What are we looking for?"

It seemed like hours had passed and Beth Anne was getting bored. The heat was sticky, and mosquitoes the size of biplanes were slamming into her calves and making her itch.

"I'm bored, Daddy."

He pressed a finger to his lips and shooshed her. Then, "Hunting isn't quick work, Bethy. It's not a dumb man's game. First, you've got to watch and get to know your prey. Watch them where they live. You gotta be so quiet they don't even know you're there."

He jutted his stubbled chin forward and Beth Anne saw where he was looking. There was a tiny shift in the tall fescue grass, something low to the ground that stopped, then shifted again. Beth Anne held her breath, her heart starting to beat.

"What is—?"

"Shh." He held his finger to his lips. "Just watch. Always watch. Longer than you think you should. That way, they won't even know you're coming." He pulled his gun closer to him, leveling it.

Beth Anne turned her eyes back to the twitch in the grass and lost her breath. A rabbit, not much bigger than one of her stuffed animals, scampered toward the clearing. His nose twitched against his nut-brown fur and he pushed back, standing on his haunches, the fur of his belly a pale, pale brown.

"No, Daddy." Beth Anne's protest was so soft she wasn't even sure if she had said it out loud.

Her daddy cradled the butt of the gun and squinted one eye. "Don't worry, Bethy. He won't even know what hit him. He's doing us a favor, and I promise, it won't bother him none."

The entire world slowed down. The rabbit's ears poked straight up. His nose swished back and forth, the tall grass moving around him like ripples in a puddle. The click of the gun's safety switching off was as loud as the shot.

"Beth Anne!" Her daddy's voice roared in her already-ringing ears.

Her eyes burned. Her nose was assaulted with the wicked stench of hot metal, of exploded gunpowder.

The gun dropped, flattening the grass, and Beth Anne's daddy grabbed her hands in his, his palms cool against her singed ones.

"NEVER put your hands on the muzzle of a gun, you hear me? You could have gotten us both killed pushing away like that. What were you thinking? Look at your hands. Look at how red your palms are!"

But Beth Anne wouldn't look at them. Her eyes were stuck on the rabbit as it scampered safely away.

Bex pressed her forehead against the carpet, trying to push the memory out of her mind. Her father had taken her hunting. Her father had told her that killing that rabbit "wouldn't bother it none." Bex shuddered. Did that prove anything? Did that prove her father was a murderer?

"Just watch. Always watch…"

Bex clenched her eyes shut and counted slowly until her breathing was at a normal cadence before pushing herself up and glancing out the window. The sedan was gone; the man watching her from the driver's seat was gone—so why wasn't the sickening feeling in her gut?

THIRTEEN

The yellow sunlight was nearly blinding when Bex opened her eyes. The man in the sedan seemed like the last remnants of a bad dream, but she checked out the window anyway, breathing contentedly when she saw that the street was empty. Her relief was short-lived when she turned around and glanced at the clock: eight forty.

"Oh my gosh!" She rifled through her clothes, jumping into her jeans and pulling on a T-shirt as she stumbled down the stairs. "I'm late. I'm so late!"

Denise and Michael sat at the table, staring at Bex with none of the urgency she felt.

"I slept through my alarm!"

"Oh, no, honey," Denise said, standing. "I turned it off. You had a rough night. We thought you should take it easy today."

"I'm not a fan of missing school, but I think Denise is right on this one. You'll have an extra day so you can just relax and…regroup."

Denise and Michael shared a glance, and Bex was struck with a sour feeling in her gut.

"I'm okay."

Michael smoothed the newspaper in front of him under his palms and Bex could see that Darla was still on the front page, the same picture of her that the media and the school had been using, the same photo that looked so much like the girl with the scarf. She had to look away.

"Are you sure?"

"Yeah." Bex forced herself to nod her head.

"Because you can stay here." Michael was gesturing to the house, but the thought of hanging around alone there made Bex even more certain that she wanted to be anywhere else—even if that was at school.

Denise looked from Bex back to Michael. "If you're absolutely sure..."

Bex nodded. "I am."

"Okay then," Michael said. "Grab a piece of toast, and I can drop you on my way to the university."

The ride to the school with Michael was long and silent but not uncomfortably so. He called the administration office on the way and told them that Bex would be there. "You're all set," he said to her, grinning as he pulled the car to a stop in front of the school.

"Jeez." He leaned forward, craning his neck to see over Bex's head. "More media. They're vultures."

Bex shuddered. "I don't know what else they think they're going to uncover here." She hiked her backpack up and stepped out of the car, leaning down toward Michael. "Thanks for the ride."

The reporters were still huddled in strange groups all over the front grounds of the school, but the frenetic bustle was gone—until

Bex stepped onto campus. They immediately started toward her as if some sort of starter gun had gone off, calling her, "miss" and "young lady" as they closed in on her. Her panic started to rise and Bex shrank back, exposed, a deer caught in the laser-sharp sight of a hunter.

She saw the school's security guard rushing through the gate toward her, barking at the reporters to get back and leave her alone, but nothing would stop them as they surrounded her, shoving microphones in her face and flicking on enormous lights that seemed to blank out the sun.

"Miss, miss, are you a student here?"

Bex felt her face flush, felt heat all the way to the hair follicles on the top of her head. Her stomach lurched and her palms were sweating. She couldn't have answered the woman even if she wanted to. Her mouth was dry, her tongue a deadweight. She was seven years old again and everyone wanted to know what she knew, whether her father shared anything other than the macabre trinkets of his deeds with her. They wanted to know what she said to indict him, when she realized what he'd done was wrong.

"Please go away." Bex was surprised by her own voice. "Please, we don't have anything to say."

It was exactly what her grandmother had said when they stepped into the big marble hallway in the courthouse after her father's pretrial hearing.

The reporters bustled there too, but all Beth Anne could hear was the reverberating sound of her grandmother's voice, half pleading, half demanding. There was the blinding flash of a camera snapping, and while Beth Anne tried to blink away the black blobs in front of her eyes, she saw her father in his nice, gray suit watching, the courtroom door just open enough for him to peer out without being seen.

Her heart swelled, and she knew that her daddy could stop it, would save her like he always did.

"Daddy!"

The horde of reporters followed Beth Anne's gaze and turned on her and her grandmother then, shoving past them to get to Beth Anne's father before his lawyer whisked him away. The last thing Beth Anne remembered seeing was the flash of silver around her father's wrists, his hands clasped together, and the awkward way he walked, his ankles shackled. She had betrayed him again.

"What is your name, please?"

"Did you know the deceased?"

"Are you a student? Are you involved in the case?"

Bex took a step back, the lights and camera flashes blinding her, cell phones shoved in her face. She held up an arm to protect herself and clamped her mouth shut against the bile that tore through her stomach and itched at the back of her throat.

"*Step back!* You all need to step back!"

The security guard had pushed his way into the suffocating circle and tried to barricade himself against the reporters so Bex could slip between them and through the gates of the school. She took a step and then another, seeing her path to blessed silence, but stopped.

A car was idling in the school parking lot, right at the middle of the horseshoe-shaped drive. It was a dark sedan with a man in the front seat. He was wearing a baseball cap pulled low over his forehead. His eyes were shadowed, but Bex didn't need a clear view to know that his gaze was laser-focused on her.

The driver put his foot on the gas, the squeal of his tires cutting through the cacophony of reporters and security guards as he sped down the Kill Devil Hills High School driveway and disappeared into traffic.

FOURTEEN

Even sitting in the school administration office, Bex couldn't shake the odd feeling she had gotten from the man in the car or the prickly memory of reporters surrounding her. The smell of office supplies and the hypnotic tapping of one of the secretaries typing should have calmed her, but she jumped each time a door opened, each time a phone buzzed.

"I'm sorry, hon." A pudgy secretary with cheeks like Red Delicious apples grinned up at Bex. "You needed a late pass, correct?"

Bex nodded.

"Do you have a note?"

Bex shook her head and cleared her throat. "No, my…dad… called about twenty minutes ago. My name is—"

"Bex, Bex Andrews."

That stripe of heat went up the back of Bex's neck once more. "Yeah…"

"You're very popular today, Ms. Andrews." The secretary leaned over and signed the bottom of the hall pass with a big, squiggly flourish. Bex could read the woman's name as Mrs. Snowbury. "You have a message."

Bex raised her eyebrows. "I do?"

Mrs. Snowbury produced another square of paper. "A gentleman called and asked if you were a student here. Naturally, we couldn't give him that kind of information but he did leave a number." She handed over the pink hall pass and the phone message, and Bex stared at them like they were about to bite her.

"He said his name was Brewster, I think. Or Schuster. It was a little hard to hear. The connection wasn't so good. We normally don't take messages for students, but it was slow and your file shows you've recently transferred so I thought…"

Bex couldn't hear if Mrs. Snowbury had finished talking because her heart was clanging like a fire bell. Who knew she was here? Who knew she was Bex Andrews? Why would anyone call the school looking for her?

She snatched the notes from Mrs. Snowbury's outstretched hand and may have muttered a thanks or an apology. She pushed out through the administration doors and speed walked in the direction of the nearest girls' room, a bead of sweat rolling down the middle of her back.

"Hey, beautiful, I hope you're rushing toward me." Trevor was in the hallway, a lazy smile on his full lips that should have made Bex swoon. He opened his arms and Bex dutifully hugged him, her whole body stiff and humming, focused on the man in the sedan, the Raleigh-area phone call, and now someone trying to contact her at school.

"You okay?"

"I just… I… No, I'm not feeling so hot. Girls' room." She pointed over Trevor's shoulder.

He looked stricken. "Do you want me to wait for you? I can walk you to the nurse."

Bex shook her head. "No thanks. Just…excuse me." She pushed past him and yanked open the girls' room door, letting out a breath she didn't know she had been holding when a wisp of cool air washed over her face. The bathroom was blessedly empty, the only sound the gentle whoosh of the breeze coming from the bank of open windows. Bex found a stall and went in.

What the hell is going on?

Her head was swimming with memories, dream images, things she'd made up. It was a consummate mess, and every image just ratcheted her anxiety up more. She stared at the note in her lap. The paper was already soft from having been balled up in her sweaty palm, and Mrs. Snowbury's swirly cursive message was starting to bleed.

Brewster/Schuster? For Bex Andrews.
Please return call at earliest convenience:
919-555-0512.

Raleigh.

"I don't even know anyone named Brewster or Schuster," Bex muttered. *Maybe a reporter?*

She thought back to the slew that had knocked on her door. It had seemed like hundreds at first, before the police made them stand back on the sidewalk. When the arraignment happened, there were fewer, most doing their harassing and postulating from the courthouse steps. The reporters were mercifully glued to the hallways of the hall of justice during her father's pretrial hearing, gasping when Jackson Reimer pleaded not guilty, all their focus on him. It wasn't until that night when news broke that Reimer had slipped custody that the cameras turned back to Beth Anne, back to her grandmother—the glare of camera lights flooding the living room from their station on the front lawn, the red record lights, the pointing fingers and hurled accusations.

Bex was going to be sick.

She whirled around, grabbing the sides of the toilet while her stomach rolled over itself.

What day is it? What day is it?

At one time, the dates of every one of her father's crimes were imprinted in Bex's mind. She knew the women's names and their birth dates too, and she carried around guilt that made her shoulders sag and alternated her thoughts between the poor women who lost their lives at her father's hand and the tiny, niggling possibility that her father was innocent. Either way, Bex had worked long and hard to erase those memories from her mind.

"September sixteenth. Melanie Harris."

Melanie had been seventeen. She had blue eyes and, in her graduation picture, a wide smile that showed off two crooked front teeth. She had been a tennis player and worked at the sports club where Bex's father played racquetball. She had gone missing on September twelfth, her naked, destroyed body found by a Food

Lion clerk on the sixteenth. Melanie had been placed in her car, which was parked in the grocery store lot, her purpled, warped hands wrapped around the steering wheel.

Bex might have worked to erase the memories but there they were—buried, not gone. She dialed the number on her phone and, with a shaking hand, held it to her ear.

Each ring made the knot in Bex's stomach pull tighter. She didn't realize she had been holding her breath until she heard the click of the phone, the gravelly voice of the man on the other end of the line.

"Beth Anne?"

Bex's fingers were numb. The phone slide through them and fell like deadweight into the toilet. The Call in Progress icon kept dancing and she stared at it, transfixed, until the screen began to blacken. The man's voice reverberated in her head.

Beth Anne.

No, she was Bex Andrews now. Beth Anne Reimer didn't exist. Beth Anne Reimer had a father who was accused of killing six women before he took off. Beth Anne Reimer had disappeared right along with him. The man's voice kept echoing in her head and she tried to focus on it. There was a slight accent. The man had pulled the end of her name up, just barely. He wasn't sure it was her.

Was he her father? Would she recognize him if he was?

The school bell shocked Bex and she backed into the corner of the stall, suddenly terrified, suddenly certain that whether or not her father had been on the phone, he was at the school. She started to shake, started to plan her escape. She could dye her hair again or maybe shave it off. She could get a wig and glasses and a bus ticket and go—where? She had eleven dollars to her name. Eleven dollars that wouldn't even buy her a ticket to get across town.

"It's still weird not having her here, you know?"

"I feel bad for getting so mad at her."

There was a clamor of chatter as the bathroom door opened and closed, but Bex could pick out Laney and Chelsea's distinct voices. She should have been calmed but anxiety tightened in her chest.

"Bex!" Chelsea's hand was on the stall door and Bex cursed herself for not locking it. "Are you okay? You look...not great."

She wanted to tell them everything. She wanted to run away from Kill Devil High and never return. She wanted to be able to speak. Instead, she pointed to the toilet.

"Phone," she offered in a croaked whisper.

Chelsea gave a cautious glance toward the toilet bowl, her face breaking into a grin. "Oh, that sucks."

Laney came up behind her. "Ew, toilet phone. Double ew, public toilet phone!"

"At least the water looks clean. It's clean, right?"

Bex nodded. "Yeah, I just... I was texting and..." She shrugged. "What should I do?"

"Put it in rice," Laney said. "Like, a tub of uncooked rice. It draws out the moisture and... How long has it been in there? Like a second or like ten minutes?"

For the life of her, Bex couldn't remember how much time had passed since she'd been in the office, since she'd received the note, since she'd heard the man's voice.

"Does it matter?"

"Well, yeah. Had they gotten to the *Titanic* in the first five minutes, it would have been a bad day instead of an international tragedy."

Chelsea shook her head, disgusted. "I think this one will be an international tragedy."

Bex actually felt a small sense of lightness.

"Aren't you going to get it out?" Laney wanted to know.

"Can't I just flush it?"

"It's a cell phone, not a goldfish. And it might still work. Or they could save the SIM card and at least get all your contacts back. But if it's already synched to your computer, you're totally fine."

"No." Bex shook her head. "Not synched."

"I forgot you came from the Ozarks or whatever."

"Raleigh is hardly the Ozarks."

Chelsea shrugged. "Are you really going to let it sit there?"

Bex slowly pulled up her sleeve, eyeing the drowned phone. Finally, Laney shoved her out of the way, snatched the phone from the toilet bowl, and handed it to her.

"Ew!" Chelsea screamed, running out of the stall. Laney chased her, flicking toilet water in her direction while Chelsea continued to gross out.

"You should wash that," Laney said.

Bex dumped the phone in the sink and turned on the tap, letting the water pour over it. She imagined the voice and the number with the Raleigh area code slipping down the drain. She'd start fresh again.

FIFTEEN

Without her phone, Bex felt insulated from the world, enclosed in her tiny circle of Kill Devil Hills—Laney, Chelsea, Trevor, Michael, and Denise. She liked it. But still her thoughts drifted to the man in the car and the man on the phone. At home, Bex looked up another number and dialed, gnawing on her lower lip as the phone rang and rang. Finally, a pickup.

"Dr. Gold's office."

Bex opened her mouth to ask for the doctor again, but nothing came out.

• • •

The Kill Devil Hills cemetery was a rolling green carpet in the center of the mostly sandy landscape. The grass was too green, almost cartoonish, and it made Bex feel uneasy.

"I can't believe we're going to a funeral of someone we know," Trevor said, shifting in the driver's seat of his Mustang. It was three days later, and Darla was still the center of every newscast, the front-page story of every paper.

Bex pulled her black skirt over her knees, smoothing it again like she had every five minutes on the car ride to the cemetery. It had taken her a while to decide what to wear that morning. She didn't have a ton of clothes, and although death seemed to follow her like a dark shadow, she had never been to a funeral. There hadn't been one for her mother, even after the Raleigh police declared her officially dead. There was no body, no note, nothing but seven years of absence, and according to the state, that was as good as dead.

There had been no money for a funeral for her grandmother, and truthfully, Bex wasn't sure anyone would have come. If they had, it would have only been to stare at the casket of the woman who raised the child of an allegedly murderous animal, who cradled the daughter of the man who may have even killed her own.

Someone had held a memorial service for all the girls after what should have been her father's trial but Bex didn't know until later, not that her grandmother would have let her go. She had wanted to, out of morbid curiosity or to make amends or pay respects in some small way, but at the same time, being there would have been a betrayal of her father and would have turned the event into a media circus.

"Have you ever been to a funeral?" Trevor asked when he pushed the car into Park.

Bex shook her head, unwilling to trust her voice.

"Hey, there are Laney and Chelsea." Trevor and Bex got out of the car and joined the girls on the sidewalk, then joined the slow procession of Kill Devil Hills' inhabitants and high school students walking into the chapel. A red-nosed woman who couldn't have weighed ninety pounds was propped next to a man in a nice suit who clasped his hands and bobbed his head each time someone walked in. Bex guessed they were Darla's parents, and a lump scraped the back of her throat.

The chapel was full. Bex recognized some of the younger attendees as students from school. She tried to look around surreptitiously, certain that everyone could read her mind and was already blaming her for bringing him—her father, Darla's murderer—to Kill Devil Hills.

A handful of football players in dark suits filtered into the church, and then behind them a girl—a woman, maybe—stepped in carefully, her cocoa-brown eyes skittering from face to face. Her hands were clasped in front of her, the sleeves of her black suit jacket short enough to show thin, pale wrists. Her eyes met Bex's, and Bex immediately looked away, feeling her cheeks flush. When she chanced a glance back, the girl had taken an aisle seat toward the back of the chapel. And she was focused right on Bex.

"Do you know who that lady is back there?" Bex whispered to Laney.

Laney made a show of looking over her shoulder, and Bex wanted to crawl into a hole. "Who? The blond in the suit jacket? She looks about our age, maybe a little older."

Bex grabbed Laney's sleeve and gave it a tiny shake. "Stop staring. Do you know her or not?"

"Negatory. Never seen her before in my life. If she's related to Darla, I never met her."

Bex should have been used to people singling her out and staring, but she was uneasy—and made more so when the heavy chapel doors were pushed shut. Bex couldn't help but feel like it was the sealing of a mausoleum, doors slamming closed, locking them all inside. Trevor reached over and squeezed her hand, and she wanted to revel in the feeling. Her heart should have swooned, but she felt nothing but the heavy stone in her gut and that made her angry. Her father had stolen everything from her, had stolen her whole identity, and now she sat at a funeral, feeling nothing but pain.

My father is gone, she told herself, her teeth aching as she clenched them together. *He didn't do this.*

She thought of the phone call, of the voice she could barely remember. Had it been deep or high? Was there really an accent, or had she just made that up?

Bex looked up when the music started to play but had to avert her eyes when the somber-looking men made their way up the aisle, all with red eyes and tearstained cheeks as they carried a slick, white coffin. The spray of flowers on top quivered and Bex lost her breath, tears pouring over her cheeks.

"I'm sorry," she said, leaning over and whispering to Trevor. "I can't... I just can't do this."

Bex knew people were watching her as she walked out of the chapel, but she didn't care. Her chest was tight and it hurt to breathe; her head thundered like a bass drum, and she thought she was going to pass out.

The fresh air just beyond the doors loosened the tension and she breathed deeply, greedily gulping air and coughing. She speed walked away, hearing the swell of the music from inside. She missed the click of the door opening and shutting behind her.

Bex wound her way through the garden but stopped at the edge of a little pathway. It opened to the part of the cemetery where the graves were, some with small stone rectangles set in the grass, others with monolithic headstones with carved angels or pictures set in corroded brass.

Death was with her at every turn.

What did you think? she scolded herself. *You're in a freaking cemetery!*

"Excuse me."

Bex turned, tried not to gape at the girl in the black suit. "I saw you in the… In there." She gestured toward the chapel.

Bex took the girl in: the black skirt that ended just above knobby knees crosshatched with white scars, the way she rubbed her hands, then her skirt, then her hands again. This girl was nervous. "Did you… Did you know…her?"

Bex opened her mouth, to say what she wasn't sure, but her eyes went over the girl's head toward the chapel doors where Trevor's head was poking out.

"I've got to go. I'll see you."

The girl looked like she wanted to stop her but thought better of it. "Uh, okay."

"Hey," Trevor said, sliding his arms around Bex's waist when she reached him. "You okay? I was worried."

Bex glanced over her shoulder to where the girl was still standing. She looked at her feet when she noticed Bex watching.

"Yeah, sorry. Just needed a little bit of fresh air."

After the service, the mourners were invited to the graveside for a second ceremony. Bex's dread mounted as they walked toward a black rectangle in the manicured lawn. It was still several yards off, but the smell of fresh earth caught on the wind.

"I can't do this," Chelsea said, her eyes starting to swell with tears again. "I can't watch them put my friend in the ground."

Laney squeezed her hand, and when she looked at Bex, her eyes were swimming with tears too. "I don't want to watch it either. It's just so…final."

Trevor shuddered. "And real."

The three started to back away. "Bex, you coming with?"

"In a second."

The grave that terrified Bex also transfixed her, and she found herself wondering what dying would be like. Not the actual death, but the aftermath. Would it be blissful darkness where there would be no feeling, nothing to worry about, no one staring or judging? She remembered a horrible old song that a kid had sung a million years ago when she went to real school and her dad was just a dad. *The worms crawl in, the worms crawl out. Into your stomach and out your mouth…*

Her stomach churned and she wondered if she'd ever feel right again.

In front of her, Darla's parents were throwing handfuls of dirt into the grave, clumps thudding, sounding hollow against the casket. When Bex turned, she nearly bumped chest to chest into the man behind her.

SIXTEEN

He was wearing a suit without a tie, and though his thick, peppery graying hair and square jaw seemed slightly familiar, something about him gave Bex the chills. She immediately stepped away.

"Excuse me," she murmured to her shoes.

"That's okay."

The sound of his voice burned through her ears, searing its way to her brain. It was gruff but smooth and deep—and shot ice water through her veins. She didn't know why, but adrenaline ricocheted through her and she started to run.

"Hey," the man said, following behind her. "Wait!"

Bex ran toward the parking lot, toward Trevor's red Mustang with its motor running. She slammed her hands over her ears as the man kept calling out to her and pressed her palms tighter so that when he said her name, she wasn't sure if he said "Bex" or "Beth." She vaulted into the front seat of Trevor's car, slamming the door hard.

"Let's get out of here," she said breathlessly. "Please."

• • •

The following morning, a small box sat beside Bex's cereal bowl when she came downstairs.

"What's this?"

Denise smiled. "Your new cell phone came."

Michael swiped his tablet and, without looking up, said, "I thought you'd be glued to that thing already."

Bex just looked at the box, phone nestled inside. It had the same number as her old, toilet-logged one, which meant that whomever that Raleigh area code number belonged to—and anyone else who had her number—could still find her. She poked at her cereal, the flakes turning into warm lumps of mush in the milk.

"I'm kind of a technophobe, I guess."

"Maybe you could teach Michael," Denise said, snatching the tablet from his hand and laying it on the table. "Make sure you turn it on today. We both have meetings, so we're not sure who'll be able to pick you up or when we'll be home, okay?"

Bex nodded, her throat bone dry.

A message was waiting on her phone the second she turned it on. She stared at the text message icon, a little green smiley face. The more she stared at it, the more the face seemed to turn sinister, daring her to look. She slid the little face over, and the machine-gun fire of her heart died down. The message was from Chelsea: Get together at my place tonight. Low key. 7pm.

"Everything okay, Bex?" Denise asked.

"Yeah, just Chelsea inviting me to her place tonight at seven. Is that okay?"

"Okay by me as long as you're home by eleven. Are you going to go with Trevor?"

"I can ask—" But Bex was cut off by the pinging of her phone. She glanced down at the face, another wave of relief flooding over her. "Trevor just asked if he could take me."

"Good deal," Michael said, inching his tablet back in front of him.

• • •

The school day passed uneventfully even though Bex's nerves were on a constant hum. She got hit with a basketball in PE and shattered her beaker in biology and was sure that she was being watched at every turn. When Trevor pressed his fingertips to her shoulders in the lunchroom, she jumped, dropping her tray on the floor.

When the final bell rang, Bex was still looking over her shoulder. She went to the front horseshoe to wait for Michael or Denise and stopped dead in her tracks.

The girl from the funeral was standing in front of the school. She started when she saw Bex and raised a hand to wave.

Bex didn't wave back. Instead, she ducked back into the crowd of kids, winding her way toward the student parking lot where she ran into Trevor. He grinned when he saw her and enveloped her in a hug.

"I was just going to text you. Need a ride?"

Bex looked back over her shoulder, sure she would see the girl standing statue still while the world pulsed along right beside her.

"Actually, yeah. That would be great." Bex set Denise a quick "got a ride" text and slid into the passenger seat of Trevor's car. She slouched down, just in case.

• • •

"Are you sure you're all right? Because I could come in and hang out with you," Trevor said, his car idling in Bex's driveway.

She wanted to say, "Yes, please stay." She wanted to curl into his arms and be a regular girl with a regular boyfriend who held her hand and made out with her on the couch. She wanted to only worry about them getting caught, her lipstick smudging, or whether or not she was kissing him right. She didn't want to think about the boogeyman, out there lurking in swaths of gray fog.

"I'm fine," she said with what she hoped was a confident smile. "Really." She pecked Trevor's cheek, and despite her fear, a rush of pleasure raced through her, making her rapid heartbeat enjoyable for once. "And I'll see you tonight."

"I'll be back here around seven. With bells on." He waggled his eyebrows, but then the smile dropped from his lips while his cheeks went red. "Oh my God, I don't even know why I said that. I don't even know what that means."

Bex giggled, allowing herself to sink into the fantasy of snuggling with Trevor at a regular high school party, someplace with a twinkly lit backyard garden and low music. It didn't matter that Chelsea, Laney, and five dozen other kids would be there. It didn't matter that the music would be blaring—something loud with a thudding bass since everyone was crazy about Death to Sea

Monkeys here—and kids would be screaming and squealing as they bumped around in someone's living room.

"Can't wait," she said simply.

Bex whiled away the hours by alternately doing her homework and rummaging through the pantry looking for something to eat. She knew she should be hungry because it was near dinnertime, but every time she thought about food, the butterflies soared in her stomach and she knew she couldn't eat. Trevor was going to pick her up in an hour, and they were going to be at a party, together.

Just like a regular couple.

Her cell phone pinged with a text from Michael: Wrping up here. Be home in about an hr.

Bex texted back.

> Chelseas party is 2nite! Might leave b4 u get
> home.
> Michael: Almost 4got. Be safe. No blankets,
> no booze, 11:30 curfew. Dad's rules.

Dad's rules.

Bex was smiling so hard her cheeks hurt. Did Michael really think of himself as her dad? His rules were lame—very dad like—but Bex loved that someone was looking out for her. She was still grinning when she heard the doorbell ring. She went to answer it, glancing at her phone to see that Trevor was more than an hour early. She shook off her nerves and glanced through the peephole, thinking if she saw him before he saw her, she would have the opportunity to wipe the puppy-love grin from her face.

But the porch was dark.

Bex flipped the light switch and looked again but nothing happened. The bulb must have burned out, she decided, as she steeled herself with a nice, not maniacal, smile.

"Hey, Trev, you're—"

The bulb from the porch light rolled across the welcome mat.

"Did you take that bulb out—?" But Bex couldn't finish her sentence. She felt the crushing weight of a hand on her chest, fisting over her shirt as she stumbled backward. The man from the funeral, from the phone call, forced his way into the house, slamming the door and whirling Bex around in one fell swoop. She heard the slam of the door at the same moment his hand clamped over her mouth.

"Don't scream. Just listen to me, Beth Anne."

SEVENTEEN

Beth Anne.

Her whole body was simultaneously leaden and made of glass. Tears sprang into her eyes as the man clamped his other arm across her arms, tight enough across her chest that he made it hard for her to breathe. Her subconscious told her body to move. Squirm. Kick. Bite. But the command died in her paralyzed body.

"I'm not a bad guy," the man whispered, his breath a mix of stale coffee and mint. "I'm one of the good guys. Promise you'll listen and you won't scream?"

Bex nodded, hating the feel of his lips so close to her ear, the way his breath broke hot and moist over her cheeks. He loosened his hand.

"You should know that my parents will be home soon. And my boyfriend."

"That's good," the man said. "You shouldn't be alone."

Bex felt herself start to tremble as he released his grip on her. She knew she should run or try to remember some of the training she'd learned at the one self-defense class she had ever taken, but her mind and her body couldn't seem to connect.

"Who are you? What do you want from me?"

The man turned her around to face him, speaking slowly. "Don't you remember me?"

Bex studied the man's face. She thought back on her father, the way she remembered him, before he disappeared and every image she saw was his mug shot on the news. She knew what he looked like—shouldn't every daughter know her father?—even if she had to search a distant memory. Shouldn't there be some innate connection that linked one of them to the other—genes or blood or—she felt her throat constrict—behavior? This man's face had just a vague familiarity.

He was still gripping her firmly, now by the shoulders, when Bex felt her knees buckle. She went deadweight, straight to the ground in a flash, crouching low before lunging for the stairs. She vaulted forward, her fingertips digging into the carpet, her socks slipping as she tried to gain traction. There was distance between her and her attacker. The air sliced as he reached out to her, his fingertips grazing her neck and sending a fresh wave of gooseflesh all the way down her spine, icy jabs to her very soul.

There was nowhere to go but up the stairs so Bex shot upward, taking them two at a time. She knew she should be formulating a plan: scream, find a phone, call 911, but all of that seemed impossible. She couldn't make her mouth move, couldn't remember seeing a landline phone in the house—and what was the number for 911 on a cell phone? She had tunnel vision, seeing nothing but an endless staircase in front of her.

"Go! Go away!" Bex didn't recognize the sound of her own voice.

"Just listen to me!"

The stairs were a blur. She was crying, sweat and tears and snot running over her lips, her chin. She felt his grip on her ankle—a single tug—and she crashed facedown, her breath whacked out of her. The man pulled her down two carpeted steps, then stood over her, pinning her ribs with his calves, one hand between her shoulder blades, pushing down firmly.

"I'm a police officer."

His admission did nothing to quell the tremors that went through her body, and her teeth clacked together. Somewhere behind her, she heard him fiddling with fabric and metal—maybe his belt buckle—and the tremors grew to quakes.

"Please," she whispered, "please don't."

The man bent over and waved something in front of Bex, then pushed it into her hands.

Leather. A wallet. A badge.

"I'm not here to hurt you." He spoke in a soothing voice as though she were a child.

"I'm Detective Lieutenant Daniel Schuster."

He slowly removed his hand from Bex's back, released the pressure on her ribs. She stayed facedown, still trembling, still terrified. Anyone could say they were a cop. Anyone could get a badge. But the name…it was vaguely familiar. A TV cop? Maybe he stole the name from a movie?

"Cops don't barge into people's houses," Bex said slowly, her mouth so dry her lips stuck to her teeth.

"You wouldn't answer my calls."

"You—" Everything inside Bex stopped when Detective Schuster dropped the yellowed newspaper article on the carpet in front of her. It had been folded and refolded so many times that the paper looked like worn fabric. The text and the black-and-white picture had been softened by fingers smoothing it flat again and again. Bex didn't need to read the article. Her stomach turned to liquid.

She was looking into the saucer-wide eyes of her seven-year-old self.

In the photograph, her mouth was covered by the belly of a stuffed animal, Princess Pig, she remembered, a bright-pink pig that her father had won her at the county fair when she was six. Beth Anne couldn't sleep without Princess Pig's soft belly pressed up against her lips. She couldn't remember what had happened to the pig, but she'd never thought she'd forget the face of the mustached man in uniform standing beside her.

"Do you remember me now?"

Disgust roared through Bex. "Where did you get this?"

"It was in the *Raleigh Tribune* ten years ago." He pointed at the date. "I kept it. That was the day we got him, the Wife Collector. That was the day we saved you, Beth Anne."

Anger replaced disgust, sparking like a white-hot flame low in her belly.

"You *saved* me?"

That day, Bex remembered, was the day her life broke in two. That was when her life became before and after, when normalcy was eaten away by news vans and police officers and social workers who took her away from her home and her father who had never done anything but love her. That day her "saviors" had shuttled her out of her house and into a squat building with linoleum floors and hard plastic furniture. They had handed her a pair of itchy pajamas and tucked her into a cot that squeaked if she dared to move, and handed her a stiff teddy bear as if that would make up for the cinder-block walls and the destruction of her life. That teddy bear didn't have a soft belly like Princess Pig did; Beth Anne knew because she had stayed awake all night staring at it.

Bex rolled over and sat up, curling her hand around the stair railing in case Detective Lieutenant Schuster made a grab for her again. Her other hand went to her neck, to the hollow at her throat, where the necklace had been all that time ago.

"You were the one who took my necklace."

"It was a ring, and it belonged to one of your father's victims. It was little consolation but the Harrises were happy to have it back. You did a good thing. I know it couldn't have been easy."

Bex stared at the carpet, her gaze laser focused, jaws clenched. "I was just a kid."

Schuster bobbed his head and rubbed his hand over his chin. "Still, if it hadn't been—"

She tore her gaze from the carpet and forced herself to look at the detective. He was much older now. The hair that she had remembered as inky black had gray at the temples, but the slope of his brow and the way he held his mouth were more familiar. His teeth were yellowed, and he bore the faint scent of cigarettes and strong coffee.

"Why are you here? How did you even find me? I... My social

worker… No one was supposed to know where I am." She pulled her knees to her chest. "Who I am."

"Beth Anne…" Detective Schuster looked away, the confidence and bravado sapped from his body. "We have reason to believe your father might be in the area."

The air was snatched out of Bex's lungs. "What?"

She saw the shackles that dragged on the ground as her father shuffled into the courtroom. She heard the sound they made: innocent, like keys rattling in a pocket, then a heavy clank when his foot hit the ground. She heard that sound in her dreams, in her nightmares. She remembered the way the silver handcuffs clenched his wrists, his hands fisted in front of him, and the thin chain that wrapped around his waist. He didn't have a belt. His sneakers didn't even have laces. Then, the next day, he was gone.

"If that were true, it would be on every news channel."

"We've been able to keep it quiet, but it's only a matter of time. He's here."

"How do you know that?"

Now it was Schuster's turn to look disgusted. "The police department has been working on tracking him for a long time. *I've* been working on it for longer. There have been signs…" He let his voice trail off before amping up again. "The more important thing is that I found you. And if I can find you, so can your father."

An image of Darla, dumped on the beach, flashed in her mind. The scent—the hideous, unforgettable stench of death—flooded Bex's nostrils as though she were back there.

"If he can find you—Bex, is it?—he can find the people you love too."

For ten years, Gran had protected Beth Anne. Since her grandmother died, she'd had nothing. Now she had someone and something to protect—her foster parents, her new friends. If her father did the things he was accused of doing and if he was truly back, he could ruin it all. Bex licked her lips.

"What do you want me to do?"

EIGHTEEN

Detective Schuster followed Bex as she rode her bike the three blocks to Kill Devil Coffee. He had offered to drive her, even insisted, but she refused to get in his car, intent on making a quick getaway if the need arose. As she rode, her mind was trilling, dropping pieces into place in her memory—the first time she saw Detective Schuster, how he looked at her father's arraignment. She trusted him, just not enough to get in the car and ride with him.

Bex rode into Kill Devil Coffee following behind the detective's car. She locked up her bike and steadied herself with a deep breath before pulling open the coffeehouse door. Her heart started to tick again when she saw the detective at the counter. *What am I getting myself into?*

"Did you want something, ah—"

Bex could tell he was trying to figure out what to call her. She had no inclination to help him. "I'm good, thanks."

She sat down and Schuster came over with a steaming cup of black coffee. Bex watched him stir in a handful of sugar packs, her tension and anxiety throbbing until it was all she could think about.

"What do you want me to do?" she said again.

Schuster sucked on the stir stick and raised his eyebrows as if the subject of their conversation hadn't been gnawing at the back of Bex's mind every minute of the last ten years. He leaned closer to her, wriggled a manila file folder from his messenger bag, and dropped it on the table, covering it with his hands.

"We're not entirely sure of the exact date your father appeared back in North Carolina."

Bex felt herself gape. "Good tracking work."

Schuster bobbed his head apologetically. "Believe me, I had the same reaction. But, again, he *did* reappear."

"You have reason *to believe* he has reappeared." Her voice was snide.

"It's been ten years, Beth Anne."

"Don't call me that."

"Sorry. Bex. It's not that easy to find someone who doesn't want to be found."

"I didn't want to be found."

Schuster didn't make eye contact while he raked a hand through his hair.

"Okay, fine," Bex said, shaking her head. "What does any of this have to do with me?"

"Nothing, we hope," Schuster said, taking a sip of his coffee. "But there is the chance that he'll contact you. I'm thinking that might be why he came back into town."

A shudder went through Bex—something between hope and disgust. Did her dad know that her gran had died, that she would be all alone? Did he want to help her—or hurt her?

"We're thinking maybe you could be the one to draw him out."

Bex's gut lurched. It wasn't a sinking feeling; it wasn't fear; it wasn't anxiety—it was something else entirely.

Would he want to see me?

A tiny spark of hope flickered but was just as quickly stamped out by guilt.

He murdered six women...

Or didn't he?

"Bex?" Schuster touched her hand. "Are you okay?"

"Yeah, I'm sorry."

"We're not sure what he's going to do—if he wants to disappear again, if he wants to make contact with you, if he wants to..." He wouldn't look at Bex.

"If he wants to kill again," she supplied.

Schuster nodded and Darla's crumpled image washed over her again. *Had he killed again already?*

"Has anyone tried to contact you?"

"You know, Darla wasn't his typical"—Bex choked on the word—"victim. Maybe it's not him, just a—"

"Copycat? Believe me, we've considered all the possibilities."

"And?"

"Has anyone tried to contact you?" Schuster asked again.

Bex picked up a napkin, rolling the fibers between her fingers. "Other than you, no."

"Anything strange, out of the ordinary happening around here?"

Bex thought about the postcard with its glaring, overly cheerful "Greetings from the Research Triangle" moniker.

"No, nothing like that at all." She didn't know why, but the words were out of her mouth before she could consider them.

Detective Schuster held her gaze and Bex felt as though he were looking right through her, reading her mind to know she was lying. She cleared her throat, looked at the napkin, and kept rolling it between her fingers.

"A body was found on the beach not too far from here?"

"Stop! What is that?"

Headlights glaring over the dunes.

A single foot, big toe buried in the sand.

"Yeah. I know. We're not certain it's him, of course, but the timing and the victimology do line up."

Victim. Darla was a teenager, a high school cheerleader who sat at the popular table and threw tremendous house parties, and now she was a victim. She wasn't a person anymore. She was a type, a specimen to be dissected and catalogued and discussed as though all that mattered about her were the things that mattered to her killer: blond hair, big blue eyes, sixteen to twenty-two years old, missing ring finger.

Bex sucked in a sharp breath. "Was her ring finger missing?"

"What's that?" the detective asked, setting his coffee down.

She pulled at the manila file folder and began pawing through it, suddenly desperate.

"Bex, you don't want to look at that."

Her gaze was steel. "Didn't you bring them for me?"

"Let me just—"

But it was already too late. The numbness started at Bex's

fingertips and deadened everything inside her. A picture of Darla, nude, with an enormous, jagged-looking Y cut on her chest, her lips lightly parted and a haunting, deep purple was at the left. To the right, a four-by-six glossy photograph of what could have been Bex's father, dressed in a slim-fitting flannel shirt, his hair unkempt and shaggy, brushing his shoulders. He was getting into a big rig, one booted foot balanced on the sideboard, the other still on the ground. The details of his face weren't clear, except for the eyes. The eyes that had once been so warm and full of security and love were cold and black and vacant as he stared into the camera and out at Bex.

"That was taken three months ago," Detective Schuster clarified, trying to close the folder. "Somewhere around Beaufort."

"South Carolina."

She snatched the picture and held it closer, squinting, trying to take in every detail. He was heavier than she remembered, with square, blocky shoulders and a stomach that was just starting to slide over his waistband. He looked much older too, with lips that seemed incapable of any expression other than the slight, disgusted frown he showed in the shot. Behind him, the truck-stop gas station had nothing to mark its character or give Bex a sense of anything but disconnection from the photo and its subject.

She took a long, slow breath, hoping that would be enough to process ten years of absence and longing and guilt. Ten years of abandonment, of hiding from the whispers and shadows and memories of what her father might have done. Finally, she shook her head.

"Look, as far as I know my father hasn't tried to contact me in ten years."

Saying that out loud hit Bex squarely in the chest. She cleared her throat, hoping to keep the wobble out of her voice.

"I don't think anything would change just because he's…" It was hard for Bex to say the word. "Here" meant that he was alive and out of hiding. He was living among his "targets"—potential victims and his accusers. And he didn't care about the daughter he had left behind. Unease rolled through Bex.

"I don't…I don't even know how I would go about finding him or"—she made air quotes—"'drawing him out' like you said. I don't really know that much about him."

It pained her to admit that she knew little about her father beyond the few memories she had of him. Anything personal— anything more than the old truck, the Black Bear Diner, and that he always called her "Bethy"—had been forgotten or blotted out by newspaper headlines and what the attorneys and reporters called "cold, hard facts" about him. He was as charming as he was ruthless. He was a pathological liar. He had an inability to feel. He hunted his prey before making a move.

"Besides, if he's trying to keep out of jail, he's probably not going to be sending up rescue flares. Even if he does know where I am, he probably won't come knocking on my door, right?" Another torrent of emotions surged through Bex. Would he come to her door? Would he want to see her at all?

Detective Schuster seemed undeterred, but there was a careful edge to his voice. "How aware are you of your father's crimes, Bex?"

She gaped, rage overtaking her. "I know what my father is accused of, Detective Schuster. I don't need a needlepoint to hang over my bed."

He didn't look at her, and for that, Bex was glad. She didn't want him to hang on the word "accused." She didn't want to have to defend her father, especially when she wasn't really certain how she felt.

"I'm sorry, Bex. I didn't mean anything by that." Detective Schuster paused and raked a hand through his brushed-back hair. "Your dad probably won't have an email address or a website, but there are lots of websites about him. Did you know that?"

Bex dug her thumbnail into the layers of veneer on the table. "I knew that."

The truth was that Bex—Beth Anne—had had a debilitating need to know exactly what her father was accused of. Once the files became available on the Internet, she had nearly lost an entire summer poring through the documents—the testimony, the crime-scene photos, the autopsy reports. Somewhere in her mind she thought that maybe the clue was there, something that the police had missed that would vindicate her father, that would vindicate her for attempting to send him to prison. The clue to absolution wasn't there. A preponderance of evidence linked her father to the sadistic, horrifying murders of young women all over the county—including the one who Bex remembered getting into her father's car and another who tucked her number into his hand.

She had run across the other websites accidentally, but then her curiosity drew her in. The sites were horrible. One showed a grinning photo of Bex's father—she remembered the shot and had herself been cropped out. The webmaster had made red flames flash across the picture with the words "The Wife Collector Should Burn in Hell." Another site rooted for her father with photographs and court documents and was populated by sickos who thought the Wife Collector was "the greatest," listing his body count and even some of their "favorite kills." Bex wasn't sure which site was worse.

"People who run these sites have followers, and while we're not one hundred percent sure, there's a really good chance that your father could be one of those followers."

The sites were bad enough. The idea that perhaps her father visited or even followed the sites made Bex's stomach turn.

"Okay…" she said slowly.

"There are forums where"—Schuster grimaced—"fans can get together and talk, like chat rooms. We think your father might frequent one or more of the chat rooms under an alias."

"So what do you want me to do?"

"I think that if you post to one of the sites, your father might respond."

She crossed her arms in front of her chest, doing her best to smother her nerves with anger. "You *think* he might respond? You want me to cyber hang out with a bunch of serial-killer groupies in case my dad decides to drop in? No"—she shook her head—"I'm not going to do that."

"You wouldn't be 'hanging out' with them per se."

"Well, whatever you call it, the answer is still no. How am I supposed to do that anyway? Why would he talk to me? Let me guess… You want me to use the screen name 'Hey, Dad, it's me?'"

Detective Schuster stared at Bex, his lips pressed together in a hard, thin line. "I think you should go public with your identity."

NINETEEN

Someone hit Bex in the chest with a sledgehammer. That was what must have happened; that was why Bex's lungs felt as if they had collapsed. That was why her heart was struggling to beat.

"You want me to do what?"

"If you come out with who you really are and publicly announce that you'd like to talk to your father, to get to know him, I think that would draw him out."

Bex's body started to shake. She gritted her teeth to avoid the *clack-clack-clack* of them banging together. Detective Schuster wanted her to make contact with her father. Ridiculous visions of the two of them relaxing at the kitchen table, sipping tea, flashed through her mind, only to be crashed by the thought of her father looming huge and turning into a monster, his hands morphing into talons that closed around her throat.

"I-I can't. I can't do that."

"You could really help people. You could help your father."

Bex snapped her gaze to Schuster. "Like I helped him before?"

"You did the right thing then, and I'd hope you would do the right thing now."

Bex wished she could name the feeling that roared through her. It wasn't simply anger. It wasn't simply pain. It was something like rage mixed with sadness and guilt, and she was feeling it more and more. She closed her eyes and pressed the pads of her fingertips against her eyelids. The girls the Wife Collector had murdered marched by in a macabre parade—lives lost, stories that never were. They were inexplicably connected to Beth Anne, and no matter how far Bex ran or who she became, they would always be connected to her.

And then there was her father.

After he was arrested, even after he was arraigned, he never spoke to Bex about the murders. She had never asked, though sometimes she had wanted to. Late at night, she would go over memories and details in her head, anything that could have been suspect or hard proof that her father had or had not committed those crimes. But the few times she had been face-to-face with him then, she had known there was no reason to ask. He was her father. He loved her and protected her. He was the greatest man in her life.

But had he been another way with someone else?

"I can't...I can't think about this right now." Her head was pounding. She felt itchy and jumpy.

"I know this is a lot to take in. But if you could just—"

Bex stood up. "I'll think about it, okay? But right now..." She looked around, not exactly sure what for, then shrugged. "I just can't do this right now, okay?" She didn't give Detective Schuster a chance to answer before grabbing her shoulder bag and disappearing out the coffeehouse door.

It was cold outside. The fog was rolling in off the ocean in a thick, gray haze. Bex zipped her sweatshirt up to her neck, trying to avoid a chill that went all the way down to her bones. Cars zipped by and a small group of girls just a few years older than her shimmied past. She couldn't help but glance at each one, taking in their features, their clothes, and their hair. She paused by her bike, staring in the direction the girls had gone.

"Always be watching," her father seemed to whisper in her ear. *"What you need is out there just for the taking. The key is finding* exactly *what you want."*

Bex couldn't remember what her father had been referring to when he'd whispered that in her ear, but now his advice took on an eerie tone. She glanced around out of curiosity. He glanced around when he was—

Something thick and heavy settled low in Bex's gut.

Her father glanced around like that when he was hunting.

Was he looking into the faces of women to find one that he liked? One with blond hair and pretty, summery features?

One that he could destroy.

A memory dislodged itself when Bex slumped against her bike, her hooded eyes trying to figure out where the gray surf ended and the sky began.

She was sitting on a park bench—no, at a picnic table—her sandaled feet nowhere near touching the ground. Her mother was there, right next to her, trying to clean Beth Anne's hand, but Beth

Anne didn't want to wait. She struggled against her mother's grip while her father mumbled something across the table.

Beth Anne was reaching, her fat, little fingers pinching... A cup. She was reaching for a cup. She felt the flimsy Styrofoam between her fingers, then felt it slipping through. She remembered the arc of the bright-red juice as the cup toppled. Her mother dropped Beth Anne's hand and tried to reach out as though she could stop the spill. But it splashed her father and Bex remembered the way the droplets hit his white T-shirt, leaving bright-pink trails down his chest.

She remembered the flash in his eyes.

The way his lip kinked up with a snarl.

His eyebrows diving down. Nostrils flaring. The red of his cheeks so much brighter than the stains on his shirt. She saw the veins bulge, stretching the skin on his neck taut. His hands seemed so big when they slammed against the picnic table. The other cups trembled. The smack of skin against skin. She was vibrating. Her skin, her teeth. The taste of blood. Sand against her cheek, peppering her lips.

What had happened?

Bex sank onto the concrete, tears rolling down her cheeks.

Was her father the kind man she thought he was—or just a kind man in her memories?

TWENTY

It was barely an hour since Bex had sat across from Detective Schuster but it felt like a thousand years had passed. She tried to curl her hair and brighten the blush in her cheeks, but no matter what she did, she looked exhausted.

Her father had surfaced. According to the picture in the file, he was officially *out*. Bex had her hand on her cell phone, ready to call Trevor and cancel, when she heard the muffled din of his engine, the thunking bass of his radio. He was pulling into her driveway. Bex did her best to push everything to the back of her mind, to hang on to what might be her last few hours of normalcy. If—*if*—her father came for her, contacted her, or made his presence known, then the whole of Kill Devil Hills—and the high school—would know who she was.

Your father has already made his presence known, the tiny voice in the back of her head taunted. *Remember Darla?*

She stamped out the thought and smiled at Trevor when he smiled at her, nodding mutely and allowing him to open her car door. She was on a date—her *first date!* Sure, they were just going to a party, but he picked her up and told her she looked nice and she had waited for this moment *her whole life.*

And once again, her father was ruining it.

Bex's mind swam as she sat in the passenger seat of Trevor's car. She knew he was talking to her, but she had no idea what he was saying. She kept her eyes focused on the dark landscape zooming by outside the passenger window. A bar parking lot clogged with shiny motorcycles. *Is my father in there?* A graveyard of school buses parked at the district bus depot. *How would he get to me? A car? A bus?* She swallowed down a niggle of sadness. *Would he try to get to me?*

A newsreel zipped through her head. *Dateline, 20/20,* "special" reports, anniversary specials, anchors, and experts talking about her father, calling him dangerous, predatory, not able to be rehabilitated.

"*Some people are born without a conscience. Quite simply, they are pure evil,*" she remembered a psychologist in an ugly tweed suit commenting about her dad. "*A monster,*" said the shaking lips of one of the victim's husbands. He "*doesn't care about anything because he* can't *care about anything*"—from a criminology expert.

"*No conscience, no capacity to love. It might seem like he was a good neighbor, a loving father, but he would have been acting. Sociopaths like the Wife Collector have a keen skill set for making people believe exactly what they want them to. This man wants a wife. He's clearly charming, good looking. He plucks these girls—because that's what they are, girls, barely women—that he wants as his own. He takes them to satisfy his own sick need to have and then kill a wife. We feel revulsion and horror. He feels nothing. There are no two ways about it.*"

Bex started blinking rapidly, rubbing her eyes.

"Hey," Trevor said, leaning over. "You okay?"

She sniffed. "Yeah. I…just got some sand in my eye or something."

Trevor squeezed her knee, his touch tender, not at all pushy or suggestive. "Just making sure," he said, his smile evident even in profile.

Again, Bex struggled. She was lying to Trevor. He was a nice boy who thought she was a nice girl, two nice kids going on a date, going to hang out at a house party and have a good time. Two kids who should be thinking about a first kiss at the end of the night—not whether one of them was responsible for luring a murderer into town.

They parked in a sand-dusted cul-de-sac already clogged with cars from the student lot at Kill Devil High.

"Wow, I thought it was just going to be a few of us."

Trevor shrugged. "It always starts out that way. We always end up on the beach, so…" He handed her a fluffy, blue comforter and hoisted his backpack onto his back. "That's Chelsea's place." He pointed to a house that seemed to meld perfectly into the sand behind it. "Ready?"

Bex wrapped her arms across her chest. "I hope they have a fire up. It's cold." Now that the car was parked and the headlights were off, the street was plunged into darkness. There was one lonely streetlight, but its sad, yellow beam barely filtered through the cypress trees dotting the sidewalk toward the sand.

Anyone could be hiding in that darkness, Bex thought. *No wonder it took so long to find Darla's body.*

She started when she felt Trevor drape something over her shoulders.

"Hey! Sorry!" he said, holding up his hands. "Just trying to warm you up."

She looked at the jacket that Trevor had draped over her. It was heavy, in Kill Devil Hills High colors.

"Your letterman's jacket?"

Even in the darkness, she could see the crimson burn on Trevor's face. "If you don't mind. It's cool if you don't want to wear it."

Bex felt her own cheeks burn as she broke out in a wide grin. "No, yeah," she said, pulling the jacket closer around her. "I'd love to wear it."

Her mind soared and the barely visible path swam in front of her eyes. *I'm wearing a boy's letterman's jacket…* When Trevor's fingertips found hers and their fingers intertwined, Bex thought she would fly away. Nothing mattered but that feeling, the way that Trevor anchored her to this spot, this moment on the beach in her new home with her new friends. She was Bex Andrews and nothing could touch her.

Chelsea threw open the door before Trevor was able to touch the doorknob.

"Hello, lovebirds!" she tweeted, shoving red party cups in their hands. "Fill up with whatever you want. There's soda and stuff in the kitchen. Martin's got some concoction brewing in a garbage can out back. Please note I am not responsible for whatever side effects that stuff might cause. And, uh, just have fun."

"The ultimate hostess," Bex said, holding up her empty cup.

Trevor took it from her hand. "What can I get you?"

Bex had never had alcohol other than a few stolen, bitter sips of her father's beer when he had passed out and the bottle sat warm and open on the counter. She remembered the bubbles burning up her nose as the liquid burned down her throat. She also remembered the airy, light-headed feeling she got when she tossed back her head like she had seen him do and glugged those first few sips. Feeling light-headed and airy was exactly what Bex wanted now.

"I'm feeling adventurous."

"Garbage brew it is."

As the party started to build, Trevor snuggled closer to Bex. "You seem happy."

She cuddled against him, tucking her head underneath his chin. "I am." She closed her eyes, loving the sound of his heart beating steadily. They were sitting on Chelsea's patio, feet in the sand, the fire pit crackling in front of them. The garbage brew tasted like a horrible concoction of cherry cough medicine and Sprite, but Bex had sucked down two cups, liking the way the booze softened the hard edges of the thoughts that barreled through her mind.

"It's like there's nothing to worry about out here on the beach." Bex closed her eyes. "Let's just stay out here forever, okay?"

Hovering there, it was almost as if she had moved past her father, past the horrible memories. She was just a kid at a party. Trevor's lips found hers, and everything else in the world fell away.

"Okay, everyone? Everyone!" Chelsea stomped out on the patio and clapped her hands, the sound sharp in the night. Bex lazily lifted her head from Trevor's shoulder and tried to straighten up.

Laney followed behind Chelsea, her arms full of white carnations that seemed to mass together in one fluffy head. Bex blinked, trying to focus, but her eyes kept going to the carnations, their powdery smell wafting over the scent of fruit juice and smoke. Something was pulling her out of the softened state of drunkenness. Something about the flowers en masse…

There must have been hundreds of them pushed together to form the limbs of the cross. Beth Anne rolled down the window and sucked in a breath of air heady with the sweet scent of the carnations. She loved everything about them, from the way they smelled to how they formed a soft, cloudlike pile, the arms of the cross reaching outward, embracing. In the center, there were more flowers—exotic and brightly colored among sprays of ferns and baby's breath.

The arrangement was at least six feet tall; it dwarfed her and looked regal and hopeful propped up on the lawn in front of the iron gates of the cemetery as Beth Anne and her gran drove by. Something was woven right into the flowers, written in sparkly silver letters that glittered in the sun. They were driving too fast for her to read—the names of all the women her father had killed.

Bex sat upright, the brew burning a hole in her stomach, the sharp pain of memory cutting through the fog of alcohol. It didn't matter if her father was looking for her—he was never far from her mind.

TWENTY-ONE

"Excuse me!"

The kids at the party—about forty that Bex knew or recognized—reluctantly stopped talking and laughing to give Chelsea their attention. Someone even turned down the speakers when she cleared her throat and pinned them with what Bex was beginning to recognize as Chelsea's patented glare of death.

"As we all know, a very dear friend passed away recently just a few dozen miles from here."

The sweet warmth and comfort Bex had been feeling dissipated as quickly as mist on the waves. Trevor must have sensed it because he pulled her in to him again, but her entire body was stiff.

"The police haven't caught Darla's killer yet, but they have some good leads. They even think they have a suspect."

Bex's heart began to thud in her throat.

"The timing, the victimology are right…"

"But we're not here to talk about her killer, we're here to celebrate her life. Since Darla touched everyone here, we thought we would send her memory out with the waves. Everyone take a flower and think of your best memory with Darla, and we'll throw them out into the water." Chelsea beamed while Laney began handing out the single-stemmed flowers.

There was some grumbling, some muffled laughter, but all Bex could focus on was what Chelsea had said: "…they even think they have a suspect."

She broke away from Trevor and zigged through the crowd to Chelsea, blindly taking the flower Laney handed her.

"The police have a suspect?" she asked, her stomach in a vice. "Who?"

Chelsea scanned the dunes as though everyone were listening. "There was a witness who saw a car pulled over on the side of the road the…the night just before we found her."

"What kind of car?"

Laney shifted the few remaining flowers. "Just like an old truck or something, but the witness got a pretty good look at the guy and actually recognized him."

"You know that weird security guy from the mall?" Chelsea asked. "He was always around us when we were with Darla. Like, always for the last six months. He was totally obsessed with her."

"Well," Laney clarified, "Darla did shoplift."

"Yes." Chelsea crossed her arms in front of her chest and jutted out one hip. "That could be what drove him over the edge, you know? Like, here's this perfect little rich girl *stealing*."

Relief flooded Bex's system. "Oh."

"Anyway, that's kind of what the police are saying."

Bex nodded and numbly followed Chelsea and Laney to the

edge of the water. It lapped at the tips of her bare feet, the water so frigid it was nearly painful—but feeling something she could actually identify felt good.

There was a lot of murmuring and sniffling as the white flowers were flung through the air and caught on the dark water. Bex held hers, spinning it around and around in her hand until her palms were heady with the carnation's sweet perfume.

"I didn't know you, Darla," she said in her head, "but…" She didn't know how to finish. If Darla was murdered by the security guard, that meant Bex's father didn't do it. He hadn't come back to taunt her, to hurt her, to murder everyone she loved. She blinked away tears. It also meant that he hadn't come back for her at all.

• • •

Trevor and Bex drove home in silence. When he reached out for her and laced his fingers through hers, Bex wanted to feel that same velvety, stomach-tingling twitter that she had felt before, but she was numb and empty. As they turned the corner, a spark of anger started low in her belly—low but big enough to fill the void. Her father wasn't going to come back for her. He probably never thought of her, while she couldn't stop thinking about him. Two hundred miles and ten years later, he was still invading her life, still snuffing out any hint of normalcy she reached for.

Bex squeezed Trevor's hand, and when he slowed to a stop and grinned at her, she leaned across the center console and pressed her lips against his, stamping out her self-consciousness.

He kissed her back. All her embarrassment faded into an

incredible, heart-pounding zing that engulfed her whole body, making every inch of her feel alive. Her fingertips were vibrating as she laced them behind Trevor's neck. His were warm and comforting as his hands snaked behind her back. They would have kept going, lost in the churning surf of that kiss and of each other, but the person in the car behind them starting wailing on the horn.

Trevor snapped away and stamped on the gas, and Bex laughed, jolting back in her seat.

"I wouldn't have done that if I'd known it would break traffic rules."

He shrugged and shot her a half smile that was as wonderful as his kiss. "Nothing in the driver's ed manual about kissing at stop signs. At least, nothing against it."

Bex's head was spinning when Trevor turned into her neighborhood. If memories of her father were still playing in her head, they were layered over by the look in Trevor's eyes, the way his hand felt in hers, the way his lips felt on hers.

"You're my first boyfriend," Bex blurted out. She immediately slapped a hand over her mouth. "I can't believe I said that."

Trevor smiled his easy smile and brushed a lock of her pale-brown hair from her forehead. "I find that hard to believe. I bet all the guys at your old school wanted to date you but were too nervous to ask. Just my luck, huh?"

Bex thought of those days when she'd curl up on her bed, filling out workbooks that were supposed to pass as "school."

"Not really. I bet you've had a ton of girlfriends though." She worked the strap of the seat belt with her fingertips, focusing intently on the grain of the blue fabric.

"Not a ton. Just one serious one…before you." He flipped on his blinker, waiting for traffic to pass. "Darla."

Bex felt her heartbeat speed up. "I didn't know you—?"

"Bex, your house."

They were still four houses down, but the flashing lights from the police cruisers illuminated the entire front seat of Trevor's car. She stared, mesmerized, mouth slightly open as two officers strode from their car and up the walk to her house. The front door was open, the lights inside blazing like day. Around them, neighbors were coming out of their houses in their bathrobes and slippers, carefully picking the way to the edge of their lawns or gathering on the sidewalk to see what was the matter.

"I wonder what happened…" Trevor started.

"Let me out."

"What?"

Bex unclicked her seat belt and tried the locked door again. "Let me out, Trevor. I have to go. I have to see what's wrong."

The sound of the doors unlocking echoed in her ears and Bex flung open the door, reminding herself to breathe as a hot lump tightened her throat.

Please be okay, please be okay, please be okay, she begged in her head.

Behind her, Trevor was yelling her name. In front of her, a looming man in a Kill Devil Hills police uniform was yelling at her to stop. Bex tried to dart past him to find Michael and Denise, but the man caught her roughly. She slammed into his chest, the itchy feel of his uniform triggering another old memory.

"Relax, little lady," the cop said, his drawl thick and drawn out.

"I won't let you take my family away again," Bex said through gritted teeth.

The man blinked at her but didn't let her go. "This is a crime scene."

"Bex! Oh thank God!"

When she saw Michael jogging down the walk, then beelining toward her, something inside Bex broke. She was coughing and crying and hiccupping as Michael held his arms out to her. She fell into them, suddenly unable to support her own weight.

"It's all right, Officer. She's our foster daughter."

"What happened, Michael? What happened? Is Denise okay? I'm so sorry. I'm so, so sorry."

Michael cradled Bex's chin in his hand. "You have nothing to be sorry about, Bex. Denise is going to be fine. She's right inside. We've been trying to call you, but you weren't answering your cell."

Bex nodded, gulping. She wiped the back of her hand across her eyes. "What happened?"

"We had a little break-in." Michael shrugged his shoulders almost apologetically and squeezed Bex's shoulder.

"Oh."

Michael led her into the house, and Bex looked around. Denise was sitting on the couch, pinching the back of her hand while she talked. An officer loomed above her, writing down everything she said in his little black pocket notebook.

"Oh, there's our daughter now." She beckoned for Bex to come over, then nearly crushed her in a tight embrace. "We're so glad she wasn't here alone."

Bex didn't have time to dwell on the fact that both Michael and Denise had referred to her as their daughter before the officer turned his notebook on her.

"What time did you leave, miss?"

Bex looked around her, trying to remember what happened before the bonfire. Then she thought of the detective lieutenant and felt exhausted. She found Denise's hand and squeezed. "A little after seven, I guess. Is this—did he do this?"

The living room where they were seated was a disaster. Pillows were strewn everywhere, drawers dumped. It was chaos but it didn't look like anything was gone. *Then again*, Bex considered, *how would I know what Michael and Denise had?*

The cops' eyebrows went up. "Who are you referring to?"

"The…the… Whoever did this… Did they…" She gestured to the mess around them.

"Yes. At nineteen hundred hours—"

Denise stood up, putting her arm lightly on the officer's arm to stop him. "Are we done here? With all due respect, I don't want to frighten Bex any more than she already has been. She wasn't even here."

The officer looked around Denise and pinned Bex with a stare that made her certain he knew exactly what she was hiding. "Did you notice anything suspicious when you left? Did you see anyone around the neighborhood?"

She wagged her head. "No, sir." Bex said it in her mind, but wasn't sure she had actually said the words out loud.

It didn't take long for the police to file out and the commotion to die down. When the last neighbor left after wanting to hear the story again, Michael closed the front door and flipped the bolt.

"Fat lot of good that thing did," Denise huffed.

"What happened?"

Michael pinched the bridge of his nose. "Sometime around nine o'clock, someone slipped into the house." He glanced back at the door. "We're not sure how. Everything was locked when we came home."

Denise shuddered, then looked at Bex. "Are you sure you locked the door behind you when you left?" Her stare wasn't accusatory, but Bex's blood ran cold.

Bex cleared her throat. "Um…" *Did I?* It was hard to remember what had happened. The afternoon seemed a million miles away. "I think so."

Michael snatched up a pillow and handed it to Denise. "The police think it was just some kids or something. Not much was taken. Just a few trinkets, mainly, and some jewelry that Denise had lying around. They didn't seem to go for any of the big stuff—TV, laptops. Seemed almost like they were just screwing around."

Denise's eyes were saucer wide but blank. "Or trying to send a message."

• • •

Bex tossed and turned, trying to get comfortable in her bed. She tried to think of the bonfire, to relish every moment of her date with Trevor, especially their kiss. But every time she closed her eyes, she saw Detective Schuster and that yellowed newspaper clipping.

"He might try to contact you…" Schuster's voice reverberated through her head. Then Denise's voice: *"…Trying to send a message."*

"No." Bex gritted her teeth and clamped her eyelids shut. She pressed her palms over her ears, but the voices rolled over and over, slightly muffled by the sound of the waves on the beach and images of Darla.

"They said it was the security guard," Bex told herself. "It wasn't him. It was a couple of kids ransacking the house. Not"—she felt the familiar lump growing in her throat—"him."

Bex was starting to nod off when a gentle rustling made her sit bolt upright. She glanced around the darkened room, sure that the ransacking kids or her father or Detective Schuster or any other manner of boogeyman was waiting for her in the blackness. Bex clicked on her bedside light, and a hollow laugh twittered in her chest. Her bedroom window was half-open, the night breeze whistling in and lifting the gauzy curtains. The wind had peeled a couple of loose pages from the top of her desk.

"I'm so paranoid."

Bex slammed the window shut and gathered up the fallen papers. When she saw the one on top, her saliva soured. Her head throbbed. She tried to focus on the page in her shaking fingers.

"Black Bear Diner!" Beth Anne slammed the heavy door of her father's old truck and ran across the dusty parking lot. She pulled open the door to the restaurant and was immediately hit with warm, familiar smells. Waffles. Pancakes. Thick maple syrup. Bacon.

"You two here again?" The blond waitress had her hand on her hip and her lips pursed, but the edges curled up into a provocative smile.

"I guess this is kind of like our place," her father said, talking to the waitress over Beth Anne's head.

"Our place!" Beth Anne repeated, helping herself to one of the coffee-stained menus.

She hadn't seen a Black Bear Diner menu in ten years, but the one in her hands was authentic, coffee stained. It smelled vaguely of maple syrup and had that sweet pancake-batter smell. It was old and crisp, the ink smeared and faded. She had no idea how it came to be on her desk, in her room.

She thought again of the ransacked house, the tortured look on Denise's face.

Detective Schuster.

The yellowed newspaper clipping.

"Our place," Bex muttered, her blood going ice-cold.

TWENTY-TWO

Bex and her father were back at the Black Bear Diner. She was still seventeen but dressed in the heavy, navy-blue dress that she always wore when her father took her out. Bex looked at her feet and saw her folded, lace ankle socks and Mary Janes.

"You never could sit still, Beth Anne."

Her father shook his head, and Bex could see that he hadn't aged at all. The planes of his face were still smooth, still relaxed back into that charming smile. His eyes crinkled at the corners as he looked down at the paper in Bex's hands.

"You shouldn't believe everything you read."

He jerked his chin toward the newspaper and Bex looked down, recognizing the article that Schuster had handed her.

"Nice to see you two again. Ready to order?"

Bex's breath lobbed in her chest when she looked up at the waitress. It was the same woman who always waited on them, but her skin was ash gray and puckered. Her milky, unseeing eyes gaped in too-big hollows. Dirt and blood were caked in her ear and along her hairline. Bex tried to avert her eyes but they were drawn to the woman's hands, to her fingers wrapped around the pencil. Her fingernails were filthy—the few that remained—jagged and broken. The nail hung from her middle finger, and her ring finger was gone.

Bex tried to get out of the booth, but her feet no longer touched the floor. She clawed at the vinyl seat, but the waitress cocked her head and smiled a gruesome, skeletal smile.

"Leaving so soon?"

Bex tried to scream but only a soundless puff of air came from between her parted lips. The woman in the booth behind them turned and smiled. She had the same zombie-ish look as she pursed her greasy, black lips and pressed a broken, swollen index finger against her lips and swung her head.

"No, no, no," she said softly. When she shifted, Bex could see that she was the woman with the scarf and she was wearing it now. But as the woman shook her head, Bex could see that the scarf was covering three thick grooves carved into her neck. The blood was glossy; it bubbled and looked fresh.

"Daddy!" The voice that came from Bex was not her own. It was desperate and breathy, childlike.

Another woman strolled into the diner, her short denim shorts revealing elegantly long, tanned legs. She wore a half shirt and a belly ring, her blond hair flitting around her shoulders. She wasn't ashy and gray like the others, but her smile was just as gruesome, just as horrifying. She pressed her finger to her bluing lips and shook her head, the action making the silver heart locket around her neck bobble and catch the light.

"Darla!"

Bex's T-shirt was soaked. So was the sheet wrapped around her. Her hair was wet and matted against her forehead and she shivered.

"Oh my God." She looked around, taking in her mint-green bedspread, the soothing pale walls, the furniture she had come to recognize as "hers." She was safe. She was home.

The sunlight started to knife its way through the blinds and Bex threw open the window, staring at the scene outside: a flat driveway. A housing subdivision. Perfectly manicured and cultivated lawns and native plants and chunks of ocean grasses. She was almost five hundred miles from where the police had last seen her father, but now she saw him in every clump of shrubbery, behind every tree. Every sigh of the wind was him, his hot breath on the back of her neck, his finger pressed against his lips reminding her to stay silent.

Bex took the hottest shower she could stand, but she was still shaking when she got out.

• • •

It was midmorning when Detective Schuster called Bex. She watched the phone vibrate its way across her desk, picking it up on the fourth ring. She wasn't sure she wanted to talk to the detective— but she wasn't sure she had a choice. Either way, she didn't want Michael or Denise to hear her phone ringing and come check on her. She didn't want this to be her life.

"Hello?"

Detective Schuster's voice wasn't jovial or light. He was all business right from the get-go. "Have you considered what we talked about?"

What you talked about? Bex wanted to scream.

"I'm not going public with my identity."

She heard the detective sigh into the phone and her resolve started to crumble. She needed to go public for Darla. For all the other girls. For her father, if he really was… She wouldn't let herself complete the thought. But going public meant going back to her old life, to staring at her shoes and pretending she didn't hear the whispers.

"Is there any other way?"

"Well, we can create a profile for you on the websites. We'll be monitoring you the whole time, of course, but we could do all the work and all you'd have to do—"

Is wait, Bex finished in her mind. *Like prey.*

"I don't know why he would even visit one of those sites, let alone want to make contact or comment on it or whatever." Bex couldn't keep the shudder out of her voice. "They're heinous."

"Do you know what a narcissist is?"

"I do."

"Well"—it sounded like the detective was shrugging his shoulders, talking with his hands—"most serial killers are narcissists. To varying extents, of course. They're intelligent and they often like to see people admiring their handiwork."

But my father isn't a narcissist, Bex wanted to scream. He was good and kind, and he would do anything for her and Gran, anything at all.

"Sometimes you'll see them taunting the police or the victims' families. They like to believe they're smarter than everyone else."

She had heard the stories of legendary killers who sent coded letters to the police working their cases, joining search parties, walking shoulder to shoulder with their victims' parents and friends while they had the missing person tucked away in some horrible lair or shallow grave. Her father wasn't like that.

Was he?

"These people are depraved, Bex. These men and women are sick."

Women?

That struck the black part deep within Bex's soul that didn't question whether or not her father was guilty. It scratched like a clawed hand, fingernails dragging through wood, piercing the back of her neck, whispering with hot, moist breath. *It's him. It's you. His depravity, his sickness, his narcissism, his need to do this runs in your own veins...*

She had seen a movie about a female serial killer once, watching it huddled under the covers while her gran slept in her chair. But it was just a movie, and the killer was a big Hollywood star who had gained a couple of pounds and wore fake teeth to look evil and ugly. She said her lines like a Hollywood starlet would, and they used computer-generated images to show a couple of murder scenes. Two weeks later, that actress was on every television station in fabulous dresses and diamond-dripping chandelier earrings because it had only been a story. The thrum of death that coursed through Bex's veins couldn't be shed like the teeth and a couple of extra pounds. Bex's ugly was in her blood.

But if Schuster was wrong...

If Schuster was wrong and her father was innocent—the word stung more than it should have, an aching reminder of what *she* did—then he wouldn't be on the sites at all, would he? Bex tried to quell her guilt, tried to remind herself that she was just a child and couldn't have known that they'd take what she said and use it against her dad.

And then the anger walloped her and the sound of Schuster's coaxing voice enraged her. *He* should have known better. He'd manipulated her, and here he was, doing it again. But no one else had ever talked to her. She was a pariah without Schuster. The emotions wheeled through her—dizzying, frustrating, lonely, painful—when all she ever wanted was to be normal.

"Bex?" Michael knocked on the door frame before slightly nudging open the door. "Ready to take a break from homework? I made lasagna. Well, not so much made as thoroughly heated up." He grinned at her, a floppy, cockeyed Dad-laughing-at-his-own-joke grin, and Bex knew that the only way to get to normal was to wade through this mess with her real father.

She pressed her fingers over the mouthpiece of her phone and smiled back at Michael. "I'll be right there."

• • •

"No. No, I couldn't. I would just die." Chelsea was shaking her head, her ponytail bobbing against her cheekbones. "I can't believe you stayed in that house knowing that someone had broken in."

Bex took a miniscule sip of her coffee and avoided Chelsea's eyes. "It wasn't really that big a deal. The cops said it was probably just kids."

Laney smacked her palms on the table, and both Chelsea and Bex jumped. "Do you hear yourself? The cops are just brushing it off, but our friend was murdered. Shouldn't they have put up surveillance or put you in protective police custody or something?"

Bex's stomach roiled. "Why me? I have nothing to do with... I mean..."

Chelsea's eyes bulged. "Are you kidding? Yeah, you do. You're a teenager. Darla was a teenager. This guy could be after any of us. Or all of us." She leaned in, hissing, "There is a crazed killer on the loose and your house gets ransacked and the police think it's just kids. Oh no, seriously, no. I'd call the brigade or the army or whatever. When you die, you should seriously sue for negligence or noncompliance or something."

Laney rolled her eyes. "I'm sure Bex is fine, Chelsea. It's not like they took anything, right, Bex?"

Bex didn't trust herself to talk so she meekly shook her head, her hands going to her backpack. She touched the zippered pouch where she had stuffed the Black Bear Diner menu, the gentle crunch of the paper giving her a strange sense of calm.

"Ladies!"

Both Chelsea and Laney groaned when Zach approached the table, but Bex was happy for the distraction. He had his GoPro camera in front of him, the red Record light glowing.

"Do you have any comments that you would like saved for

posterity? Perhaps some advice or information for the incoming freshman of, say, 2089?"

"Hopefully, the people of 2089 will be so advanced that they'll have done away with high school."

Laney cocked an eyebrow. "You realize 2089 isn't that far away, right, Chels?"

Chelsea batted at the air. "Whatever. We're all going to be dead by then."

"Anything to add, Bex?"

Bex had suddenly gone cold, the din of the cafeteria noise overwhelming.

"I-I've got to go."

TWENTY-THREE

Bex paced a worn spot in the grass behind the gym. She was only about twenty feet behind the school, but the thick, tall brick wall of the gym separated her from the rest of Kill Devil Hills High and all of the students inside.

If there really were a brick wall between me and the world, Bex thought, *then no one else would get hurt.*

She pulled out her cell phone and dialed, counting the rings, waiting for the overly cheerful receptionist to pick up the receiver and announce she had reached Dr. Gold's office. She would talk to Dr. Gold, and Dr. Gold would remind Bex that the only thing she *had* to do was take care of herself. Dr. Gold would make everything okay with her psychology speak, and Bex would hang up the phone and cut the line to Detective Schuster and her father and get to work pretending that nothing had ever happened.

But Darla... Bex's mind kept humming even as she tried to stamp out the voice and concentrate on the ringing phone. On the fourth ring, a series of chimes and an automated voice came on to tell Bex that the number had been disconnected. The disembodied voice suggested she check the number and call again. Bex did just that, only to be greeted with the same message. She frowned at the phone, then swiped on her browser, groaning when an emoticon frowny face popped up telling her that she was out of Internet service range.

When the bell rang, Bex jogged to chemistry class, arriving out of breath.

"Hey," Trevor said. "I was beginning to think you changed schools again."

Bex offered him a weak smile. "No, I'm just…super busy with an assignment." She saw the hurt and confusion in his eyes but turned away anyway. "Mr. Ponterra, I'm really behind on my assignment. Can I go to the computer lab and finish up?"

Mr. Ponterra nodded and scribbled off a pass.

Bex was the only person in the ancient computer lab. She fired up one of the machines and tapped her fingernails on the desktop, waiting for the thing to load and connect to the Internet.

"Come on, come on," she groaned.

Finally, she pulled up a search engine and typed in Dr. Gold's information, desperate to find a new phone number for the office. The old machine seemed to practically chug and spit out smoke, taking way too long to pop up Bex's results. But when the page started to load, Bex wished that it never had.

Social Psychologist Elliot Gold Found Murdered near Wake County Home

Social psychologist Dr. Elliot Gold, who had been reported missing two weeks ago, was found dead on the banks of Harris Lake on Sunday afternoon. Her body was discovered by two Raleigh-area residents who had gone fishing.

"We nearly couldn't recognize what it—what she—was at first," said Tucker Spayeth, one of the fishermen.

Gold suffered antemortem blunt-force trauma, but authorities say that she was killed by asphyxiation, strangled by a scarf that the murderer left tied around her neck. Her left ring finger was removed. Though that is the signature of North Carolina's infamous Wife Collector, whose case Gold was closely involved in before he went missing ten years ago, the work was likely that of a copycat's.

Bex felt her lower lip tremble as tears burned in her eyes.

"Why did he do this?" The words were out of her mouth before she had a chance to consider them.

When authorities went to search Dr. Gold's place of work, they found that her office had been ransacked, her personal files upended and unorganized. Missing files lead police to believe that Gold's killer was likely a disgruntled patient.

Bex shook her head, the words on the screen blurring. "He wasn't a patient," she mumbled to herself. "He was searching for one."

"Um, hello?"

Bex jumped, her thighs slamming against the underside of her desk.

Zach blanched.

"I'm sorry. I didn't mean to scare you. You were just talking"—he scanned the room—"to yourself, I guess. I didn't want to interrupt."

Bex frantically wiped at her face and sniffed. "No, sorry," she said, trying to exit the newspaper site. The fan on the old machine spun as an icon whirled around, telling her to wait. She saw Zach's eyes drift to the page on her screen, then back to Bex.

"Everything okay?"

"Yeah," she said. "I was just…coughing…and my eyes were watering." She stood, shouldered her backpack, and clicked off the computer. "I'm done here if you needed this machine or something."

She stomped out of the room, head held high, hoping that her facade wouldn't crack. Once she was out of the building, she pulled out her cell phone and dialed. The phone didn't even finish a full ring before it was answered.

"How do I do this?"

"What's that now?"

"I want to find him," Bex said. "How do I… There are so many websites. How am I supposed to be sure which one he'll go to?"

There was a long pause before Detective Schuster answered. "Thank you for doing this, Bex. I know it can't be easy—"

"Just tell me, please. Before I change my mind."

"Do you have a pen and paper handy?"

• • •

Bex stared at the blinking cursor on her screen, then at the torn-off piece of notebook paper in her hand. She had carefully written down everything the detective told her, then folded the paper and put it in her jeans pocket. She had touched it throughout the day, certain that if she were to lose it, it would somehow be linked back to her. Every hour or so she had smoothed it between her fingers, rolling it in her palm so much that now it almost felt like cloth. The blue lines had started to bleed their color, the red to run. The black ink from her ballpoint pen didn't smear though, and the websites looked permanent and menacing, like black tattoos across the white paper:

WifeCollectorFanatic, FreeWTC, SerialLover/ WifeCollector

She slowly typed the first entry into the search bar, studiously checking each letter against the paper, then hovering her finger over the Search button.

She didn't really want to know…but soon the guilt was consuming her—guilt for Darla, guilt for her father, guilt for bringing her hideous, warped world to Kill Devil Hills. She hit Search.

The results seemed to take ages to load, then suddenly it was too soon. The pages cascaded down Bex's screen, each one flashing gory pictures or grainy black-and-whites of her father and splashed with all manner of icons—from bloody butcher's knives to barbed-wire-wrapped hearts. With each new *ping!* of the computer, Bex's resolve chipped away. This wasn't an attorney doing his best to prove her father was responsible for every reprehensible crime splayed in gory photographs; these were people who believed—and *reveled* in the fact—that her father was the Wife Collector. Again, the guilt, the slight bit of terror, and that hideous thought: *If he's guilty, you're guilty too.*

Bex bit down hard on her lower lip, the surge of pain a welcome distraction.

"I'm doing this for Darla," she muttered.

She closed all the other pages, leaving only the first one from Detective Schuster's list open, her fingers trembling as her cursor circled the Forums menu. She clicked and the page loaded, sterile and white compared to the previous one. Bex watched a list populate questions and topics from tiny, thumbnail-sized avatars of people named GOBLIN, PATDRAGON, or GAMECREATOR with trending subjects like "What would you do for a million dollars?" and "Does this make you sad?"

They were basic questions, but posted on a site created by and populated with people who adored serial killers, these took on an ominous, dark edge and goose bumps trailed along Bex's bare arms. She slid into her hoodie and pulled the hood up, somehow in need of the extra comfort and protection the fleece cocoon gave her.

"Here goes nothing."

The detective had given her a list of things to do and write—even the best time to post and what her subject line should say. Bex typed from the paper, focusing only on the letters and not the words they were making up. It was better that way; she wasn't part of it then. She was just a receptionist, just typing a slew of letters that formed themselves into words that formed ideas without her. She had barely hit Post Topic when the first response pinged in. It was the same cheerful ping she got from every other website on the planet. Somehow she thought a notification from a serial killer page would have a more apropos tone, like a chain saw revving or a woman screaming. Bex's stomach rolled into a tight knot.

1player1 has responded to your posting BLACK BEAR CUB.
Would you like to accept?

Bex could feel the hot breath pumping through her nostrils and burning the tips of her lips. She didn't want to accept. She didn't want to accept any of this. The animated question mark throbbed. She clicked.

Hi BETHANNER (great name by the way, true fan, huh?!)!
There is another guy that usually posts here—his screen name is IMHIM_HESME. He knows all about the Wife Collector's family life. More than I do. What exactly do you want to know about?

More messages popped up, one after another in a terrifying deluge. Some responded to Bex's question, and most referenced Beth Anne—Bex—in horrible, stomach-sickening references. Bex felt their poison sink into her, making her eyes sting as tears rolled over her cheeks. To some of these "fans," Beth Anne Reimer was a legend with "royal" blood.

They estimated that she was probably "as bad as her daddy, if not worse" and had not only the benefit of her father's genes but his tutelage too. One responder stated that Beth Anne diligently visited her father every other weekend, knowing exactly where he was, and took notes. Another said she was probably in an institution. Still a third said that he emailed the Wife Collector's daughter frequently and that they'd even had a fling.

Bex could feel the sick at the back of her throat as she scanned each message, trying to only find keywords, the things and patterns that Schuster had told her to look out for without actually reading the text.

Two hours later, Bex felt like a wrung-out dishrag. Her head throbbed, her throat felt raw, and it felt as though her tears had run divots down her cheeks. The messages had slowed to a trickle, and Michael and Denise had poked their heads in to say good night and warn her off the computer. Bex had nodded mutely and mumbled, "Almost done," but kept clicking on each new response. She stopped when she got to the message from IMHIM_HESME. It was simple:

WHO ARE YOU?

It was an email response. Three silent words sent through cyberspace, but Bex felt like they were in her house, in her room, throbbing, growing, suffocating her. It felt like IMHIM_HESME was screaming at her, his breath hot, his hands talons, clawed, coming for her.

He was in the house.

No, Bex told herself, shaking her head. *"He" is no one. A name. A jerk. Probably some ten-year-old kid from some country she had never heard of.*

WHO ARE YOU?

The words burned Bex's throat and she whirled in her chair, blinking at the darkness that blanketed her. At some point, the

streetlights had gone on. At some point, the cars had stopped drifting up the street and the yellow lights in the neighborhood had
clicked off one by one.

It was like Bex was the only one awake in the world. A warning
gnawed at her. *You brought him here. You have to make sure they're safe.*

She glanced at her phone, ready to text Trevor, Chelsea, and
Laney—but what would she say? "Hey, guys, just want to make
sure my potentially-a-serial-killer father hasn't butchered you?"

She tried to laugh at her pitiful joke, but her heart pounded
and that unrelenting voice kept saying, *Not them…* Bex thought of
Michael and Denise, poking their heads in and wishing her good
night before they ambled across the hall. She cocked her head,
hoping for the comforting sound of the television turned down
low or one of the Michael's curtain-sucking snores.

There was only an overwhelming, deafening silence.

No.

Bex jumped out of her chair so fast it fell to the floor behind her,
catching on the edge of the bed and sliding to the ground slowly,
soundlessly. She picked her way across the heavy pile carpet, each
creak and settle of the house sending a shock wave of angst down
the back of her neck.

She could hear him breathing.

No! Bex scolded herself. *That's Michael. Or Denise.*

But something about the computer in her bedroom, the screen
glowing like a beacon, seemed like an open door inviting the Wife
Collector and all his weird groupies into her world—into Michael
and Denise's *home*. Bex brought evil.

You're a traitor.

Michael and Denise's bedroom door was open a crack and Bex racked her mind, trying to remember if that was the way they always left it at night. Or did they close it, and someone had gone in and…

Bex's heart lodged in her throat.

Blood pulsed through her ears.

She pushed open the door with a single, trembling hand, waiting for her eyes to adjust to the near-pitch-darkness. She didn't dare call their names. She couldn't turn on the light, that old urban legend about killers hiding in the darkness under the bed bearing down on her.

Bex could see them then, Michael and Denise, their bodies outlined under the sheet. She stood in the doorway, watching them breathe, needing to make sure that their chests rose and fell rhythmically, even while she felt as if she was betraying her father and Denise and Michael all at once.

I don't want to be here, Bex thought. *I don't want to do this.* She had already changed her name and her looks and moved across the state. She was sure now that anywhere she went, Beth Anne Reimer and the Wife Collector would follow her. For Bex, there was no way out.

She stepped out of the doorway slowly, carefully pulling the door closed as she did. Bex let out a long breath and took another, stepping into her own room and doing a cursory scan. She smacked the lid of the laptop shut and was about to scold herself for letting her eyes play tricks and her imagination run away with her when a slight breeze pulled the edge of one of her curtains. Her breath hitched when she noticed the shoes. Big, heavy boots with rounded toes. Jeans with dirty, fraying hems pooling around the ankles.

Beth Anne was seven years old, and for the first time she could remember—maybe for the first time in her whole life—there was a blanket of cottony white snow on the ground. It was thin but it was there, delicate flakes clinging to the bare branches of the half-dead dogwood in the front yard, its gnarled branches made elegant by the glistening snow.

"Jacket on. And SHOES!" Beth Anne heard her gran trill.

Beth Anne was still in her nightgown. It was warm, flannel, the wrists gathered and puckered, a peplum around her ankles. Her father's boots were in the hallway, rounded toes pointed toward the door. She slid her stockinged feet into the giant, clunky things, the tops reaching nearly to her knees. Beth Anne picked up one foot, then the other, each boot as heavy as a melon, but they stomped great tracks in the snow. Hard edged, defined.

"What in Sam heck are you doing out there in my good boots, little girl?"

Her father was framed in the doorway, hands on hips, eyes narrowed, but a hint of a smile on his lips.

"I'm playing a game!" Beth Anne yelled back.

"You don't know any games!"

Stomp. Stomp. Stomp. "I made it up!"

"You're making tracks. In my shoes."

He did a high-kneed jaunt out into the snow, swiping the girl up

HANNAH JAYNE

and nuzzling her close. "You made it look like I walked around this place all silly. Tracks here and tracks there."

Beth Anne giggled, waggling her feet in the boots. Her father leaned in close. "That's a good girl. They'll never find me with tracks like that!"

"You like my game, Daddy?"

"It's my game, Bethy. I make them up. I make them all up."

Bex woke like a drowning woman breaking the surface of water: panicked, coughing, gasping for breath. Her whole body seemed to move in slow motion, that dreamlike state between dreaming and waking up where you *have* to move, *have* to run, or whatever was chasing you in your nightmare will cross over into your waking life. She blinked at the computer in front of her, the screen gone black.

The curtains. The boots.

Bex was still sitting at her desk, arms thrown in front of her, but her entire body was tense, a coiled wire. She forced herself to turn around before he approached her, before he crossed the room and put his hand on her shoulder, dragging her back to the web page or to Darla's dump site or into one of the horrible things his "fans" suggested.

Finally Bex forced herself to turn around, her fingers fumbling over the desk, looking for something to swing.

This is my dad. This is a monster. A criminal, a joke, a dream, my mind playing tricks on me.

She grabbed a handful of Bic pens and slowly crossed the room, each silent step on the carpet like a screaming beacon for evil to come get her. She reached out her arm, her fingers playing in the lacy edge

172

of the curtain, her hand with the pens pulled back and ready to stab. She yanked the curtain open.

There was nothing there.

There is nothing there!

"Oh God," Bex murmured, pressing her fingers against her temples. "I'm going crazy. Seeing things. I'm absolutely going crazy."

That snowy day in Raleigh crashed back on Bex. It wasn't the boots. It was the game. *"It's my game, Bethy. I make them up. I make them all up."*

Bex went to her computer, though everything inside her told her to stop. She clicked the message icon.

GAMECREATOR has requested a private chat.

????

GAMECREATOR has logged off.

TWENTY-FOUR

"Hey, Bexy!"

Denise gave her a kiss on the top of her head, and Bex smiled at the linoleum. She felt silly for liking the way Denise sometimes babied her.

"How'd you sleep?"

Bex couldn't remember *if* she'd slept, but she found that she was getting better and better at stamping down the tsunami of feelings she had every day. The chat request from GAMECREATOR hung on her periphery, but she reminded herself that there were thirty-eight other messages from people with provocative names—like RALEIGHRAIDER and THEREALWC—who seemed to be nothing more than rabid Wife Collector fanboys. There was no *real* reason to suspect that GAMECREATOR was any different...*right?*

She'd had thought the same when Detective Schuster sent a text this morning—simple, to the point, very Schuster.

Schuster: Any contact?

Bex had hesitated for a half second before hastily typing, Nope.

Now she absently touched the phone in her pocket as she shrugged at Denise. "Good, I guess. You're back from your run already?"

"Slow day in the track shoes. Just been puttering around here, baking cookies, doing the nineteen-fifties-wife thing." She held out a plate stacked with badly misshapen cookies and frowned at them. "I haven't really perfected it."

Bex took a cookie. "I never judge a cookie by its shape." She bit. "Mmm, good."

Denise handed her a glass of milk and Bex turned, catching a snatch of television screen in her peripheral. She froze, her saliva going sour and metallic. The chill of the glass froze her fingers and the cold went all the way up her arm; then the glass was going down, slow, slow, slow until it thunked on the floor and spattered the icy liquid against her calves, the remainder of the milk pouring out of the now-shattered glass at her feet.

From somewhere, she heard Denise calling to her, but all she could focus on was her father. His smiling face beamed out at her from the television screen. Bex had seen the picture they used a dozen times on screen, then a thousand times in her memory. Every time was a punch in the gut—a pang of memory, a starburst of rage, and that overwhelming, crushing guilt. That man wasn't a murderer; that man was her father.

The news ticker scrolled underneath his picture:

Breaking News: Possible Sighting of Jackson Reimer, Alleged "Wife Collector" Murderer in Beaufort, South Carolina.

A parade of the Wife Collector's victims followed his picture as it always had. The girls, blond and smiling, frozen in some other time; then shots of the dump sites; and finally, a body in a carved-out rectangle of earth, bare knees hugged to her chest. The news always blurred out the body, but Bex knew who it was—the Wife Collector's sixth victim, Amanda Perkins.

Her stomach rolled over on itself. *You did that. You let that happen. Just like you let it happen to Darla.* Bex was shaking her head, the tips of her too-short hair prickly against her cheeks. "No," she whispered. "No."

"Bex!"

She could feel Denise's hands on her shoulders, leading her to a chair. Bex sank into it.

"What is it, honey?" Denise glanced at the screen, grabbed the remote, and clicked off the television. "Are you worried about that? The Wife Collector? Oh, honey, how do you even know about that? He was way before you would have known about such things. No one is going to get you here. I will never let anything like that happen to you." She offered a reassuring smile, brushing Bex's hair from her forehead. "Beaufort is more than four hundred miles away. You're safe here with us."

"I-I guess." Bex stopped, sucked in a long breath, and tried to gather herself. *Denise would understand*, she thought quickly. Then, *Denise can never know. They won't love you anymore. You are the child of a serial killer…and even if you're not, you're the child who drove away her own father when you provided the police with evidence.* She gritted her teeth, forcing that voice down. "I guess I just got a little freaked out is all. Let me clean up."

Denise waved Bex away. "Why don't you go change? You've got milk all over your shoes."

Bex nodded, hoping Denise wasn't watching as she took the stairs two at a time, pressing the pads of her fingertips against her temples. Somewhere between the first bite of cookie and seeing her father's face, her head had started pounding and her stomach roiling. The news was out. Everyone would know. Her father had resurfaced and—*and what?*

Bex's eyes started to sting. In the ten years that he'd been gone, her father had never tried to contact her. She used to pretend that he did, that one day she would move a bureau or open a closet and find a stack of old, unopened letters that her grandmother had never given her. There would be birthday cards and Christmas wishes, her dad asking about school and boys, and apologizing. Hoping his daughter was okay. After her grandmother's death, Bex had scoured the house, both hoping that he'd left her something and that he had not. She could never be sure if it was better that her father distanced himself from her rather than keep her close. For Bex, it hurt either way.

It was Christmas Eve, and Beth Anne had just turned thirteen. Everything around Raleigh was decorated with swaths of pine, red bows, and giant, round ornaments, and bell-ringing Santas were outside stores. Every commercial on TV showed a family rushing into one another's arms, having been separated by long flights or college or snow. Not one of them showed a father in a holding cell, gathering up his motherless daughter in his arms. Not one showed a little girl fingering an old, knitted stocking, wondering if she should bother to put it next to hers.

Every day the world reminded Beth Anne that her family wasn't normal, but it was always worse in December. There were no holiday cards in the mailbox, no Christmas letters to read, no snow-laden family pictures to tack up. There was a flimsy Christmas tree wrestled from the attic and adorned with a string of half-working lights. A couple of brand-new ornaments bought from the Walgreens because Beth Anne's family had nothing to hand down. And there was one photograph that Gran trotted out every year and put on the mantel.

From a distance, it looked like a normal—if slightly stiff—family portrait. Gran stood on one side of Beth Anne, her father on the other. Her mother, like a shadow, hovered behind. It almost looked like they were smiling but there was no joy in the slightly upturned lips. Every year Beth Anne studiously avoided the portrait, but that year, she rolled up on her tiptoes and pulled it from the mantel, scrutinizing it. There was something sad in her grandmother's eyes. Something empty in her mother's. And her father's…well, they were sharp and black, searing and defined, daring you to look away.

Beth Anne, six, at best, was clutching a square gift box wrapped in red and green, the only indicator of the season. Her grandmother's hand rested gently on her shoulder. Her mother's hands were clamped around Beth Anne's arms as if holding on for dear life. And her father had his hands by his sides, slightly fisted, two inches of space between him and his family. Beth Anne wondered why she had never noticed the distance before.

In her room, she tried to block out the images of the victims, but they flashed in front of her eyes, seeming to lurk in every corner: Amy Eickler with a necklace of ligature bruises in the closet; Isabel Doctoro, bloodshot eyes wide and accusing, hunkering by the bed; Melanie Harris, hands bloodied as she clawed for her life in that Food Lion parking lot. Even as the sunlight streamed in through the windows, Bex turned on every light and pushed open every drape until her bedroom nearly glowed. She could still hear their voices. She could still hear his. She pressed her hands against her ears.

"Stop, stop, please stop," she whispered.

Dr. Gold had talked to her about "the phantoms" once. Had told her that they were figments of her imagination, manifestations of her guilt for not turning her father in sooner. *Then why was he talking too? Why was he begging me to remember, to set them straight?*

Suddenly Bex was shaking.

"Maybe he'll want to tell you his side of the story." She remembered Detective Schuster's trailing words.

Maybe...

Bex sat down at her laptop, her fingers hovering over the keys.

"W-W-W," she started. She paused, tapping her finger against her bottom lip, everything inside her a churning mass of confusion. She wanted to talk to her father. She wanted to tell him to run. She wanted to tell him to disappear, to never bother her again, to never have been in her life. She wanted to see him locked up. She wanted to never exist.

"*W-W-W*," she said again, her voice soft, "*W-C-F-A-N*…on fire."

It was the same page from the night before, but this time there weren't a dozen others blocking out the home page. It popped up immediately, joy and terror populating her whole screen. There were pictures, screen grabs of old headlines and newspaper clippings. Repeated shots of her father glancing over his shoulder, his eyes fierce and black, his lips pressed together hard, the slightest hint of a contemptuous grin.

Bex wasn't sure she was breathing. She wasn't sure her heart was still beating.

Her mouse hovered over the main menu, page titles like "Kills," "Court," and "Crimes" magnifying. She knew she should go straight for Forums because she was doing what Detective Schuster had said: she would find her father and trap him. The overzealous "Dangerous Serial Killer Surfaces in Beaufort" headlines would vanish, and maybe, if she was fast enough and smart enough, she could disappear back into her life as Bex Andrews, back into Michael and Denise's family, back into her plain high school social life at Kill Devil Hills High.

A girl was murdered there after you came, that horrible voice hissed. *You'll never be normal. You'll never disappear…*

Bex didn't even try to blink back the tears.

"*You and me, Bethy girl. We're special. There ain't any like us. We stick together. We take care of each other. We're special, Bethy. You and me.*"

Her father's voice was a smoke-filled whisper in her ear. The memory of her sitting on his knee, his big palm wrapped around her rib cage, was just a slice, a tiny vision.

TWISTED

"I'm helping Detective Schuster," Bex said, jaws clenched.

But was he really the one who needed help?

Bex knew she should drop another bit of bait, but the page Beginnings caught her eye. She wasn't sure she had seen it the night before. She clicked and the photo-heavy page loaded slowly. As the connection lagged, the picture came up incrementally, half-inch-thick bars creeping horizontally across the screen. She saw the top of her father's head first, some caught-forever-on-film breeze casually lifting a few strands of hair that used to be the same color as Bex's.

The page kept going and she was struck still, staring at a photo of her family—mother, father, daughter—that she never remembered seeing. There was another photo inset, a smaller one of her father and Gran, and finally, the same picture that had sat on the mantel every Christmas. This one had text across the front and a bold, red circle around Bex's smiling mother with her hands protectively gripping her daughter. Someone had scrawled "Victim zero?" with three big question marks and a typed parenthetical: "(first wife)." The text along the bottom read:

Did our serial have a practice vic or "victim zero" in his own wife? He married nineteen-year old Carrboro, NC, resident Naomi Lee who he met at his job at Joe's Tires. Lee was pregnant. The couple moved to Raleigh where daughter Beth Anne was born.

Bex's heart began to thud. She scrolled with the text, and a black-and-white square popped up showing a picture of her parents,

181

younger than she ever remembered, smiling while sitting on the back of a car. In it, her mother held a tiny bouquet against the slight bump at her belly. Bex had never seen the picture, had never known that her mother was nineteen or from Carrboro, or that she herself had been a bump straining against her mother's lacy, white shift dress the day her parents married. She didn't know any of this but a stranger with a fake name did. A complete stranger was filling in the gaps in her history, stocking it with pictures, even.

Bex felt sick. She continued to read.

Naomi "abandoned" her family when her daughter was barely six years old. Or did she? She shares a lot of the same physical traits as the Wife Collector victims.

Bex couldn't read anymore. She slammed the lid of her laptop down, pacing. She tried to turn on the TV, but every channel was running and rerunning what seemed to be the same photo series of her father and the victims. Doe-eyed anchors looked concerned while news reporters peppered the broadcast with general serial killer "facts." She started to play music but every song seemed to be specifically chosen to make her feel guilty, to remind her that she was no good. She couldn't be good; she likely shared the blood of a serial killer.

The tiny ribbon of hope inside her, that inkling of thought that maybe he wasn't guilty, was beaten to a pulp by the websites, the pictures, the reminders that she didn't really know him at all. That should have made her feel better. It should have made her more resilient, more determined to send him to prison where he belonged. But all it did was turn her into a quivering heap lying on her bedroom floor and feeling hopeless and horrible.

She was through crying and half-asleep when Detective Schuster called.

"I guess you've seen the news."

Bex nodded, then mumbled, "Hard not to."

"Have you gotten anything from him?"

A sob lodged in her throat and burned at the edges of her eyes. "I don't want to do this anymore."

The detective paused on his end, and Bex could hear him suck in a long, slow breath. "I know this is hard, Bex. But this is so, so important. Especially now. He knows that the world is looking for him. He's going to need help. He's going to be looking for someone who will sympathize with him. Your dad's smart. You could very well be our only hope of catching him before…"

Bex knew what he was going to say: before he kills again. He had to say it, had to pin her with it because all she wanted to do was tuck her head in the sand and fall into a dreamless sleep that would last until the whole ordeal was over. But saying no was as good as becoming a monster herself.

"Let me think about it," she whispered.

TWENTY-FIVE

Bex stayed after school to make up the geography test she'd missed when Michael and Denise let her sleep in. When she finished, she slipped the paper into her teacher's wire basket, said good-bye, and stepped out into the hallway. It was completely deserted. The floors looked like they had just been cleaned, and the smell of chlorine and industrial cleaning products stung Bex's nose.

Her footsteps echoed throughout the hall, as did the footsteps of the person behind her. Bex casually glanced over her shoulder, then stopped.

It was the girl from the funeral, the girl who had waved to her.

Tension pulled Bex's shoulders up to her earlobes. "Can I help you with something?"

Clearly startled, the girl blinked her deep-brown eyes.

"I-I…" The girl swallowed and blinked again. She straightened. "I'm the girl whose mother was killed by your father."

Someone had sucked all the air out of the room and Bex couldn't move, her mouth open, eyes wide. In her mind's eye, she doubled over herself, oofing from the sucker punch to the gut.

"Wh-what did you say?"

"I'm Lauren." The girl looked as uncomfortable as Bex felt, taking a step and then stepping back, offering a hand, then pulling it away. "I just…"

"Oh. Oh," was all Bex could say as a million things crashed over her: Apology. Grief. Guilt. Blame.

Blame?

Your mother shouldn't have made my father kill her.

The thought—a fleeting one that was in as quickly as it was out—made Bex sick to her stomach.

"I just wanted to…see you…I guess," Lauren was saying, the fabric of her skirt swooshing into a colorless blur.

"My father… He never… It was alleged…"

But Lauren just stared at her, eyes wide, intent, curious.

Bex took a step back. "I can't… I've got… Excuse me." She turned and pushed in the door to the girl's bathroom, making it to the first stall just as she started to wretch. She was sweating, a burning stripe going from the back of her neck all the way down her spine as she vomited. Each time her stomach convulsed, a new wave of images shot through her mind—gruesome, haunting, slasher-movie scenes that made her sick all over again.

When there was nothing left to throw up, she grabbed a handful of toilet paper and blotted her eyes and nose as she cried a silent, body-racking sob for this strange girl Lauren and the mother that Bex's father had snatched away. She cried for Lauren and for herself, and begged for forgiveness for thinking that the woman's murder could be anything but her father's fault.

You don't know that! that inner voice told her.

He's your flesh and blood, another one countered. *Like father, like daughter.*

Bex wasn't sure how much time had passed but she'd cried everything out, her entire body feeling hollow and light. She splashed water on her face and pulled her hair over her eyes and cheeks, trying her best to hide the red splotches and smeared makeup. When she pushed back out into the hallway, it was blessedly silent.

"It's Bex now, isn't it?"

Lauren was still there, and Bex felt herself start to tremble.

"How did you know who I am?"

Lauren shrugged her thin shoulders. "I…know people. I went to the same juvenile detention center you did. I guess I kind of kept tabs…"

"I'm sorry," Bex said.

"Me too," Lauren said.

Bex started. "What are you sorry for?"

Lauren crossed in front of her. "I shouldn't have just… I wasn't even going to talk to you." She looked at her shoes. "I really just wanted to see you, see what you looked like."

Bex sucked in a slow breath. "Did you want to see if I looked like him?"

Lauren glanced at Bex, then stared at her shoes. "You do, kind of. I mean, the pictures."

Bex nodded, unsure what to say. She really didn't know what her father looked like, other than the pictures, and in them, she couldn't see much more than a slight and passing resemblance: same hair color, similar expression.

"Do you mind if we sit down?" Lauren asked.

Bex wanted to say no, but something drew her. Whether she thought she owed Lauren something or not she wasn't sure, but she pushed open the double doors and led her to a bench in the quad.

"Is it true that he gave you things—things that belonged to—"

"Yes." Bex couldn't bear to hear Lauren say the words. "I didn't know…"

"Did he ever give you earrings?"

"No, but I never had pierced ears."

Lauren pulled the sleeve of her cardigan up revealing a thin chain that looped around her wrist. On it was a five-petaled gold flower with a tiny pearl at the center. "This?"

Bex shook her head. "It's really pretty though."

"It was my mother's. Her earrings. They only found the one. He took the other one."

They were silent for a long while. Bex noticed that Lauren wouldn't look at her. She stared straight ahead while they sat shoulder to shoulder, barely blinking, talking without a breath, but focused like there was something in front of her to see.

"I think I came here… I wanted to see if maybe you knew."

Bex was walloped. Surprise, shame, anger, pain. She snapped her head to Lauren. "Knew what?"

Lauren swallowed and her voice was barely a whisper. "Why he did it."

Bex knew she should argue. Set this girl straight. It was alleged that her father was a murderer, but it had never been proven. A sob lodged hard in her chest. She shook her head slowly, her breathing shallow and painful.

"My mom had one of those giant personalities. And your dad…" Lauren went to tuck a strand of hair behind her ear. "He's just a man, you know?"

Bex nodded again, although she didn't really know. Her father was a distant memory. Her father was a two-dimensional picture in the newspaper, a man with a dark beard and a shaggy haircut. He was a gray man and a legend with a made-up name. He was the Wife Collector. Her father died a long time ago.

"I'd look at his pictures. I was obsessed with them." She let out something between a snarl and a laugh. "I couldn't believe it was him. I wanted him to be bigger. A monster maybe, with claws. Someone—something that couldn't help what it was, so a real person wasn't responsible for seeing my mother—hearing the way she would laugh out one high-pitched squeak before giggling without making a sound. The fact that she was a mother who read *Horton Hears a Who!* with a crazy voice and her arm in front of her nose like a trunk just because it made me laugh.

"I wanted your dad to be a monster who couldn't understand that my mom was a woman and a person with an awesome chocolate-chip cookie recipe and a daughter because really, how could a *person* do that to another person?"

Bex didn't have to look at Lauren to know that tears were pouring over her cheeks. That they were the kind of tears that took with them a tiny bit of Lauren's hope and joy and heart.

"I think I came here hoping that he would be here with you."

"He's not." Bex didn't mean for it to come out a whisper. "I don't know where he is either."

Now Lauren shook her head and used the palms of her hands to wipe at her tears. "I don't know what I was thinking. I shouldn't… You don't…" She paused, and a fresh torrent of tears started. "I guess I thought maybe you owed me something but"—she sniffed—"you're out a parent too."

Bex wanted to apologize for her father. She wanted to tell Lauren that even at home he was shy and mostly kept to himself, but she didn't know the man that Lauren talked about.

• • •

Bex spent the rest of her week avoiding Detective Schuster and trying not to think about Lauren, about her wide, flat brown eyes. But by Saturday, the thoughts consumed her as she sat in front of her laptop.

"Hey, Bex. You okay? You've been up here all day."

Bex blinked at Denise as she stood in the doorway. Her head was cocked, her voice soft. "It's Saturday. I think by law we're supposed to make sure you get at least one hour of sunlight each day."

"Yeah," Michael said, coming up behind Denise. "Don't let anyone say that we're raising veal."

Bex rubbed her eyes. "Um, I was thinking of going to a movie with Laney and Chelsea."

"Sunlight! Fresh air! Stretch your legs! Stop watching that little screen and go watch the big screen. In the dark. While sitting down." He looked at Denise. "Pretty sure we're nailing this parent thing."

Denise shot him a high five and Bex smiled. "You guys are so weird."

They left the room and Bex glanced back at her computer, hoping Denise and Michael hadn't noticed the way she'd blanched when they came in the door. She was still on the Wife Collector fan site, still trying to avoid the photos that popped up. She had already seen most of them, but they never ceased to make Bex's stomach drop into her shoes. She was going to close the laptop when a chat bubble popped up.

DETECTIVE LT. SCHUSTER is requesting a chat.

Bex clicked Accept and a tiny, smiling picture of the detective appeared in one corner of the gray box, his typing scrolling across the screen.

LT SCHUSTER: How is it going?
B*AND: Not gr8
LT SCHUSTER: Be patient. He's going to be cautious.

Bex felt slimy talking to Detective Schuster about trying to trick her father.

B*AND: Maybe he's just not on there.
LT SCHUSTER: What sites have you tried? Our link to your computer isn't up yet.
B*AND: Tried them all. Nothing. Maybe UR just wrong.

Anger and annoyance simmered low in Bex's gut. Anger, annoyance, and…joy? *If he wasn't on the site, maybe that proved that he wasn't guilty…*

LT SCHUSTER: Just—

SCREEN NAME B*AND has left this discussion.

She dialed Laney.

"Bex! Still up for a movie?"

Bex rubbed her eyes, yawning. "I was going to ask you the same thing."

"Is that why you yawned? To demonstrate your interest in the exciting social lives of Kill Devil Hills' finest?"

"Aren't a town's finest supposed to be the police?"

"I don't know. Anyway, you coming with?"

"You'd better be coming with!" Chelsea chorused in the background. "Unless you're throwing us off for Trevor, but you'd better not be!"

Bex laughed. "Yeah, I'm coming with, and I would never throw you guys off for a guy."

"That's good," Laney said, "because we're outside your house."

"Woooo! The call is coming from outside the house!" Chelsea burst into hysterical laughter. Bex wished all spooky stories could end the same way.

"What were you going to do if I *had* decided to ditch you guys and go out with Trevor?" she asked, opening the front door.

"We knew you would never do that," Laney said, following her into the house and hanging up the phone.

"We have intimate faith in you," Chelsea said.

"Imminent, Chels. The word is imminent."

"Whatever. Don't take this the wrong way, Bex, but you look awful."

Bex was dumbstruck for a half second. Her friends were in her bedroom, less than three feet from her open laptop and the heinous pictures and the throbbing forum of weirdos craving blood. Her two lives were about to crash into each other.

She slammed the laptop shut.

She didn't hear the ping of a new message alert from the fan site.

She didn't see the single line in the subject box from GAMECREATOR.

Is it really you, Bethy?

TWENTY-SIX

"Okay, the movie sucked. Capital S. U. C. K," Chelsea said as she, Bex, and Laney shuffled out of the Cineplex late that night. "I'm almost sorry I gave you that makeover."

Bex blinked her heavily made-up eyes and smacked her lips together, tasting the waxy residue Chelsea's borrowed Bombastic lip color had left. "It may have been a lousy movie, but I looked great watching it."

"That's what counts!"

"I bet he liked it." Laney jutted her chin toward a crowd of kids in front of them, Zach taking up the rear. He turned and looked just as Bex did, their eyes locking, then falling away immediately.

"He left the theater, like, three times," Laney said.

"Probably to go run and film himself saying that he loved the movie because it was 'based on actual events.'"

"'Inspired by,'" Bex corrected. "And I didn't think it was that bad."

A sly smile spread across Laney's face. "Like you even saw the movie! Your eyes were glazed over the whole time in Trevor-loves-me-land."

"Oh, let her be in love. We all could be serial-killer fodder in five minutes."

The jovial conversation immediately died. Bex wondered if Laney and Chelsea were thinking about Darla. All she could think about was her father, the screaming headlines, the talking heads on the news.

"Um, we should get to the car," Bex mumbled.

"Ladies…" A beat-up convertible BMW nearly ran over the girls' feet as the driver slowed to leer.

"Screw you!" Laney yelled to his taillights.

"Do guys think that actually works?" Bex asked, thankful for the subject change. "Like, how many girls climb into a complete stranger's car?"

"I don't know," Chelsea said, squinting in the direction the car had gone. "If he was cute…"

"Chels! That guy was, like, a hundred."

"And he doesn't seem all that picky." Bex pointed to where the BMW had pulled to the curb, another group of high school girls drifting toward the passenger-side door and giggling.

"I didn't mean that guy. And besides, if those girls get in that car, they deserve whatever they get. Herpes, scabies, whatever."

Bex looked away, briefly wondering if the women who had gotten into her father's car deserved what they got. The thought immediately made her blood run cold. *No one deserves that kind of death!* she screamed in her head. But then, that horrible voice: *They deserved it. You know they did. You think like he does. His blood is yours…*

194

Bex tried to shake the voices from her head.

Chelsea touched her arm. "You okay?"

"Yeah, just spaced for a minute there."

"Guys?" Laney had stopped in front of them, pointing at her car. It was the only one left on that side of the lot, and it was covered in paper.

"Lane! Someone left you, like, a thousand love letters!" Chelsea started toward the car, but Bex hung back, certain the pages weren't left for Laney.

"What is this?" Chelsea asked, peeling a paper from the windshield.

Bex pulled one out as well. They were slighter bigger than standard size, and when she leaned into the light to read one, her heart stopped. She held her breath as she stared at the others, hoping they weren't the same—but each one bore the same headline, the same inch-high, bold, red letters: MISSING. Under each heading there was a full-color picture.

"Oh my God." Laney pulled one from the windshield, squinting at the photo. "Who is this? Bex, do you know who Melanie Harris is?"

"Or"—Chelsea snatched a poster from the roof—"Amanda Perkins?" She pulled another one. "Kelly Hughes? Who are these people? Why did someone plaster these all over your car?"

Chelsea and Laney were plucking off the sheets, uncovering new photos—Amy Eickler, Katrina Wendt, Isabel Doctoro.

Bex knew them all.

They were all her father's victims.

"Oh no," Chelsea said, her voice shaking. "This one is just a little girl." She plucked off more of the pages to show a new smattering of posters below. They were all the same picture, all the same girl.

"Who is she? What's her name?" Laney asked.

"Beth Anne Reimer," Bex said, her voice a choked whisper.

• • •

Chelsea and Laney removed most of the posters. Bex tried to help, but her hands were shaking and her brain couldn't seem to command her arms to do anything but flail around uselessly.

"Jeez, Bex, you're white as a ghost. It's okay. It's probably just some stupid prank," Chelsea said, rubbing her palms over Bex's arms.

Laney frowned at the last of the fliers. "Some kind of disgustingly morbid prank. Get in, the car is mostly clear."

Bex nodded, unable to pick the proper words from the ones that drove through her head. *Who? And why?* When her cell phone chirped, she dropped it twice before swiping to answer.

"Hey, Trevor."

"So? Did you get it?"

Bex pressed her palm to her forehead, liking the cool feel against her hot skin. "Did I get what?"

"I left you something outside the theater. You couldn't have missed it."

Bex frowned. She felt her throat as it closed tighter and tighter. It was hard to breathe. She felt like she was already crying, but her eyes stayed dry and she was statue still.

"You did this?" Her voice was a faint whisper.

"You did this?" Beth Anne couldn't keep the incredulity from her voice. "I can't believe you did this."

Gran swelled with all the pride her ninety-eight-pound body could muster and dangled a key ring, two keys jangling together at the end. "You're sixteen, Beth Anne. Did you think I'd forgotten?"

"No." Beth Anne shook her head. "I didn't think you'd forget but I-I… We can't afford this, Gran."

Gran scoffed. "It's not exactly a Rolls Royce, dear."

It was a Ford Escort and it was at least twenty years old. The paint was chipped off the roof but what remained had been lovingly shined up. The seats were covered by a funky leopard-print blanket that had been carefully folded and cut to fit. "The original interior was not in the best of shape but—"

"It's beautiful, Gran. Thank you."

Gran folded the keys into Beth Anne's palm. "Well, go ahead. Take it for a spin."

There were exactly three places that Beth Anne knew to drive to, the only three places in town she ever went: the library, the grocery store, and, when she could see from the street that it was blessedly empty, Deja Brew coffeehouse on Falls of Neuse Road. She'd tuck her feet underneath herself in one of their half-hidden wingback chairs and spend hours reading and sipping the bitter brew. It was one of those places where she thought she could blend in. She was wrong.

She remembered walking out to the parking lot just before closing. There must have been people in and out of the coffeehouse, but she had been so engrossed in her book that she had never noticed. Now, when she saw her car, Beth Anne wished she could crack open the book's hard spine and climb in. Hers was the lone car in the lot. The one that Gran had scrimped and saved for, even though it was "not exactly a Rolls Royce."

Someone had spray-painted the side.

The letters were huge, glaring red, and crudely written. Now the car bore the same stain that she did: MURDERER.

She had abandoned it then and there.

There was a rush of cold air over Bex's cheeks as Laney swiped the phone from her. "Hello? Who is this?"

"It's Trevor, Laney. Put Bex back on."

"Did you say you did this? You did this to my car?"

"Wait, what are you talking about?"

Bex turned to Laney and clawed for the phone. She wanted to smash it, to step on it, and then do the same with this life—smash it into a thousand obliterated pieces. She had thought Trevor liked her. She thought that he...

"I left flowers on your car for Bex. What are *you* talking about?"

Bex could see Laney's jaw drop open just slightly. "So you didn't plaster my car with Missing posters?"

"What? Who the hell would do that? Let me talk to Bex."

Laney tried to hand the phone to Bex but she waved it away, numbly walking to the passenger's side of the car and settling herself in. The sound of the seat belt clicking was reassuring, but for a second Bex thought about unbuckling it, sliding into the driver's seat, and driving away. She wouldn't go anywhere. She wouldn't stop anywhere. She would drive into the surf, a tree—anything that would stop the pain that was coursing through her body, stinging with every beat of her heart.

Everywhere she went, she brought death and destruction. Even when she tried to get away, it found her, making its presence known. That was who she was. That was who she'd always be. Bex couldn't end Beth Anne, but Beth Anne could end Bex. She pressed her index finger to the seat belt button and heard it click. She started to slide toward the driver's seat...but Laney beat her there. She was shaking a slim bouquet of cellophane-wrapped flowers in front of Bex's nose.

"Trevor left these, Bex. These flowers. There were no posters here when he left these. They were under all the paper on the windshield. It wasn't Trevor."

Chelsea slid into the backseat and Laney started the car, the purr of the engine sending a warm shimmy through Bex. They drove in static silence for blocks before Chelsea cleared her throat and spoke in a hoarse whisper.

"How did you know the name of the little girl in the poster?"

Bex didn't answer and Chelsea fell silent for a beat. Then, "I know who it was." Chelsea snapped her fingers. "Zach."

"Zach?" Laney asked.

"Yeah. Isn't it obvious? He was at the movie, so he had the opportunity."

Bex felt her breathing slightly regulate. "Zach? Why would he do something like this?"

"Because he's Zach," Chelsea exploded, eyes rolling. "He wants a story. He was probably behind us filming the whole thing. Like one of those hidden-camera pervy things. He probably just googled 'kidnapping,' found pictures on some creepy-assed 'people who love weird crime shit' sites, and slapped together a whole bunch of Missing posters. He knew we were going to the movies…"

"And there is only one Cineplex in this shoe-box town. It's not like he'd have to drive around looking for us," Laney reasoned.

Bex chewed her bottom lip. "I guess he'd know your car."

"Asshole," Laney fumed.

"Jerk," Chelsea added.

But Bex just sank back in her seat. She wanted Zach to be the culprit and this whole stupid stunt to be a prank. But how did he know about the Wife Collector? How did he know to choose all his victims? And how did he get the picture of Beth Anne Reimer?

TWENTY-SEVEN

"Are you going to be okay?" Laney asked when she pulled into Bex's driveway.

"Yeah," Bex said, waving at the air. "You're probably right. It was probably just some dumb prank."

"We can stay here if you want us to," Chelsea said as they got out of the car.

But Bex wanted them to leave. She'd wanted them to leave the second she saw Beth Anne Reimer's Missing photo. It wasn't a coincidence. Someone wasn't just playing around. Beth Anne Reimer had never gone missing. Whoever had stuck the posters on Bex's car knew who she was and had spent the time creating Beth Anne's poster. The thought burned a hole low in Bex's gut and she chewed the inside of her lip, going through a mental contacts list.

Had Zach found out who she was, and the posters were his reality-show way of making her admit it? Did Detective Schuster think she needed an extra nudge to cooperate? Had someone on the Forum figured out who she was and where she lived? Bex shivered, the last possibility driving a knife-sharp icicle into the center of her heart. Was it her father, playing some kind of sick game?

"You guys should go," Bex said quickly. "I mean before it gets super late."

She wanted them to get in Laney's car and drive for as long and as far as they possibly could. She wanted them to drive out of Kill Devil Hills, out of the last weeks of her life. She wanted her friends to be out of danger. Again, the image of Darla on the beach floated back to her, and Bex shuddered.

"Only if you're sure," Laney said carefully.

"She's fine, Lane. It was a bunch of stupid posters. Paper can't hurt her. Unless it's a paper cut, and those things can hurt like—"

Laney grabbed Chelsea by the arm. "We'll go."

Bex let herself into the house, slowly creaking the door open and looking around like a criminal. She felt as though she were a trespasser in her own home. *No,* that horrible voice whispered, *your home is with your father.*

Once she was in her bedroom, Bex glanced at her laptop, pinching her upper lip.

"I tried," she whispered to herself. "He's not looking for me."

Or maybe Detective Schuster had been wrong all along about her father, and he didn't really kill all those women. Maybe her father fled because he was innocent. Maybe Zach had discovered who she was and just wanted a great story. Bex was nodding her head as hope swelled inside her. Maybe everything had just gotten turned around, and Bex—Beth Anne, rather—could have a real and regular life with a father and a mother and a home and without the need to lie. Maybe…

"Phone," she said while rummaging through her purse. "Phone, phone, phone…" The readout on the face said 12:41. Too late to call Detective Schuster.

"Laptop."

Bex opened it, running her fingertips over the track pad to wake up the screen. When she did, she saw the message.

GAMECREATOR: Is it really you, Bethy?

That hope that had swelled from a flicker to a flame in a few short seconds was snuffed out just as quickly.

No one else called her Bethy. Not when she was Beth Anne Reimer, not ever.

There was no joy. There was only terror, tinged with anger and hate.

Once again her father had turned her life upside down. He was on the site just like Detective Schuster had said he would be—because serial killers crave praise.

But-but-but… that little voice started. *He was looking for me! He made the connection!*

"No." Bex licked her lips. "So he knows a pet name. He's not real. He's another imposter."

She clicked the message icon and a single meager line toppled out.

What do you put on your pancakes?

Bex didn't think. She typed.

Powdered sugar. By the bucketful.

She hit Send before she second-guessed herself. She waited for a response.

She waited all night.

• • •

Bex was poking at the soggy remains of her cereal when Denise came in the front door. Michael fixed a mug of coffee for each of them while Denise popped out her earbuds and sat down across from Bex.

"I'm telling you, Bex. A morning run feels amazing. You should come with me sometime." She glanced at her husband and smiled. "Unless you're like Michael here, who prefers to get his exercise by osmosis."

Michael feigned offense. "I'll have you know that whenever I go to the grocery store, I park very far from the front door!"

"That's actually a great way to get extra steps in. Do you do that at work too?"

Michael globbed a knifeful of butter onto his bagel. "I'm not trying to be a hero."

"What about you, Bex? Join me sometime? We could make it a girl thing."

"Yeah." Bex nodded. "That might be fun."

"Oh, hey. How come you aren't wearing your new necklace?"

Bex's hands went to her throat but she didn't answer.

"The silver heart," Denise clarified. "That Trevor gave you."

Bex felt her cheeks warm. "Trevor said he didn't leave it."

Michael crossed his arms in front of his chest. "Do you have another admirer? Am I going to have to buy a shotgun?"

"I actually don't know who would have sent it. It's weird."

Denise snaked Michael's bagel and took a bite, licking the butter from her fingers. "It was probably one of the girls then. You should wear it to school today."

"I don't know. It just seems—"

"If it's not Trevor, it's got to be Laney or Chelsea. Wear it. Show it off. It looks great on you."

Bex shrugged but climbed the stairs and slipped the necklace on anyway. It did look nice on her, the silver a pretty contrast against her skin. Bex smiled at her reflection and slid her backpack over her shoulders, bounding down the stairs when Michael called for her.

• • •

Bex expected the same circus of reporters, news vans, and cop cars when Michael dropped her off in front of the school, but they were gone. Nearly two weeks and it was as if Darla's murder had never happened.

"That was quick," Bex muttered.

"For the best, don't you think?"

Bex nodded, hoping her intense relief wasn't so obvious. "Yeah, definitely."

"Now you guys can try to get back to normal."

"Whatever that is," Bex said, kicking open the car door.

She walked across campus, slowing at the quad. One of the trees had been taken over and was now a makeshift memorial. Purple ribbons were tied around the trunk, with "RIP Darla" written in puffy silver paint on the tails. Bex's eyes burned as the ribbons caught the wind, blowing across a smiling picture of Darla in her cheerleading uniform. There were letters and notes surrounding the picture, prayers and missives to her. Stuffed animals, flowers, and candles in tall glass vials were gathered at the base of the tree.

"Pretty intense, isn't it?"

Bex glanced at Zach, his GoPro camera slung around his neck.

"Yeah," she said. "It's terrible."

"A tragedy," he said, his eyes holding hers.

Bex blinked several times, trying to ignore the cold sweat that had started at her hairline. "*A tragedy. A real tragedy.*" That word was used in the newspaper every time another one of her father's victims was found. No matter the circumstances or the woman, the event was always classified as "a tragedy." Bex realized now how empty that word was, being used to describe everything from a poor fashion choice to the end of someone's life. Darla's murder was more than a tragedy; it shouldn't have happened.

"Yeah," she said, stammering. She glanced down at the camera, remembering the intense burning of the red light that night on the beach. "So, did you get some good footage?"

Zach followed her eyes to his camera. "Of this? I mean, I got a few pictures but—"

"No, at the beach that night."

Zach's eyebrows went up. "What are you talking about? I wasn't there."

She pointed to his GoPro. "Yeah you were. I saw you. Or I saw that. The red light. You were filming from across the street when the cops came."

"Look, I don't know what you thought you saw or anything, but"—he grasped his camera protectively—"it wasn't me. I'm not the only guy with a camera." Zach walked away, and Bex stared after him.

"That dude is weird."

Now it was Laney at Bex's other shoulder.

"Zach?"

"Yeah." Laney's lip curled up in something like disgust. "I don't know what it is, but something about him gives me the creeps. And he's always staring through that stupid camera. Can't be normal to live your life staring at other people, right?"

"I guess not."

"By the way"—Laney thumbed over her shoulder toward the tree—"Darla would have hated this."

"Too much?"

Laney chuckled. "Not enough."

"Hey." Chelsea approached them, staring down at her phone.

"You're going to walk into a Mack truck staring at that thing, you know."

Chelsea shrugged and slid her phone in her pocket. "I am perfectly aware of my surroundings at all times, thank you very much. Hey, Bex." She took a step closer, squinted her eyes, then picked up the silver chain. "Ooh, something sweet from *mi amour*?"

"*Ton amour*," Laney corrected.

Chelsea stopped when she got to the bauble. She held it up, and they all watched the silver heart slowly spin on the chain.

"Where did you get this?" Suddenly, there was a cold edge in Chelsea's voice.

Bex slid the necklace from Chelsea's fingertips and laid it flat against her chest. "It's not a big deal."

"I'm serious, Bex. Where did you get that necklace?"

"I don't know. I figured one of you left it for me."

"What do you mean 'left it for' you?"

"Someone left it on my doorstep. I thought it was Trevor at first, but he said it wasn't him so I thought maybe one of you…"

Laney put her hand on Chelsea's arm and the two shared a look.

Bex's saliva soured in her mouth. Her breakfast sat like a cold rock at the pit of her gut. Images of television mean girls flashed in her mind, and she thought back to that first moment she'd met Chelsea and Laney, when she thought they would be horrible and mean to her. Maybe they weren't her friends. Maybe they had been playing a part. Maybe they knew who she was all along.

She swallowed even though her throat was bone dry. "It's not from you guys? It was wrapped up in a box, and there was no note or anything." She could feel the tears starting and tried to steel herself, to will herself not to cry.

"That necklace was Darla's. She wore it every day. She never took it off."

Bex was reeling. Chelsea, Laney, the tree, the school—everything blurred out of focus and became fish-eyed. Bex took off running, clawing at the bauble around her neck. With every step the thin chain seemed to tighten, the once-delicate links like barbed wire digging into her skin. She lost her breath and felt the pressure on her chest, against her windpipe. She coughed, gagged.

She pushed the bathroom door open and made it to a stall just in time to vomit. She was crying, her shoulders shaking, her lips bitter and trembling. When she turned around, she saw her reflection in the mirror: eyes wet and blackened by dripping mascara. Cheeks hollow and pale. A hair color she didn't recognize. And around her neck the heart sat, now edged in blood from the scratches from her own clawing fingernails.

She thought of her father, the way he must have looked down at his prey, at their milky, sightless eyes, their lips, the pinkness of life giving way to deathly blue. He must have looked at them and thought of her. She imagined his fingertips brushing aside Darla's blond hair, his rough fingers working the delicate clasp on the necklace.

Bex gripped the pendant and broke the chain.

TWENTY-EIGHT

Bex avoided her laptop all night. She unplugged it and tucked it under her bed as if those extra precautions could somehow cut her off from any response GAMECREATOR could have left or any more references to her "celebrity" father.

The next morning, she was poking at the peanut butter sandwich on her plate when Denise walked into the kitchen, her face half-obscured by the cardboard box she was carrying. She dropped it on the table with a slight thud and a puff of dust.

"Okay, Bexy, red or black?"

Bex blinked, half her sandwich in her hand. "What?"

"Red"—Denise peered over the box, shaking a red pom-pom that looked like it had seen better days—"or black?" She shook a similarly shabby black pom-pom in the other hand.

"What is all this stuff?" Bex stood, peering into the recesses of the box. "Is this a boa?"

"Ah!" Denise curled the feathery thing around Bex's shoulders. "This was from the senior talent show!"

"Senior? Like college senior?"

"High school." She shook the poms. "Rah, rah, rah! Kill Devil Hills!"

"You went to KDH? Why didn't I know that?"

Denise shrugged and continued rifling through the box. "This thing has been in the garage for ages. I thought maybe you'd want some of this stuff for the big game."

"Big game?"

"Big game." Denise dropped two strands of red and black beads over Bex's head. "Tonight. Last game of the season. Football?"

Bex slapped a palm to her forehead. "I can't believe I forgot."

"I noticed you've been kind of distracted lately. Everything okay?"

Bex nodded sharply, her lips pressed together in a tight, bloodless smile. "What else is in here?"

"Just some old school stuff of mine and Michael's. I thought the KDH stuff might be cool for you to have."

"Yeah, thanks. So, did you and Michael meet in high school then?"

Denise shook her head. "No, we didn't meet until after college. It took a while, but I was eventually able to lure Michael out of the city and out"—she spread her arms wide—"to the beach."

"Oh. What city was that?"

"Raleigh. Seems like a lifetime ago, but it was only about nine years ago that we moved."

Bex's face must have blanched because Denise's eyes darkened and she put a hand on Bex's arm. "Hon, are you okay? You went kind of pale."

Bex thought about Michael and Denise in Raleigh, living and breathing and being in the same town where she had lived, where she was Beth Anne Reimer, daughter of the "most prolific serial killer" in North Carolina's history. They must have seen the papers, probably followed the story on the news. Everyone else did.

They may have even read her name or seen her, Beth Anne Reimer, in that stiff velvet dress, the kid who turned her own father in, the kid who was raised by—and therefore shared the same tainted blood as—a serial killer. Bex's heart did a double thump when she thought that Michael and Denise could have recognized her from then to now. Something about them living in Raleigh and living with her now tugged at her, ratcheting up the slight tremor of anxiety that never seemed to fully go away.

Bex tried to force a smile, to put some nonchalance into her voice, but it came out high and slightly cracked.

"Nothing. I was just thinking about the game." She took the pom-poms. "These will be great. I'll just have to find something school colored to go with them."

Denise checked her watch. "Well, you've got about nine hours until kickoff. Plenty of time to pillage the closet or"—she rifled through her wallet and handed Bex some bills—"the mall. Call the girls. Get out."

The girls.

That same newsreel spun again in Bex's head. The girls. The victims. Unseeing eyes; hollowed, dirty cheeks; cracked, once-pink lips now an ugly headstone gray.

"Going to the mall is still a thing, right? Bex?"

Bex snapped back to attention. "The mall? Yeah, totally. I'll do that. I'll call Laney and Chels."

Denise stared at Bex, who remained seated. Then she added, "I'll call 'em now."

Bex took the stairs two at a time, her anxiety not lessening even in the relative calm of her bedroom. She yanked out her cell phone and zipped right past Chelsea's and Laney's numbers, stopping at the entry for Detective Lieutenant Schuster. Her thumb hovered over the call button, the animated telephone-receiver icon bouncing up and down. What would she say to him? Everyone knew that the Wife Collector was out there, escaped.

Bex thought of the request flashing on her computer screen: GAMECREATOR has requested a private chat...

She hesitantly pushed the button, counting the rings until Schuster's voice crackled over the line.

"You've reached Detective Lieutenant Schuster. I'm currently leading a training session and will have limited access to email and messages. If this is an emergency, please hang up and dial 911. If this is a pressing matter, please call my assistant, Sheila, at..."

Bex held the phone to her ear, wondering if she should take down Sheila's number or dial 911. Connecting with someone who might be masquerading as her father wasn't an emergency. Was it even pressing?

She hung up before the message tone signaled.

• • •

The ride out to the mall in Nag's Head was quick, and with Laney driving and Chelsea cranking up the stereo, Bex was able to let go and sink into the Outer Banks sun streaming through the open car windows—almost. Each time traffic slowed and they pulled alongside another car, she found her eyes cutting to the driver. The rest of the time, she was eyeing the passengers in the cars around her, wondering if maybe *he* was in one of them, having stolen his way out of Raleigh, and was now doing his best to blend into the last remnants of beachgoers and tourists in the beach town. It wouldn't be hard, Bex reasoned, as she eyed a box-shaped SUV with tinted windows, the driver wearing dark sunglasses and a low-pulled East Carolina hat.

"Are you going to get a dress, Bex? You should get a dress. Something with sequins or something."

Bex's eyebrows rose. "We're still talking about what we're wearing to the game tonight, right?"

Chelsea sighed. "Yeah…but Trevor *loves* you. He's so into you! And that's so romantic." She growled at her phone. "I need my new boyfriend to be romantic!"

"You have a new boyfriend?" Bex asked.

"She wishes," Laney said. "She got some dude's number at the coffee place and is all whipped."

"I'm not whipped. If he would text me, then I could be whipped. Anyway, dress. No chick looks sexy in a football jersey."

"I'm pretty sure Bex wasn't planning on wearing an actual football uniform to the game." Laney caught Bex's eyes in the rearview mirror, then rolled hers. "And because Trevor loves her, that's all the more reason she should totally be herself and dress like herself. If she showed up in an evening gown, Chels, Trevor wouldn't even know who she was!"

Chelsea and Laney laughed and Bex wanted to. But all she

could think about was the fact that Trevor wasn't really into her at all. He was into Bex Andrews, and with each thought of the Wife Collector fan forum, with each memory of her father, with each callback from Detective Schuster, it was becoming more and more obvious that she was and would always be Beth Anne Reimer. There was no Bex Andrews.

The mall was packed, but Laney seemed to find the last spot in the parking garage. They got coffees and people watched, then Chelsea yanked Bex by the arm to a store displaying a series of funky shirts that just happened to be in the Kill Devil Hills High colors.

"These are amazing, right? You'll look incredible but also not like you're trying too hard."

Laney rolled her eyes.

"Try this one. And this one."

Bex did as she was told, throwing an impromptu fashion show, feeling better and lighter as Chelsea tried on a half dozen dresses that made her look like a Las Vegas lounge singer and Laney clomped around in a pair of hot-pink, sky-high stilettos.

"I never really thought I was a stiletto person, but I'm kind of digging these," she said, crossing the store with an awkward walk. "Seriously."

"They cost more than your house. So you're getting that, right, Bex?" Chelsea wanted to know.

"Yes." Bex rifled through her purse. "Crap. My wallet. It probably fell out in the car."

"No worries," Chelsea said, picking a credit card from her wallet. "You can pay me back."

Bex bit her lip. "Thanks, but I feel weird without my wallet. I'm just going to run back to the car. I'm sure it's there. Five minutes."

Laney tossed Bex her keys and Bex zipped out of the shop, making a beeline for their third-floor parking space. The air was hot and still, the parking garage eerily silent after the dramatic din of mall voices and canned music.

A man stepped out of a car just across the aisle from Bex and locked eyes with her. Her hackles went up, tension shooting up her spine like a live wire. The man slammed his car door and locked it, then slipped into the mall without looking back.

Bex pinched the bridge of her nose. "I have to stop freaking out."

A couple rolled down the aisle in a dark sedan, slowing as they got close to Bex. Her heart started to thud, and she could feel the lactic acid slipping through her muscles, tight and taut, waiting for flight.

The car stopped, the passenger-side window rolling down. Bex's heart thudded in her ears.

"'Scuse me. You leaving?"

Bex stared at the keys in her hand, then back at the woman whose lips were pursed impatiently, one brow cocked.

"Well?"

"Uh, no, sorry. Not leaving."

The couple sped away with an irritated squeak of their wheels. Bex slumped against Laney's car, her palm pressed against her jackhammering heart.

"I'm going to die," she mumbled to herself. "Whether or not my dad comes around, I'm going to give myself a heart attack and die."

"What about your dad and your heart attack?"

Chelsea was standing behind Bex, hands on hips, shopping bag slung around one thin wrist. "And why are you talking to yourself?"

If it were physically possible for Bex to jump out of her skin, she would have. "You scared the crap out of me."

"You were taking forever so we got you this." Laney held out a bag to Bex, the T-shirt she had decided on wrapped in tissue paper inside. She rolled up onto her toes and waved, calling, "See ya, Mr. Pierson!" Then, to Bex, "Were you not supposed to go out or something?"

Bex looked dumbfounded, staring in the direction Laney was waving. "Did you see Michael?"

Laney frowned. "Didn't you? You were talking about your dad giving you a heart attack, and he was right there." She pointed. "He was looking right at you."

Again Bex looked. There was a vacated parking space and a pair of taillights disappearing down the garage driveway.

When Bex let herself into the house after Laney dropped her off, Denise and Michael were sitting on the couch watching television.

"Did you get something good?" Denise asked.

Michael turned and smiled, ready to inspect Bex's shopping spoils.

Bex held up the shirt Laney and Chelsea bought for her, a feeling of unease overwhelming her. "I'm sorry if I just stared at you in the parking lot, Michael. I…guess I didn't recognize you."

Denise's eyebrows rose when Michael turned to Bex. "Which parking lot?"

"At the mall just now. Laney saw you."

Michael and Denise shared a look, and Michael's eyebrows knitted together. "Wasn't me."

"We've been here all afternoon."

Michael gestured toward the TV. "Denise has me fully enthralled with this home decorating network. Apparently, I'm supposed to be taking notes on something called 'tinning.'" He stood up and patted Bex's shoulder conspiratorially. "Maybe it was my super-lucky doppelgänger that you saw. Enjoying his non-house-remodeling freedom."

Denise hopped up after him. "It's adding an antique tin ceiling and you'll love it!"

Bex blinked, watching them go. Were Michael and Denise lying, or was Laney just mistaken?

"My God," she mumbled, pressing her palms against her temples and making little circles. "I've got to stop freaking out over every little thing."

Of course Laney was mistaken. She and Chelsea had only met Michael once.

Bex glanced down at the bag in her hand, at the coffee table where Denise's red and black pom-poms were discarded. She wanted nothing more than to skip the game and crawl into her bed and pull the covers up over her head. "If I could wake up sometime around senior year of college, that'd be excellent."

Sighing, Bex climbed the stairs to her room, glancing at her laptop tucked silently under her bed. She thrummed her fingernails over the closed lid, curiosity pulling at her.

GAMECREATOR *is probably some crazed fanboy*, she reasoned. *He's not my dad. He's not. And the memory? Just happened to fit. All little kids played games. All dads said stupid things like, "I invented the game." It was nothing.*

She glanced again at her cell phone. Not a single missed message or call from Detective Schuster.

But still that little voice inside Bex's head said, *What if?*

She sat down at her desk, opened her laptop, and touched the trackpad, and the screen flicked to life.

She navigated her way to the fan site, no longer shuddering when the page pulled up, no longer flinching at the macabre pictures. Her Forum inbox was bulging with a series of post replies and private message requests, but not one from GAMECREATOR.

Bex slammed her laptop shut, not sure whether to be disappointed or relieved.

TWENTY-NINE

The closer Trevor and Bex got to campus, the more thoughts of Detective Schuster, her father, and anything Wife Collector related faded away. With each stoplight, the energy of Kill Devil Hills High seemed to pulse and throb more.

"Oh my gosh," she said as they reached the school. "Is the whole school here?"

"Try the whole town," Trevor said as he smoothly coasted the car into the lot. "There's not a lot to do around here if you haven't noticed. Ooh, spot."

Trevor continued to chatter, but Bex was focused on the crowd streaming by the car. They made a fairly solid red-and-black mob, girls with Red Devil pitchforks on their cheeks and ribbons in their hair, guys with football jerseys and faces painted red and black.

"I can't believe that everyone gets so into it."

He gestured toward her shirt. "Looks like you got a little school spirit too."

Bex could feel her cheeks redden. "I had to go out and buy it today."

"Good choice. Anyway"—Trevor shrugged—"football is life."

"So, why don't you play?"

"Ugh…football is also guys who are a lot bigger and faster than I am. Besides, the high school team was basically formed before I got here."

Bex felt her eyebrows go up. "Got where?"

"KDH."

"I kind of thought you were born here like everyone else."

Trevor pushed the car into Park. "Thanks…I think. We actually moved here just after eighth grade. From Chicago."

"Is that where you were born?"

He nodded. "Uh-huh. So I kind of know what you must feel like being the new kid."

Bex clicked off her seat belt and glanced out the window to where the students seemed to be moving together in one hulking mass. *If you only knew…*

"Yeah," she said.

• • •

Kill Devil Hills High was ahead by a single field goal, which meant that the stands were thundering. Laney, Chelsea, and the other cheerleaders were stomp-clamping and screaming themselves hoarse, jumping and cheering and urging the Red Devils to Go-Fight-Win. Corolla's Fighting Mustangs were doing the same—cheerleaders chanting, crowd roaring, team huddling together. It was only a fluke that Bex happened to glance down at her purse and see the blinking light from her ringing cell phone. Caught up in the moment, she grabbed the thing from her purse, slid the answering bar, and said, "Hello?"

She could barely make out the caller's words. "Hello?" she said again. There was a sound like crinkling paper on the other end, like the caller was hanging his head out the window while he drove on the freeway. If the caller did try to speak, Bex couldn't hear on her end. The Red Devils were gaining yardage, and the bleachers pulsed with whoops and cheers.

She hung up the phone, then glanced at the readout. The number was from the same Raleigh area code—Detective Schuster.

"Everything okay?" Trevor asked when the crowd roar died down.

"I'm good," she said, shrugging. She didn't realize that a thin sheen of sweat was covering her upper lip and brow until a breeze swept over them. Again, Bex glanced at her phone, this time seeing that she had two missed calls from the detective and had three messages. She chewed the inside of her lip and tried to focus on the game. Each play seemed to morph into a swirl of red and black and screaming and stomping, but all she could think about was what the detective might be trying to tell her.

Maybe they had found her father.

Maybe he was headed to prison and the whole mess was over.

"Actually, I'd better get this message." She paused for a beat. "It's my mom."

"You could probably get better service down there." Trevor pointed to the bottom of the bleachers. "Might be a little quieter back there too. Do you want me to come with? I won't listen or anything."

Bex liked the way his cheeks flushed a sweet pink and he barely made eye contact with her, suggesting that he wouldn't eavesdrop.

"I can manage," she said, giving him a quick peck on the cheek and pointing to the field. "You just make sure we win this one."

Bex took the steps two at a time, the anxiety about Detective Schuster's message drowned out by the kids she passed who grinned at her and said hello, who called her by name and punched at the air screaming, "Go, Devils!" Bex Andrews was part of something so normal and so real and so far removed from Raleigh and Beth Anne Reimer and the Wife Collector that nothing could reach her, nothing from that old life was big enough or real enough to change who she wanted to be.

When she set foot on the ground, she hit the voice mail button, thumbed in her password, and listened while the automated lady told her about her saved messages, that she had three new messages, and when the first was sent. Bex leaned up against one of the huge pillars that held up the top row of the bleachers and mashed a finger into her free ear, trying to hear the voice on the message. The crowd swelled and screamed right when the caller began speaking, so Bex ducked her head under the bleachers, trying to get some quiet.

The crowd roared again.

Bex hit Replay and breathed in the cool darkness underneath the bleachers, most of the sound of the football game and its revelers blotted out by the thick concrete architecture. Other than some garbage and a littering of cigarette butts, there was nothing under the bleachers but a wide expanse of dark, cavernous nothing. It was vaguely creepy but with an entire town's worth of people just over her head, Bex stepped in deeper, finally able to hear her phone. The automated lady took an achingly long time to replay the recording.

"*You have six saved messages. You have three new messages. To replay messages, press seven. To erase this message, press eight. To hear more options…*"

Bex groaned at the annoyance and mashed her finger against the seven button, holding it down.

"*I'm sorry, your entry was not recognized. To replay this message, press seven.*"

"Ugh!" Bex pulled the phone from her ear, squinting at the lighted numbers. Behind her, a twig snapped or a plastic cup popped. She whirled, her heart thundering, then giggled at her own stupidity when she saw a plastic cup rolling along the hard-packed dirt.

She hit the number seven.

"*Sent at seven-oh-one p.m.…*"

There was another sound like someone walking, a footfall on the heavy earth, crushing the wadded pieces of garbage. The hollow, echoing sounds under the bleachers gave Bex the creeps, and she glanced over her shoulder, expecting to see another abandoned cup rolling along the dirt.

There was nothing.

"Hey, Bex, it's me, Detective Lieutenant Schuster. Can you give me a call when you get this message? It's kind of important. Uh, thanks."

The crowd up above let out a muffled roar as Bex erased the message and moved on to the second one.

"Uh, Bex, Schuster again. Look, I really need you to give me a call the second you get this message, okay? It's urgent. It's Detective Schuster."

Bex kicked at the dirt while she erased the second message.

She started when she thought she heard someone clear their throat behind her. She slowly turned, letting her eyes adjust to the darkness, trying to study every corner and crevice.

"Stop being a paranoid freak," she mumbled to herself. "Probably just some kids making out…"

She hit the button to play the third and final message.

"Bex, you need to call me. Jeez. Look…"

"And it's another touchdown for your Kill Devil Hills Red Devils!"

The structure all around her throbbed with cheers and foot-stomping fans. The ground seemed to shake. The clang of hundreds of pairs of shoes thunking against metal, hands clapping, cheers, and the din of the announcers seemed to engulf her. It rattled around her.

"Beth…"

She blinked at the phone, pressing it hard against her ear. Did Detective Schuster call her Beth?

"Hey—"

There were fingertips on her bare arm, someone reaching out for her.

"…Could go all the way!"

Another raucous surge: *"Go, go, go!"*

Bex whirled but no one was there. She stepped toward the light at the end of the bleachers and pressed the phone against her ear. "Hello?"

"…you need to call me right away."

"The Devils are closing in, folks!"

Bex was sure that someone was under the bleachers with her. Even with the crowd raging above, her consciousness picked up a slight movement, a light sound. She took another step and squinted in the darkness. It looked like someone was pressed up against one of the pillars, trying to remain motionless under the bleachers.

"If you'd like to erase this message, press eight. To save…"

Bex pinched the bridge of her nose and pressed seven to repeat Detective Shuster's message.

"Bex, you need to give me a call. Jeez. Look…" There was a labored sigh. "It's your dad."

The crowd noise died down. Bex's heartbeat sped up. Everything around her dropped into a deafening silence, as if the entire world, every single person in the stands, had ceased to exist. She heard the sound of a match head being dragged slowly across concrete. The desperate breath of a flame catching air. He was behind her, taller than she remembered, his hand cupping the throbbing orange-red flame as it singed, then caught on his cigarette. Bex watched the way the flame swallowed the pure-white edge, burning the paper.

Detective Schuster's message continued to play on the phone. "He's here, Bex. Your father is in Kill Devil Hills."

THIRTY

Bex wasn't sure what happened first.

The Red Devils held off a Fighting Mustangs play that brought the crowd to its feet, whooping and hollering and stomping and cheering.

A rough hand closed on Bex's upper arm.

She screamed. Deep and loud, ripping from the pit of her soul.

The crowd roared.

The hand around her arm tightened.

She gripped the cement pillar in front of her with her free arm, her hand wrapping around, fingers clutching at the rough concrete.

"Please!" Bex shrieked.

"Please," came the gruff voice.

She almost recognized the eyes in the darkness. Were they his?

"Dad?" Bex's voice was a choked whisper.

"Bex?"

Bex blinked, feeling like a wild animal caught between hunters.

Finally, Trevor chuckled and touched her softly on the shoulder before pulling her in to him.

"Hey, I'm so sorry. I didn't mean to scare you. You were gone for a long time and I thought—are you okay?"

Bex realized that her mouth was hanging open, her body stiff even as Trevor's fingers trailed up her arm.

"Are you okay?" he asked again.

She forced herself to pump her head, her eyes scanning the space.

"Did you see someone else here just a minute ago? A man?"

"A man? I saw Rod Delveccio giving Tabitha Collins a hell of a mouth check back there, but I wouldn't say he was a real man about it."

"No," she said. "A guy, a man. Right here"—she patted the air—"by me. He had his hand on my arm."

He cocked his head, gave an eyebrows-up frown. "There was no one else down here that I saw. What do you mean, he had his hand on your arm? Are you okay? Did some guy try to hurt you?"

Trevor seemed to puff up in the chest, his cheeks flushing a hint of crimson as he whipped around, looking for some imaginary Lothario.

"No, Trevor, I guess I was just…" Bex looked around again, feeling exposed, feeling watched. "I guess I just thought I saw someone. Must have been nothing."

"You ready?"

Bex swallowed hard, Detective Schuster's message burned in her head. *He's here, Bex.* She looped her arm through Trevor's and held on tight, trying to get as close as possible.

Here in Kill Devil Hills? Here at the game?

She scrutinized every face she could, paying extra attention to those who glanced at her, but it was futile: there seemed to be thousands of people, and half of them were wearing baseball hats pulled low or had their faces painted red and black. It should have been impossible to spot someone, but Bex was sure she could feel eyes on *her*, that she was pinned under someone's unfaltering gaze. When she turned, she saw Laney and Chelsea deep in conversation with a clutch of other cheerleaders. Zach was at the top of the bleachers staring down, but was he looking at her or at his GoPro?

And halfway down, arms crossed in front of her chest, was Lauren, staring passed Bex with flat eyes that looked vacant, unfocused. Bex's stomach seized as the chatter and noise went on around her. People approached her, chucking her shoulder, fist-bumping Trevor, jumping up and down. All around her, people moved forward while she seemed to wind down, slipping into some sort of vortex where everyone but her swirled and blended. She stood out like the hard-lined oddity.

Trevor tried to convince Bex to come with him out to the beach where Laney, Chelsea, and the rest of the spirit squad were setting up a bonfire and a keg, but Bex's nerves were a jangled mess. She slid down in Trevor's car, not sure whether she was hiding from her father or Detective Schuster, not entirely sure whether she wanted to sit by Trevor's fire or pack up all her things and run.

Once home, she didn't bother turning on the lights. She went straight from the front door up to her room without checking in with Denise or Michael. She undressed in the dark, using a bath towel to rub off the pitchfork tattoo that Chelsea had insisted she wear since halftime, then folding herself into the relaxing cool of her mint-green sheets. She pressed her eyelids shut even as Detective

Schuster called and texted her. She glanced at the first text, "Did you get my message? Has he contacted you?" then thumbed the phone to silent and pushed it under the bed.

Her father was in Kill Devil Hills. She thought that he had come for her, that he was there under the bleachers but—but what? Had she made the whole thing up? And if she hadn't, what had happened to him? Bex's heart skipped from thrilled to terrified to guilt-ridden to sick. The filmstrip of girls... Detective Schuster, convincing Bex she was doing the right thing.

But what if I'm not?

Bex pulled her laptop from her desk and opened it. She began to type:

BETHANNER has requested a private chat with GAMECREATOR.

Immediately, GAMECREATOR accepted.

BETHANNER: Who is this?
GAMECREATOR: You put buckets of powdered sugar on your waffles. At least you did whenever we went to the diner and your gran wasn't around to stop you.

Bex's head started to buzz. Her palms started to sweat. Could this really be him? She kept typing and continued with a question-and-answer session that lasted deep into the night, that convinced her that if GAMECREATOR wasn't her father, he was someone very close. That was the last conscious thought Bex had before falling off to sleep.

"Shouldn't they have to pay us for this or something?" Chelsea whined. "School's been out for an hour. We should get overtime."

Bex unfurled another loop of red crepe paper and Trevor cut it off. "If you're getting paid to go to school, I need to know," Trevor said.

"It's one day," Laney said.

"It's a week," Chelsea corrected, holding up the appropriate number of fingers. "Three days to decorate these ugly halls, one day to make the 'Yay parents!' posters, and one day to hand out punch and cookies. All after school hours."

"In other words, it's Back to School Night."

Bex smiled thinly. For the past two days, she had been emailing GAMECREATOR. She was sure now that he was her father, and she refused to allow herself to think of anything else—not Darla, not Detective Schuster. She would draw him out when the time was right, but for now, Bex was enjoying their e-chats, her father asking her about Gran and bringing up memories—ones that no one but her father could have known.

"Are your foster parents coming?" Trevor asked.

"Michael and Denise are the coolest. I wish my parents would give me up for adoption. I'd sign up to stay with them."

Laney shot Chelsea a murderous look and Chelsea shrugged, sticking a piece of tape to the crepe paper and smacking it to the wall.

"Um, I guess," Bex said. But in her mind she pictured her father here, talking to her teachers, impressed at how quickly she caught up, examining the series of ocean paintings she had done in art class.

"Bex! Bex!"

Bex snapped to attention. Trevor was standing directly in front of her. "I don't know where you've been all day, but it sure isn't here." His voice was playful, but there was an edge to it that made guilt flutter through her.

"I'm sorry. I've just got…a lot on my mind." She unfurled the last of the crepe paper, and Chelsea stuck it to the wall. "Are we good here?"

• • •

When Trevor dropped Bex off, she was ready to race to her room to start another chat with her father, but Denise met her on the landing.

"I was just going upstairs," Bex said.

Denise gently turned her around and led her down the stairs and into the kitchen where Michael was chopping vegetables.

"You've been holed up in your room every day for a week now."

"Yeah," Michael said. "What have you been doing up there? Running a meth lab? A salamander-fighting ring?"

Denise stole a stalk of celery from Michael; he waited for her to turn around before handing Bex a cookie.

"Just a lot of schoolwork," Bex said, her mind going to the web forum, to her father who was probably waiting to talk to her.

"Well, tonight schoolwork can wait until after dinner. You're starting to get computer screen pallor." Denise pulled out a chair. "Sit, talk, interact."

Bex did as she was told, answering questions about Trevor and school and whether she was interested in any school activities. She tried to be as social and as normal as possible, but she wanted to talk with her father. When dinner was mercifully over, she bounded up the stairs and sat in front of her screen, frowning at the only message in her inbox:

GAMECREATOR has left this conversation.

A beat passed before the icon showed GAMECREATOR logging back in. Bex started to type, but stopped when GAMECREATOR's message came through:

Don't have access to computer much longer. Can I talk to you?

Bex tried to swallow the boulder in her throat. Slowly, she watched her hands settle on the keys. She watched herself type the three letters that would make GAMECREATOR and her father real.

BETHANNER: Yes.

She gave him her phone number, then stared at her phone, feeling beads of sweat running down the back of her neck. She jumped at every little sound, certain it would be an incoming call.

And then the phone rang.

She stared at it, dumbfounded. Her hand shaky, she slid the phone on.

"Hello?" Her breath came out a strangled whisper.

There was no sound on the other end of the phone, just a dull static and Bex could feel herself straining to hear if there was someone there. She pressed the phone hard against her ear, listening for a wisp of breath or the peals of laughter from a prankster screaming that, as always, the joke was on her.

"Bethy."

The man's voice plucked her from her surroundings and dragged her back ten years to the last time she heard it. Bex wondered how she could have ever thought she'd forget. It was as if he'd never stopped talking to her, never stopped calling her Bethy.

Bex's uncertainty about what to call him, how to address him went out the window and the word rolled out. "Dad!"

She hadn't meant to cry. The tears rolled over her cheeks. "Dad."

Her father sniffed and chuckled on his end of the phone. "I've dreamed of hearing your voice for ten long years."

Bex nodded her head in agreement. "Me too."

"I can't believe it's really you."

She remembered she was supposed to be skeptical, analytical, on guard, but all she could think was that she was on the phone with her father—her *dad!*—and he was crying and sniffling and as stunned and happy as she was.

He did miss me. He does love me.

"Bethy, I don't have much time."

"Where are you?"

A slight pause, a sound like he was sucking air through his teeth. "I can't tell you that."

"I can help you, Dad. I know I can. And Michael and Denise—"

"That the couple I saw you with?"

Bex's heart dropped into her gut. "You saw me?"

"We're family, Bethy. The first thing I did was come and find you."

THIRTY-ONE

Joy swelled through her. She wanted to scream at all the talking heads that had accused her father, that said he was unfeeling and unable to form attachments. He wasn't a sociopath. He wasn't a serial killer. He was her dad. Bex wanted to tell him everything, but caution dulled the sharp edges of her glee.

"Can I ask you something?" Bex stared straight ahead, her father's breathing a steady in-out, in-out, heavy in her ear.

"Anything, Bethy."

"There were...signs."

"Signs?"

She could hear her father shift on his end of the phone. She tried to imagine where he was. She could hear the faint whooshing of cars or waves, but Bex couldn't tell if that was on her end or his. There was nothing else, no telltale squeak of furniture or din of coffeehouse chatter.

"When I first got here to school, there was something in my locker." She swallowed. "A postcard." She pressed her eyes closed, and even though she hadn't looked at the card since, the cheery greeting, the ominous scrawl on the back was forever burned in her mind. "It said, 'Daddy's Home.'"

There was a long, pregnant pause, and Bex counted the seconds. "Did you put it there?"

"No, sweetheart, I didn't."

"Are you sure?"

"Of course I'm sure, Bethy."

"And there were Missing posters."

"Were those in your locker too?"

Bex pressed her palm to her forehead. "No, they were on my friend's car. Hundreds of them. They were all…" She took a deep breath. "The victims."

"Victims?"

She gritted her teeth. "The Wife Collector's victims."

Her father cleared his throat. "I didn't do that."

"Who would? And why would someone?"

"I can't explain everything right now. There's not enough time. I can't stay here."

A sob lodged in Bex's chest. "You just… I just found you. You can't just go."

"It's not safe right now. I'll make contact with you. I promise I will."

"Dad, I—"

"Look, Bethy, I've got to go." A siren wailed long and low in the distance. "I'll call you again soon, okay? I've got to go."

He hung up the phone and Bex stood there, her phone pressed to her ear, listening to the dull silence. Finally she hung up, wondering why she felt so empty inside.

Bex walked through the next day in a daze, checking her cell phone call log to make sure that the previous night's phone call had actually happened, that she hadn't imagined it.

She remembered talking to Laney and Chelsea but couldn't say what it was about. She remembered sitting down and having lunch with Trevor, then kissing him good-bye when she slid into Denise's car.

"Good day today?"

Bex nodded, her hand still on her cell phone.

Denise was silent until they were nearly home. "Is something going on, Bex?"

"What do you mean?"

"I mean you've been holed up in your room. You barely talk when you do come downstairs, and it's been like pulling teeth to even get you to go out with your friends the last few days."

Anger swelled in Bex's chest. Denise wasn't her mother. Denise had no idea what she was going through, what she had gone through. Her father did.

"We're going to talk to your teachers at Back to School Night. I hope they're not going to tell me you've been out of it in class too."

Bex shook her head, then forced the words out of her mouth. "No. I'm doing okay. I'm just distracted. Schoolwork and—"

"You've played the schoolwork card a few too many times, hon. And the distraction one. You need to let us know what's going on with you. Is it something with Laney and Chelsea? With Trevor?"

Bex gritted her teeth, feeling annoyed and violated. What right did Denise have…?

"I'm fine," Bex said.

Denise pulled into the garage and Bex slung her backpack over her shoulder, deliberately lingering a few extra minutes in the kitchen so Denise would get off her back. She unwrapped a granola bar and sat at the table while she ate, and she and Denise at a frosty standoff.

"Can I go upstairs now?"

"You can go upstairs whenever you want. I'm just worried about you, Bexy."

"There's nothing to worry about," she said, pushing past her foster mom.

Bex padded up the stairs, not bothering to check the readout when her cell phone rang.

"Hello?"

"It's Detective Schuster. I'm just checking in—"

"No," she said, "he hasn't made contact." Bex hung up without waiting for Schuster to respond. She threw her cell phone onto her bed and dumped her backpack, then opened up her laptop. She had no new messages. She stared at the bright screen and her empty mailbox until she drifted off to sleep.

• • •

"Beth Anne! Beth Anne!"

She knew that voice, remembered that voice. It was far off in her dreams, in her memory, coming from somewhere deep. "Dad?" she heard herself murmur.

"Yeah, Beth Anne, it's me. It's your daddy. Now I'm going to put my hand over your mouth here. Don't you scream, okay? Don't you scream."

"Why would you—"

Bex felt fingers on her cheeks pressing carefully but firmly. A thumb on the bone just under her eye socket. The heavy, far-off scent of tobacco and old sweat was overwhelming.

"Now don't scream."

Her eyes flew open.

His grip tightened across her mouth. She blinked. His eyes widened, round, black marbles in the darkness.

"Promise me, Bethy."

Bex could feel the tears running over her temples and pooling in her ears as she nodded her head. She wouldn't scream.

Her father took his hand from her mouth, his dry lips cracking into a smile.

"It's been such a long time, Beth Anne. Just look at you."

Bex didn't dare move. A man was beside her, hulking, bigger than she remembered, with a face that was familiar but more lined, more seasoned than the one she saw in her memory, in her dreams. She was in her mint-green bedroom in Michael and Denise's house where she was Bex Andrews, and her father was right there, kneeling by her bedside. Her two worlds crashed together.

"How did you get in here?"

Her father's eyes went round, hurt and surprise playing in them. "It's been ten years, Bethy. Look at you. You're like a young woman now. So pretty."

Bex's heart hammered, thoughts streaming at record speeds. This was her father. This was a murderer. This was a man who came to find her against all odds. This was a man who broke into her house and slammed a palm over her mouth and told her not to scream. *This was her father.*

"Dad?"

She could see him blinking in the darkness, the faint light from the streetlight outside catching the glisten from his eyes as he blinked back tears. "I've missed you so much, Bethy."

He scooped her up in a rib-crushing bear hug, and Bex could feel his shoulders shaking as he cried, as he murmured into her hair, "My sweet Bethy girl, how I've missed you." Bex wanted to hug him back. Tears burned at her eyes, and she wanted to cry and fall against him and tell him how much she'd missed him too, but her body wouldn't relent and she remained still, her eyes dry.

"What are you doing here, Dad?"

He held her at arm's length, his whisper hoarse and choked with emotion. "I came for you, Bethy."

"In the middle of the night?"

"I had no choice. I tried…I tried to get to you earlier, but there was always someone there. It was too risky."

Bex thought back to the football game, the throaty voice calling her name under the bleachers, the burning touch on her arm.

"We can't talk here. Those people are asleep in the next room. We can't risk them finding me—finding us." He held out a hand. "Come with me, Beth Anne."

She thought of her father staring down at sleeping Michael and Denise, and she felt anger, violation, suddenly protective.

"You can't just come in here…"

Her father kept his hand outstretched to her. "Just talk to me,

Bethy. That's all I want. I know you must have questions, hundreds of them, and I'll answer them all. What happened when you… When they…" He glanced at her, his face contorted in pain, then looked away as if he couldn't bear to see her. "It was all wrong."

Bex's breath hitched, her throat burning. She'd done it. She'd turned him in. "I'm sorry."

"Come on, Beth Anne."

She stared at his outstretched hand, watching her own, shaking, unsteady, reaching out for him. Bex wasn't sure what she expected to happen—lightning sparks or one of those bright-light, hair-blown-back movie montages where she would see everything her father had done over the last ten years, but it was simply her hand slipping into her father's.

"Put some clothes and shoes on. I'll wait for you downstairs."

"I'm not going with you."

Her father let out a long sigh that seemed to have ten years of angst and hope built up in it, and it broke Bex's heart. "I know, honey. I wouldn't expect you to up and run off with me. It's been a long time. You don't even know me anymore. I'll be waiting outside for you."

Bex watched the careful way her father moved across her floor, the gentleness he used when closing her door behind him.

"I'm just going to go talk to him," she reasoned, mumbling. "Just talk to him outside and come right back to bed and…"

Bex pulled the laces on her sneakers and avoided her own questions. "I'm just going to talk to him." She stood and Lauren's voice pulsed in her ear: *He was just a man, you know?* Bex swallowed hard, a tremor rolling through her.

The night air was a wild, cold burst when Bex opened the front door, and she zipped her hoodie up to her neck. Her mind spun: *He came for me! He wanted to see me!* Why, *why would he want to see me? He wants something; he did something; he's an animal who can't make connections, can't feel.*

She looked around, hissing in the darkness. "Dad?"

The only answer was a dull silence pierced by the vague sounds of trucks on the highway and waves crashing somewhere in the distance.

"Oh my God," she mumbled, sweat pricking the back of her neck. Her hands tingled, and this time she couldn't control the tears. "I'm going crazy. He was never here. I was dreaming…" She plopped unceremoniously to the ground, her tailbone thunking the cement hard when she heard the hum of an engine, saw the faint shadow of white parking lights.

There was a truck at her curb, and her father was in the driver's seat. She looked at him and she was seven years old again. The wrinkles and the gray hair that she had been so focused on were obscured by the darkness, and it was as if no time had passed as he curled a finger out to her, his grin wide and welcoming. Still, Bex was tentative, hesitantly walking toward the car and approaching the driver's side.

"Well, come on. Get in. Wait. Do you want to drive?"

She shook her head. "I thought we were just going to talk."

"We are, Bethy. But it's almost four in the morning. I think we're going to be a little conspicuous sitting out front of your house, don't you? And as much as I'd like to keep all this on the up-and-up…" He screwed up his face into some approximation of apology or shame.

"O-okay, but we're not going too far."

Her father threw open the passenger side door and Bex looked up at him, a daughter seeing her dad. He was innocent. He was harmless. He loved her.

"Aw, Bethy," he said, shaking his head slowly. "Don't tell me you believe all the lies they've fed you."

Cold betrayal shot goose bumps down Bex's arms, and she shook her head again, then stepped into the car, belting herself in.

"He was just a man, you know?"

They drove in silence for a few moments, until the truck's tires began to spin under the dusting of sand on the blacktop of the beach parking lot. He pressed the car into Park and killed the engine.

"Is this your car?"

He shook his head. "You know…my circumstances, don't you, Bethy?"

Bex bit her thumbnail and looked away, nodding curtly.

"I was so glad when you reached out to me."

She turned back with a start. "When I reached out?"

"On the site." He touched his chest.

Bex's tongue went heavy in her mouth, her muscles liquid. She knew that he was GAMECREATOR, but somewhere in the back of her mind, she'd hoped it wasn't true, hoped her father wasn't lurking on a page that praised a madman. "So that was definitely you."

"Well, yeah."

"He's a narcissist, Bex. He'll be trolling the sites, enjoying that people worship him."

"Why?" There was anger in her voice, and Bex could feel her nostrils flare.

"I wanted to find you."

"That's not why. You had no idea that's where you would find me."

He shrugged, his shoulders bigger and meatier than Bex remembered. "But I found you just the same."

They stared at each other in dark silence for a beat until her father unclicked his seat belt. "What do you want to know?"

THIRTY-TWO

At first, Bex didn't answer.

"You want to know if I'm guilty? You want to know if I did it?"

She didn't know her father well enough to read the intonation in his voice—was it angry? Exasperated? In the darkness, the planes of his face were shadowed and Bex couldn't read him at all. It didn't matter because she couldn't look at him. She stared at her hands in her lap.

"Did you?"

"Of course not! You know me, Beth Anne. I'm your daddy!" He touched her shoulder awkwardly, trying to get her to face him. "You know I couldn't do something like that."

But Bex didn't know. This man was a stranger to her.

"How come you never wrote to me or tried to call?" The anger was softening, her words going from sharp and deliberate to a softer, more needy tone. Bex hated it.

"I thought it would be better for you if you just forgot about me, you know? Got on with your life. Tried to be normal and all."

"So why now? Why did you decide to show up and come

find me now?" Again, Bex was getting worked up. She could feel the hot blood pulsing through her veins, her every cell on high alert.

"I heard that your gran had died. I knew that they were going to put you in the system. I couldn't let that happen." He slid a single finger under her chin, edging her head up to face him. "I couldn't let that happen to my little girl."

Bex didn't realize she was crying.

"If you didn't do this, Daddy, why didn't you fight? Why did you run?"

"You don't think I was going to try that? I couldn't afford a good lawyer, and they had the best and the fanciest lining up to have my head based on what they said I'd done. I knew then that you can't fight the law, Beth Anne. They wanted to put someone in jail. And I just happen to fit in wherever there were holes. I had to go."

Bex inched back. "What are you talking about?"

Her father looked down at his hands, then up at Bex. There was moisture in his eyes. "You know I'm innocent. I was framed, Beth Anne."

Bex felt like someone had sucked all the air out of the truck's cab. "What?"

"I was on that website because I was looking for the real killer."

"They're masters of manipulation…"

"I know who it is. I was sure that he would show up on one of the sites, but of course, I got distracted."

"Dad, if you know who framed you… I mean, this is huge. This could change everything." Bex got up onto her knees on the bench seat, feeling herself bounce as excitement mounted. "We can go to the police and—"

"Bethy, Bethy, hey. Settle down. Look, I'd love nothing more than to do that, but I can't just go to the police. I've been on the run for ten years, and in their book, that makes me guilty."

"I can go. I can tell them that I talked to you… Maybe, like, say you emailed me and then you can come out of hiding when they catch the guy and, and—" The tears rolled steadily now and Bex could taste them on her lips. "Dad, this is great."

"We can't go to the police. The man who did this—the man who killed all those women and framed me for it, Bethy—he's a police officer."

Bex was struck dumb. Though her tears were hot and she was covered in the sheen of a nervous sweat, she shivered. "What?"

"The detective—shit, you probably don't even remember. You were just a little kid. You talked to him, told him some story…"

Bex felt herself coming apart, piece by piece. She was the reason he had to run. Her father wasn't guilty; *she* was.

"He was some young buck cop trying to make a name for hisself."

"Detective Schuster."

"That's the guy! Schuster."

Bex closed her eyes. "He framed you."

"He killed those women, Bethy. I didn't know it at the time, not really. But when my DNA started turning up—I knew it wasn't right. I wasn't there, Bethy. I wouldn't have hurt those women. I wouldn't do that. This Schuster guy, he's sick. I had to find you before you disappeared into the system because I was afraid he would be able to track you down and, and maybe"—he looked away, squinting his eyes at the dark ocean in front of them—"he might try to do to you what he did to those poor girls. I couldn't let that happen. I couldn't."

"He did find me." Bex's voice was a barely audible whisper. "He wanted me to find you, to draw you out."

Her father's profile was sharp in the low light.

Bex went on. "So you risked coming out... You did all this... for me?"

He pumped his head. "I'd do it again for you, Bethy girl. I'd do anything to keep you safe."

Bex felt herself teetering. Could Detective Schuster really be responsible for the murders, framing her father all those years? When her father reached out and squeezed her hand, Bex felt herself falling over the edge. It made sense. Detective Schuster had handled all the evidence in her father's case. The eyewitness reports were all people that Schuster had tracked down. The murders all happened within the Research Triangle, which was her father's trucking territory—and wouldn't be that far for a rookie cop to travel. She thought of the detective in his leather jacket, the way his lip curled downward and his nostrils flared each time he talked about Bex's father.

Then she thought of Dr. Gold.

"Dad, did you know Dr. Gold?"

He frowned, his fingers going up to pinch his chin. "Dr. Gold?"

"She was a psychiatrist."

He wagged his head slowly. "No, Bethy, I can't say that I do."

Bex remembered the first time her child advocate had steered her toward Dr. Gold's office. Detective Schuster had been there, his eyes grazing over her as she was ushered through the door.

Is that how Schuster found her?

"Bethy, I don't know—"

"The necklaces and the jewelry," Bex said quickly, shaking her dad's hand from hers. "How did you get the necklaces?"

He shrugged. "Different ways. The ring that I gave you? I found it in my truck. I'd give ladies a ride from time to time, hitchhikers, you know? I thought one of them must'a dropped it, and I thought it'd be something that you like. A couple of the necklaces and stuff I just picked up here and there, found 'em when I was on my route, but now I know that Schuster must have planted them there for me to find."

Bex bit her bottom lip. "So he was framing you all along?"

Her father held out his hands, palms up. "I don't know about that. I just know that I was in the wrong place at the wrong time, and I was the type of guy they were looking for. They thought the person who did that must have been nomadic, you know, on the road a lot? Well, I was. The guy would have been big and pretty athletic, and they supposed that he didn't have a lot of connections keeping him in one place—like he was probably not married. That's me too. I think I just fit and this Schuster guy jumped at the chance to get himself off the hook and look like a big hero at the same time."

Her father shook his head, eyes downcast. Even in just the sliver of moonlight streaking in through the window Bex could see how tired he looked, how downtrodden—like a man who knew he never had a chance.

"I couldn't fight him, Bethy. I just couldn't."

Bex scooched closer, for the first time in ten years feeling her father's warmth beside her, feeling the smooth pull of his arms around her. She breathed him in, his soap and seawater smell, something she didn't remember but was already starting to love.

"We could end this, Dad. I could help you and then"—she sniffed, tearing up again—"and then we could really be a family."

He rested his chin on Bex's head, squeezing her tightly. "That's all I've ever wanted, Bethy. You and me to be together as a family." He pulled away, a small, wistful smile on his face.

"Detective Schuster came here, you know. He came to my house. How did you find me, Dad? How did you find me here?"

"So you've seen him."

"Yeah."

"You got a cell phone on ya?"

Bex nodded, showing it. Her father took it, popped the little compartment open, and took out the SIM card. "He's probably tracking you with this."

"No." Bex shook her head, guilt crashing over her again. She wouldn't lead Schuster to her father a second time. "I don't think so." She pushed the SIM card back in and showed her father as she turned off all location markers.

Her father looked pained, his shoulders slumping. "I can't stay around here, Bethy. They're going to find me."

"No they won't. I'll hide you."

He shook his head. "I gotta move on."

"Tonight? Right now?"

There was a pause, the air in the cab of the truck heavy and electric.

"Come with me, Bethy."

She blinked.

"Come with me. Tonight. Right now. We'll find some town where no one'll ever know us and become new people and live out our lives. Whaddya think about that, Bethy? I could be, I don't know, called Howard or Matthew or something."

"And we could work on your case."

"Sure."

It sounded like a good idea. But then Bex thought about Trevor and Laney and Chelsea, and everything else she was leaving behind. "I can't go with you tonight. I have to say good-bye to someone."

"Bethy—"

"Friday. It's Back to School Night. I'll leave with you on Friday." She paused, then put her hand on his arm. "Then we can be a family."

"If only your mother were here to see it."

Bex felt like she had been punched in the gut. "Mom? Do you think…?"

His eyes were steady on hers, and her voice dropped to a low, terrified whisper.

"Do you think Detective Schuster was the reason Mom left? Do you think he…" Bex couldn't bring herself to finish the sentence, to say the words, but a new flare of anger raged up inside her. It was Detective Schuster who had taken everything from her, who had started to dismantle Bex's family before she was even old enough to read.

She thought of the way he'd removed the lightbulb on her porch and pummeled her, hand over mouth, his calves pinching her rib cage, tightening like a corset, just waiting for her bones to snap. An honest detective wouldn't have had to trick her. A respectable police officer wouldn't have wrestled her to the ground in her own home.

She thought about how she'd lain, chin pressed against the carpet, as he dropped the newspaper clipping in front of her. He said he kept it in honor of her. Was it truly a remembrance—or a trophy?

THIRTY-THREE

Pink fingers of sunlight were starting to scrape against the sky as Bex crept back into her house.

"Were you outside?" Michael was standing on the landing, hair ruffled, eyes bleary with sleep.

"Uh…" Bex stammered. "I woke up early. Couldn't sleep." She thumbed over her shoulder. "I thought maybe a walk would be good."

Michael nodded, yawned, and brushed past her. "You want coffee?"

"I'm actually going to try to see if I can get back to sleep now. Get in another hour before I have to wake up for school."

She padded up the stairs, the thunk of her heart mirroring the thunk of her footsteps. She peeled off her clothes and slid into bed, for the first time that she could remember, feeling light.

Bex's phone went off before her alarm clock did.

"'Lo?"

"Bex?"

She sat up ramrod straight, all thoughts of drifting back into sleep-filled oblivion gone. "Detective Schuster."

"You didn't call me back last night. Are you okay?"

"Uh, yeah." She coughed into her hand. "I'm fine."

"I want you to know that we're protecting you, Bex. You're not on your own in this. We're going to find your father. So there still has been no contact?"

Bex gnawed on her lower lip, her heart speeding up and doing a breathless double thump. She thought about her father's downcast eyes, the earnest way he pursed his lips when he was telling her—admitting to her—that he wasn't guilty, that Detective Schuster was framing him. She shifted in her bed. "Uh, no. He hasn't reached out."

The detective blew out a breath. "Okay, well. Let's keep each other posted."

"Okay."

"Hey, Bex?"

"Yeah?"

"You're doing a great thing here. You're helping to take a danger-ous man off the streets."

Bex hung up the phone without answering. She let a beat pass before pulling her laptop into her lap.

"Bexy?" Denise knocked, pushing open the door a half inch. "You awake?"

"Yeah."

Denise opened the door, sitting on the edge of Bex's desk chair. "Everything okay?" Her eyes were searching.

"Totally. Yeah."

"Michael said you were out really early this morning."

A stripe of heat burned the tops of Bex's ears. "Uh, I was just having trouble sleeping so I went for a walk." She shrugged, trying to act nonchalant. "No big deal."

"Not really, no." Denise looked away, seemed to think better of it, then fixed her gaze on Bex. "It's just that—I mean, I want to be cool and all, but I'm still your mom. Your foster mom. I'd like it if you wouldn't just go out like that. At dawn. Or at night. They still haven't caught Darla's killer and…"

Bex nodded, wondering when Darla's name would stop triggering that awful memory—her broken body on the beach, those milky, unseeing eyes. Then she thought of Detective Schuster suddenly showing up in town. Had he really been looking for her, or was he hunting for Darla?

Bex's stomach started to churn, pinpricks of heat burning through her nightshirt.

"I'm really sorry, Denise. I won't slip out without telling you. And about everything else lately…" But even as Bex finished her statement, she knew it was a lie. "I'm sorry."

Denise stood up. "Hey, no problem. We never really set any ground rules. We're new at this, you know."

Bex forced a smile she didn't really feel. "Me too."

She really did like Michael and Denise. There probably weren't cooler or nicer foster parents in the entire system but Bex's father— her dad!—was *back! Maybe,* that same tiny voice cautioned her. *Maybe…* She thought of the psychologist, the eyewitness testimony. *Serial killers are master manipulators…*

"You should probably hop in the shower or you're going to be late for school."

As soon as Denise closed the door behind her, Bex flipped open her screen and went directly to the fan forum. GAMECREATOR was already online.

Bex clicked the private chat icon and GAMECREATOR accepted. She started typing, her fingers stopping after just two letters: *H-I*. Did she say "dad"? Did she call him by his screen name? His first name? Finally, she hit Enter and watched her piddly "Hi" fill the screen.

> GAMECREATOR: Thanks for talking with me last night.
> BETHANNER: I still can't quite believe that was actually you.
> GAMECREATOR: You don't think it was your father? The one who ordered two waitresses to bring more powdered sugar that one time at the Black Bear Diner? Oh, man, was your granny mad at me when I brought you home. Said you kept her up nearly all night!

Bex grinned. She remembered that dinner. She had wanted pancakes for dinner and her father had indulged her, stopping first their waitress and then another to bring Beth Anne another white bowl mounded with powdered sugar. That second waitress had lingered after setting the bowl in front of her, had leaned one bony hip against the torn Naugahyde booth and talked to Beth Anne's daddy in a slow drawl that didn't sound like it came from North Carolina.

Because she was from Texas. She was Amanda Perkins. Three days later, her body was found mostly undressed in a ditch, what was left of her pink Black Bear Diner uniform streaked with reddish-brown blood and dirt. Bex remembered how the sodden uniform had looked, rolled up in a Ziploc bag and held aloft by a man in rubber gloves.

> BETHANNER: I remember that night. I remember the waitress.
> Her name was Amanda Perkins. She was murdered 3 days later.

There was no response from GAMECREATOR.

> BETHANNER: She talked to you. Did Schuster know her?
> GAMECREATOR: Probably. Lots of cops ate at that place. It was
> kind of a hangout.

Bex couldn't remember that, but her simmering anxiety was almost snuffed out.

> BETHANNER: One of the other women—Amy Eickler, I think—
> we gave her a ride.
> GAMECREATOR: I don't remember that, but OK.
> BETHANNER: She was murdered after.
> GAMECREATOR: She was hitchhiking.
> BETHANNER: Schuster could have picked her up.
> GAMECREATOR: Yes.

Bex's phone blared out Trevor's favorite Death to Sea Monkeys song and she glanced down at it, seeing his grinning face on the home screen. She smiled to herself but sent the call to voice mail and grabbed her towel.

• • •

Chemistry was bad enough when she could concentrate, but on this day, it was excruciating. Bex had spent her day e-chatting with her father and her night tossing and turning, hearing him whisper to her, seeing him in the dark recesses of her mind. Was he right? Had Detective Schuster framed him? And if so, why? When she had asked her dad, he gave her this simple explanation:

> Schuster is a psychopath. If he pinned the murders on me, then he's also the hero who caught the big bad wolf. I go down and he moves up in his career, and really, he can keep doing what he's doing. Killing them girls. He didn't think anyone would ever figure him out. He's like that. Narcissistic.

Narcissistic.

That's what Schuster had called her father. That's what "all psychopaths" were. But did her father know because he was one?

When morning came, Bex was cranky and jumpy at the breakfast table and in class, her mind constantly wandering, trying to figure out a way to help her father, trying to decide what to do about Detective Schuster. Turn him in? Set him up? Her father was stern—as stern as someone could be in writing—telling her to let him worry about Schuster. But Bex knew she had to help. She had helped incriminate her father away; now she could help to free him.

She told her dad that Schuster was in town, that he had been texting and calling her. Her father had called him a dangerous man and urged her to stay away. And in the last twenty-four hours, her phone had been mercifully silent, not a text or a call from the detective. It should have made Bex feel better, but instead she found herself studying everyone now, squinting at the barista who poured her coffee, sweeping her gaze at the team of gardeners huddled in front of the school. Now Bex wondered if Schuster was in every crowd, watching her, holding back, waiting.

Something hit her square in the lap and she glanced down, staring dumbly at the folded piece of notebook paper. Bex looked up and Trevor cocked an eyebrow, a hint of a smile on his lips. He jutted his chin toward the note and Bex looked up surreptitiously, watching Mr. Ponterra's fat bottom jiggle while he wrote equations on the whiteboard, completely oblivious to the yawning class behind him. She snatched the note and smoothed it open on her lap.

> Does this class make you want to die? Check yes/no.

There were boxes to check next to "yes" and "no." Bex pulled out her pen, marking the "yes" box with a thick blue check and underlining it three times. She crossed her eyes and stuck out her tongue at Trevor before folding the note and handing it back to him.

There was another beat, then another note in her lap.

> What should we do about it?

Bex replied.

I don't know. Stage a walkout??

He tossed the note back.

Or maybe...

She looked up when Trevor stood, waving an arm. "Mr. Ponterra?"

Bex could feel her heart flutter. Was Trevor actually going to stage a walkout?

Mr. Ponterra turned, eyebrows raised as if surprised to see an entire class behind him.

"Yes, Trevor?"

He paused, then opened his mouth at the exact moment the fire alarm started to wail from the loudspeaker.

Mr. Ponterra clapped his hands for the class' attention. "Fire drill, fire drill, everyone! Now line up and—okay, orderly lines. Okay, okay…"

The class stood and interpreted "orderly lines" as "meandering cluster heading toward the door." Bex grabbed Trevor's arm.

"Did you do that?"

"Would you believe it was a lucky break?"

She hiked her backpack over her shoulder and narrowed her eyes. "No."

"Okay, then let's just say I have friends in low places." He winked, his fingers sliding down her arm, then linking with hers. Bex squeezed his hand, enjoying the pinprick-like shivers. They followed their class into the hallway, carried along with the shoulder-to-shoulder crowd. Bex tried to keep her focus on Trevor, on the way his thumb stroked the back of her hand, on the way their hips bumped as they walked but she still searched the crowd, examining every face for her father as the crowd wound out to the designated meeting spot on the back forty.

"Is there really a fire?" someone asked. "Oh my God, did something really happen?"

Nobody answered immediately, and Bex felt a niggle of fear at the back of her neck. Someone jostled between her and Trevor, and he broke hands with her while a line of students trudged through. She whirled when someone called her name, but Trevor still wasn't there.

"Trevor?" Her voice was swallowed in the din of students talking and the far-off wail of the fire alarms. "Trev?"

She began to walk, then blinked when two teachers rushed by her. She didn't recognize them. She didn't recognize the boy who bumped into her or the two girls behind her. Bex turned, anxiety starting to swell.

"Bex?"

She turned, trying to find the person who said her name. It wasn't Trevor. It wasn't Mr. Ponterra. The voice was rich and deep, but it was familiar.

"Bex!"

Had he said Bex or Beth?

A man was coming toward her, fast, but he turned before she got a good look at him. But the profile, his hair, his broad shoulders…

Dad?

Another alarm blared. Someone stood up with a bullhorn. Someone was cheering—or was it screaming?

She stumbled over her feet, thought she heard someone mumble, "sorry" or "'scuse me."

Bex pressed her palm over her chest, felt her heart slamming against her ribs. She was breathing hard, her cheeks and eyes burning. She started to walk blindly toward the school, weaving through the crowd that seemed to swell and push against her.

"Hey, hey, you can't go in yet. That way." Someone grabbed her by the shoulder and steered her toward the left. Someone turned, elbowing her in the chin. She stumbled backward and tripped. Bex hit the ground, her tailbone smacking against the packed dirt. She saw a snatch of bright-blue sky before the crowd closed in around her, legs and backpacks and arms closing in on her. She was crying, trying to push herself up, but each time she did someone pushed past her and she felt back down again.

"Trevor!" She stared to sob. "Stop, please, I'm down here! Don't!"

"Bex?"

Trevor pushed between the crowd, his face appearing at her eye level. He reached out and slid his arms around Bex's waist. "Move, assholes! Someone is down here!"

A few kids stepped away, looking stunned. Most looked annoyed but still moved.

"Are you okay?"

Bex looked around, blinking in the too-bright sunlight. "I-I fell." She tried to shake Trevor off, feeling instantly embarrassed. "I just tripped and fell, that's all."

Trevor kept a tight hold on her, leveling her chin with a finger. "Hey, it's okay. I'm not big on crowds either."

Someone came on the bullhorn again, and this time, Bex could hear the order. The fire alarm had been cleared; students were told to return to the building and go to their next class. It was now her lunch period. She raked a hand through her short hair.

"God, you must think I'm the biggest idiot."

Trevor brushed a clump of grass from the knee of Bex's jeans. "Not the biggest idiot," he said with a soft smile. "Actually, I kind of think you're one of the coolest girls I know."

She felt herself blushing. "Thanks. I guess I don't really feel all that cool. You know...ever."

"You're pretty hard on yourself."

Bex cocked her head. "There's a lot you don't know about me, Trevor."

He shrugged. "Like your locker number or ATM code? I figure that's more of a second semester of dating thing."

"I'm serious."

The smile dropped from Trevor's lips. "You are? Are you an ex-con? An undercover cop? Really a man? Because all those things are okay with me. Well, most of them are. If you're a dude, I probably won't take you to prom, but we can still hang out and catch a few games together."

Bex shoved her hands in her back pockets and smiled. "Is there anything you're not cool about?"

"Narwhals," he deadpanned. "They don't get the respect they deserve."

Bex rolled her eyes as she and Trevor strolled away from the school and toward the football field, where they slid onto the lowest bench on the bleachers. Trevor took both of her hands in his, his eyes soft.

"Seriously, you can tell me whatever you want, Bex. Or you don't have to tell me anything. I mean, I want to know everything about you. But only if you're cool with that. There's nothing you can say that's going to make me think less of you."

"Unless it's something derogatory about narwhals."

Trevor nodded solemnly. "Well, obviously."

Bex stared at the toes of her Converse sneakers tapping against the bleacher floor. She shot Trevor a sidelong glance, taking in the slant of his nose, the way his chin poked out just slightly. Behind him, Kill Devil Hills High looked like any other high school anywhere in the world: kids were milling around, and there were streamers and GO BIG RED! posters plastered all over the exterior wall of the gym. There was nothing different about the scene, and Bex was a part of it. For the first time she could remember, she was part of something normal. And she was about to ruin it. As much as she wanted to shrug off her father and Detective Schuster and just kiss Trevor and go to prom and forget about anything else, there was one other poster on the gym wall that gnawed at her: the grinning picture of Darla, the letters *R.I.P.* emblazoned across the front of her cheerleading uniform.

"You know—do you remember when we were kids, there was a serial killer out in Raleigh?"

He cocked an eyebrow. "You mean the Wife Collector? He's, like, local legend there."

Bex kept her eyes on her toes. "He's real. Everything he did… It was real."

"Okay…" Trevor drew out the word.

"The man they accused of being the Wife Collector had a daughter, you know. A young daughter." Bex's heart slammed against her rib cage. She tried to keep her breathing steady and even, but it was like her insides wanted to implode.

Bex couldn't bring herself to look up. She was sure that if she did, Trevor would be gone, a trail of smoke and laughter behind him as he ran to tell Chelsea and Laney and the rest of the school that Bex Andrews was a lying freak. She didn't want to see the hate and disgust on his face, the way his lip would curl if he spat on her or slapped her. If the Wife Collector was her father, what did that make Bex?

Trevor was silent for a beat that seemed to stretch on for a year.

"I think I remember reading that. Talk about a kid who's going to need some serious therapy."

A stabbing pain arched through Bex. "You mean because she's probably psycho too."

Trevor shrugged, considering. "Not necessarily. But if you found out your dad was a murderer, don't you think that'd mess you up, even a little?" He held her eyes and she wasn't sure if he was asking her or challenging her. She wanted to sputter out the whole truth, who she was, because even if Trevor ran from her, it would be better than the lie she was living. If she was truly the Wife Collector's daughter, it would always be a stain on her soul. Therapy couldn't fix her. She would never be normal. But either way, she was the daughter of the man who was accused of committing those crimes.

"I guess."

"So?" Trevor's sneaker slid toward her, then lightly kicked her toe. She glanced up and he reached out to lightly stroke her cheek. "You're not the kind of girl who needs a ton of therapy, baby."

Bex wanted to cry. Or run. She'd thought that telling Trevor the truth might peel the weight from her shoulders and maybe he would understand. Except she knew that everything she feared about the way people thought of her as Beth Anne Reimer—messed up, in need of help—was true. She may be Bex Andrews now, but she was still the accused Wife Collector's daughter. Tears played at the edges of her eyes, and Bex was far too tired to try to stop them when they overflowed and rolled down her cheeks.

"Why are you crying?" Trevor jammed his hands in his pockets and fished out a brown Starbucks napkin. "I'm so sorry. I didn't mean to make you cry. Bex, are you scared of something? Are you scared of that killer coming here?"

She silently shook her head, took the napkin, and blew her nose. "I don't know. I don't even know why I started to talk about it."

"I'd like to believe it's because you trust me." His hand found hers. "And hopefully because you know that I love you."

The air was sucked out of Bex's lungs. She stared at Trevor, stunned. He squeezed her hands.

"Bex?"

"Did you just—?"

No. She had heard wrong. Trevor didn't love her. No one did.

She was unlovable. She was the daughter of an alleged murderer, and that blood—that horrifying blood—flowed through her veins, so no one could love her. No one should. No one could ever know—not Trevor, not Chelsea or Laney, not Michael or Denise. Even her own father didn't love her to fight for her.

"Did I just say that I love you?" Trevor nodded. "Yeah, I did. I do."

Bex knew she should talk. Acknowledge him somehow. Tell him that she loved him too, because she really thought she did. But all she could do was open her mouth, then close it again dumbly. She was the child of a *murderer*, and this good, decent guy didn't know that and now he thought he loved her. He *said* he loved her. But he didn't really know her.

"Did you want to tell me something else, Bex?"

Trevor's eyes were intense and drew Bex in. They were gorgeous but at the same time terrifying. The sun broke though the clouds, and she squinted in the light. When the sun was bright enough, you couldn't see the darkness, but the second the wind changed, the clouds shifted and the gloom was there again. That was the story of her life.

"Um, just that I love you too."

THIRTY-FOUR

Bex shifted the weight of her backpack from one shoulder to the other. The coffeehouse was populated with a half dozen people who didn't look up when Bex walked in and Lauren, looking especially out of place in her boho chic dress and flats. She waved when she saw Bex, and Bex's stomach dropped. Now she couldn't disappear back out onto the street and pretend that Lauren never existed.

"I was afraid you weren't going to come," Lauren said.

Bex nodded curtly and offered her a soft smile. "To tell you the truth, I wasn't totally sure either. This is…"

"Weird. I get it." Lauren pushed out a chair for Bex, who sat quickly.

"But thank you so much for talking to me again. I don't really know what I'm hoping for, just…" Lauren looked out the window, watching the waves crash, her blond hair standing out like a golden halo around her head. "I guess I'm weird. Or obsessed. I… You probably wouldn't understand."

Curious, Bex leaned forward. "Try me."

"It's just that my life was very different. Growing up, people either pitied me or feared me. I mean, not only was I the girl whose mother was killed by the Wife Collector, but my mother was the one who made him a bona fide serial killer."

Bex dug her teeth into her lower lip. She knew what Lauren meant: a killer was just a killer until at least his third kill. Then he was a *serial* killer. Bex felt the acid burning through her gut.

"Her picture was in the paper all the time. And her story…" Lauren shook her head and pushed a lock of hair behind her ear. "I swear I've heard every iteration of it. Some of them say my mom was a dedicated young wife and mother; others say she was loose and practically a prostitute."

"What?"

"My dad… He was pretty abusive. I don't really remember much, but I remember being scared. My mother was trying to leave him. She had taken me with her, and we were living in an apartment. People said my mother was cheating and that's why she left. She didn't say anything. I guess in her mind being thought of as a cheater was less humiliating than being a domestic violence victim. Your dad started coming around. Just once, maybe twice to the apartment."

Bex swallowed down the lump in her throat, the urge to protest.

"You're sure it was him?"

Lauren nodded.

Suddenly, Bex blurted, "Did you know Detective Schuster?"

"Schuster?" Lauren frowned, then pressed a piece of her hair between her lips. "I think so."

Bex felt her eyes widen. "Did your mom know him too? Before she met my dad?"

"I'm not really sure."

"Think!" Bex's voice was louder than expected and Lauren sat up with a start. "Sorry, Lauren. Just—do you remember?"

She shook her head. "I'm pretty sure I didn't meet the detective until late—wait." She paused, her eyes getting a faraway look in them. "He knocked on the door. He was going door to door with another guy, and they talked to my mom about coming to some kind of meeting."

"A community meeting to talk about public safety and the murders."

"Yeah, I think so."

Bex's heart started to thud.

Always be watching, Bethy.

She felt the adrenaline flood her muscles, making them tight and hot. "I think…I think there might be a possibility that the police got the wrong man."

Lauren blinked. "What?"

"What if—"

"I saw him, Bex. I saw your dad. He came over to the house."

"So did Detective Schuster."

Bex could see Lauren's face fall. She blinked, trying to hold back tears. "No, Bex. The detective was helping."

But Bex wasn't dissuaded.

"What's up, party people?"

Both Bex's and Lauren's heads snapped toward Chelsea as she dragged a chair up to their table and plopped down, grin on her face, phone in her hand. "I don't know you," she said to Lauren. "I'm Chelsea."

Lauren stared blankly at Chelsea's outstretched hand and then at Bex. "I…" She stood up quickly. "I need to get going."

Bex and Chelsea watched Lauren speed walk to the door, Bex's gaze following Lauren across the parking lot and into her little black Honda Civic.

"Pleasant lady," Chelsea said. "Friend of yours?"

Bex chewed her bottom lip. "I'm not sure."

• • •

Bex got home just as Denise was tying Michael into an apron. He clapped a pair of tongs at Bex and grinned. "I'm making my famous charbroiled burgers tonight, Bexy Boo. Up for helping?"

"Don't you mean charcoaled, dear?" Denise cocked an eyebrow, shooting Bex a wicked smile. "You hungry?"

Bex couldn't remember the last time she'd eaten, but it was the last thing on her mind. She patted her stomach. "Actually, Chelsea and I just came from getting coffee. I've got a latte and a muffin sloshing around in here." She turned and headed for the stairs before Denise or Michael could say anything. "Maybe in a little bit."

She knew that Denise and Michael must have shared a slightly worried-looking glance. But they weren't her parents. Bex jogged into her bedroom and slid her computer onto her lap, throwing on her headphones and bypassing the home-page images of pretty blonds and shallow graves as she went directly to Forums, searching for GAMECREATOR.

Hi, Dad. You OK?

It seemed like less than a second that her father typed back.

Good, just gathering some information.

She imagined her dad in some nondescript motel room, stretched out on some god-awful bedspread with pages and newspaper clippings all around him as he diligently pieced together the time line and clues that would prove his innocence. Then, she would appear in court with them and they'd have a father-daughter movie montage of tears and hugs when he was finally vindicated and Detective Schuster was led away in chains. People would send letters to their house apologizing for treating Bex so poorly or saying that they'd always believed in her father's innocence. Maybe even Michael and Denise would be at the courthouse…

Bex felt a slight pinch of guilt when she thought about Michael and Denise downstairs cooking dinner without her, when she thought about leaving them to move back in with her father. But at the same time, she got a hollow-stomached feeling when she thought of sharing breakfast with her dad for the first time in ten years, seeing him across the breakfast table, making a life together. Just a regular dad and his regular daughter.

"Bex!" Michael's call came from downstairs. "We got burgers and your buddies down here!"

Her fingers shot across the keyboard.

Friends are here, Dad. School project for lame Back to School Night on Friday! Talk to you later!

She waited for him to write her back. When he did—Have fun, xoxo Love, Dad—Bex could feel a big grin pushing up her cheeks.

"Well, isn't someone bouncy?" Denise asked when Bex came downstairs.

"Dude, your dad makes some killer burgers!" Laney said, holding up a half-eaten one.

Bex felt her eyebrows ride up, and Denise nudged Michael. "I may have suggested a cooking tip or two."

Chelsea dropped a handful of potato chips onto her burger patty and smashed the bun with the palm of her hand, the chips crunching underneath. She took a bite that bulged her cheeks.

"I have no idea how you eat like that and never gain an ounce," Bex said, sliding into a chair.

"She's super-active. Texting and running away from her mother," Laney said.

Michael helped himself to a second burger while sliding one on Bex's plate. "Why are you running away from your mother?" he asked Chelsea.

"Cell phone bill," Chelsea with her mouth full. "She says I text too much."

"It's her new boyfriend."

Bex sat up. "I didn't know you have a new boyfriend."

Chelsea pointed a chip at her. "You would have known if we ever saw you anymore. Even at school you're, like, in la-la land."

Denise and Michael exchanged a look, and Laney put her hands out. "But Bex is totally fixated on school, I promise."

"You're not giving away any secrets, Laney. Denise and I are both going to Back to School Night. We'll be scrutinizing Bex's teachers and learning about this la-la land of which you speak."

"Well, spill, Chels. Who's the new guy?" Bex clapped a hand to her forehead. "Ohmigosh, is it Brenden? You've been crushing hard on him since I met you."

Chelsea looked disgusted. "It is *not* Brenden. He acts like a toddler."

"I can't think of anyone else I've seen you with at school lately."

"He doesn't go to KDH."

Denise stood up, collecting Michael's plate and then hers. "Come on, hon. Let's give the girls a chance to talk."

Michael looked wounded but stood up anyway. "Don't we get to know about Chelsea's new beau?"

"The fact that you used the term 'beau' should answer that question." Denise looked over her shoulder, winking at Bex. "We'll be upstairs. Make sure you get your project done, and, Bex, don't stay up too late."

Once Michael and Denise were safely out of earshot, Laney leaned forward. "Your parents are so cool."

But Bex barely heard her, mentally calculating how long it would take to make the posters for Back to School Night, how long it would take before she could get back online to talk to her father. Maybe by now he had come up with more information about Schuster or a plan on how to catch him. Maybe he could even come to Back to School Night if…

"Bex!" Chelsea snapped her fingers. "You're not even listening to me."

Bex blinked. "I totally am. Was."

"Then what did I say?"

Bex frowned. "That Laney should start opening the paints?"

Chelsea rolled her eyes. "I was talking about Dan. Danny." She brushed her long hair back, sweeping it up into a high ponytail. "Now you don't get to know."

"No. Danny... I totally heard you."

"Can we just get to work on these things, please?" Laney looked annoyed. "It's bad enough we have to waste an entire Friday night standing around handing out that nasty orange punch to our parents while our teachers bad-mouth us. I don't want to lose a whole other night on these things."

"I'm pretty sure teachers don't bad-mouth the straight-A students, Lane." Bex grinned, then glanced down at her phone. A text message from Detective Schuster: Please get in touch.

A wave of anger burned through her. Schuster wasn't her father. He was... She wanted to call him no one, but that wasn't true. Schuster was the man who had taken her father away from her, who had taken daughters away from several fathers. Bex was pulled back into the courtroom all those years ago when one of the victim's fathers had wanted her to stay in the room, yelling, "She should have to see what he done to my little girl."

A lump, hard anger and sadness, sat in Bex's gut. Schuster had been sitting right there in that courtroom when shame and bewilderment had exploded through seven-year-old Bex. He hadn't flinched. He hadn't cared. He was a monster.

It was almost midnight when Bex stood the posters up in her garage to dry and Laney and Chelsea went home. Though sleep was pushing her eyelids closed, Bex pulled her computer into her lap after washing her face and brushing her teeth. She went to the Forum page, waited for GAMECREATOR to find her. He didn't.

IMHIM_HESME did.

> IMHIM_HESME: Hi there.

Bex ignored the message, scrolling through her last chat with her father. IMHIM_HESME popped up again.

> IMHIM_HESME: Are you there?
> IMHIM_HESME: Beth Anne?

Bex blew out a sigh and started to type.

> BETHANNER: I'm logging off.
> IMHIM_HESME: WAIT. Please.
> BETHANNER: Good night.
> IMHIM_HESME: You're not safe.
> BETHANNER: Go away.
> IMHIM_HESME: You have to listen to me.

Bex knew she should just log off, stop typing, and shut the laptop. But something bothered her and she typed on.

> BETHANNER: I don't even know who you are.
>
> IMHIM_HESME: A friend.
>
> BETHANNER: Sure you are. Bye.
>
> IMHIM_HESME: I promise. Talk to me.
>
> BETHANNER: Blocking you now.
>
> IMHIM_HESME: Then someone you love is going to die.

THIRTY-FIVE

Bex slammed the laptop shut and skittered away, pressing herself up against the side of her bed and breathing hard.

Someone you love is going to die.

The pounding of her heart metered out the words: *you're* (thump) *going* (thump) *to* (thump) *die* (thump). She stared at her computer in abject horror, waiting for it to ping out the sound of a new message, to open itself up, the ominous silver screen glow coming after her.

"Just a weirdo freak," she panted, her heartbeat thudding in her head now. "He's just stupid."

She clicked out the lights and curled up on her bed, pressing her eyes closed tightly, but the words were behind her eyelids too, tattooed there, stark and black and deadly. She opened her eyes and blinked as though she could erase the words from her mind. Then she stared into the darkness, letting her eyes adjust. A breeze lazed through her open window, pushing back her curtains. A car drove slowly down the street and Bex dove to the window, certain the car was looking for her.

Who is IMHIM?

Her father was safe; he was on her side. But the site was populated by the Wife Collector's crazed "fans," morbid rejects who thought murder was cool and treated killers like rock stars. And wanted to be like them.

"He's probably just some stupid kid, trying to scare me."

Bex tried to believe it, but something ominous made her uneasy. Something that told her IMHIM_HESME wasn't joking. Something that told her that he was closer than she wanted to believe.

She wasn't sure when she fell asleep, but when she did, she slept fitfully, dreaming of old newspaper clippings and of the hollow, haunted look in Lauren's eyes, and of her father and Detective Schuster, and the sound of the dirt falling on Darla's coffin: heavy, smothering.

• • •

"It's just unnatural being at school at night," Chelsea was saying as she and Laney walked just ahead of Trevor and Bex. Trevor squeezed Bex's hand in his and shot her a heart-melting smile. It made the lump in her throat feel that much more raw. She shifted her purse. It was weighted down with an extra set of clothes and a thick handful of underwear, socks, and bras, as well as a toothbrush and the least amount of makeup she could get by with.

She and her father would leave tonight.

Bex still couldn't believe it. As much as she wanted to be with her dad, to see him vindicated, she didn't want to leave Trevor— and she didn't want to leave Detective Schuster to terrorize more women. She planned to call the police when she and her father were safely out of town.

"This is where I get off," Trevor said. "I have the awesome job of opening and closing the curtain for the drama showcase."

Bex gave him a lingering kiss, holding on to his hands and trying not to cry.

"Let him up for air, Bex!"

Trevor didn't seem to mind, but Bex broke the kiss anyway, pecking him one more time and watching him sprint toward the drama department.

"Someone needs to turn a hose on you two," Laney said.

Chelsea rolled her eyes and tossed a perfectly coiffed piece of her blond hair over her shoulder. "You're just mad because you're the only one of us not in love." She did a twirl. "My boyfriend is amazing and makes me feel so safe. Dating a cop will do that for you."

Bex stopped. "You're dating a cop?"

"A detective, actually." She wrinkled her nose and held her index finger and thumb a half inch a part. "He's a weensy bit older but doesn't look it."

"Because you're sixteen pushing forty-five." Laney smirked. "My stop. See you later."

Bex stepped closer to Chelsea. "He's a detective?" Heat spiraled up her spine. "Chels, what's his name?"

"I told you, Ms. Never Listen. Danny."

Bex blinked. Detective Schuster. *What was his first name?* Then it came to her: Detective Lieutenant Daniel Schuster.

Someone you love is going to die.

Bex snatched Chelsea by the arm and gave her a hard yank. "Chelsea, you can't see him. You can't see him ever again."

The delight on Chelsea's face turned to anger. "And why not?"

"He's bad, Chels. Please, you've got to believe me."

Chelsea rolled her eyes at Bex. "You're just jealous that your boyfriend is a little boy when mine is a man. Get over it, Bexy."

"I'm serious!"

People were starting to fill the campus; a din was starting to reverberate through the halls as kids escorted their parents around, pointing out lockers and classrooms. A crowd cut between Chelsea and Bex.

"You have to listen to me!"

But Chelsea had already dismissed her and was pushing her cell phone to her ear. It was then that Bex noticed the charm hanging from Chelsea's cell phone case: a tiny, jeweled flower. It hung from a loop of silk floss, but it wasn't a charm—it was an earring.

A small, gold, five-petaled flower with a pearl in the center. Just like the one that Lauren wore. Just like the one that the Wife Collector took when he killed Lauren's mother.

Bex grabbed Chelsea's wrist, her breath a terrified whisper.

"Where did you get that charm?"

Chelsea glanced at the flower, pink rushing over her cheeks. "Danny."

Bex's entire body turned to ice. "No, Chelsea, no. That belonged to... That's an earring. You can't—you can't see Danny anymore. Please, Chels, please listen to me."

Chelsea's eyes narrowed and she shoved the phone in her back pocket. "I'm done with you." She spun on her heel and started to walk.

"He killed Darla, Chelsea!"

But by that time, the overhead speaker had crackled on and the principal was in the middle of his welcome speech. Bex saw Chelsea's arm raise above the undulating crowd, her wrist flipping dismissively.

Bex wasn't sure Chelsea had even heard her.

The crowd split and jostled by, then closed on her, and Bex was bumped from side to side.

"'Scuse me."

Bex looked up to see Zach, his GoPro slung around his neck.

"Pardon me."

Another jostle, another ear-splitting announcement over the PA. Bex felt hopeless as she allowed the crowd to pull her down the hall.

No.

She wasn't alone anymore. She dialed her father.

"I'm here, Bethy."

"Dad, I think Chelsea is dating Detective Schuster. Or she thinks she is. We've got to stop him." The tears were falling freely now and Bex was hiccupping. "We've got to stop him before he hurts her."

"Do you know where she is?"

Bex scanned the hall. "I can't see her, but she was headed down to D hall. It's the classrooms closest to the parking lot."

"I'll help, Bethy."

The second she hung up her phone, it rang again.

Detective Schuster.

She stared at the readout, her hand trembling. She watched the phone light up with each ring, finally letting out her breath when the missed call icon flashed. And then the phone started ringing again. Bex paced, her stomach playing the accordion. She answered before the final ring.

"Detective Schuster?"

"Bex, thank God you answered. Where are you right now?"

She looked around, certain he could hear the swell of voices. "I'm at school."

"I think your father is on his way there. Stay put. Hang tight and I will be there in five minutes. Don't do anything until I get there, okay? If you see him…run away." Then the call ended.

The hall started to clear as parents followed their kids into classes. Bex was determined, speed dialing her phone as she jogged toward Chelsea and her father in D hall.

"Pick up, Chelsea!" When Chelsea didn't, she tried Laney, Trevor, and Denise. No one answered. "Where are they? Where are they?"

Detective Schuster's text came through as Bex rounded the corner into B hall. My men are two minutes from campus. Where are you?

Bex spun, looking at the hall of closed doors around her. The C hall was mostly metal shop and electives, classrooms none of the parents visited. The hall was dark. Bex's heart thundered and skidded. She dialed Chelsea again and again and was greeted by her voice mail. She was about to dial her father when she heard voices.

They were muffled but still audible. And she knew they were girls, and then a boy spoke. One of the girls laughed out loud, and Bex's stomach went to liquid.

THIRTY-SIX

It was Laney.

"Trevor! Stop, you're hilarious!" Laney said.

"You'll laugh at anything, Lane." Chelsea.

Someone mumbled something that Bex couldn't make out, and the laughter rang out again. Her heart thumped painfully, slamming against her rib cage, but relief gave her breath.

"Guys?" Bex called.

The voices immediately stopped, and Bex's own voice echoed back to her. She continued walking, sliding her hand along the wall between the banks of lockers, looking for a light switch. The voices started again, but they were heavy whispers and low murmurs. Bex was certain they were whispering about her.

"Bexy!" It was Laney, her voice cheerful and friendly.

"Where's my fox?" Trevor chimed in.

Bex glanced over her shoulder, her fear starting to fall away. Her heartbeat slowed to its normal rate. "Guys?" she called again.

She could see a light coming from one of the classrooms up ahead; it was where the voices were coming from.

"Oh thank God."

Bex ran toward Mr. Rhodes's room and stopped in the doorway, her blood turning to ice in her veins. Her friends weren't sitting in the classroom waiting for her. They were projected on the movie screen in the front of the classroom.

"What?" Bex walked toward it, then away again, following the light from the projector.

"I love you, Bexy!" she heard Chelsea call.

"The Wife Collector has struck again."

Bex stepped back as Loretta Harris, the Raleigh Super Eight news anchor's concerned face flooded the screen. A picture of Erin Malone flashed on the screen over her left shoulder. Bex could feel the bile at the back of her throat.

"Bexy!"

The image on the screen flashed back to Laney, Chelsea, and Trevor sitting on the beach, the bonfire illuminating their faces. But now Bex was in the scene too, wrapped in Trevor's letterman's jacket, curled underneath his arm. She was mesmerized, watching as Trevor leaned close to her, laying a quick kiss on the part of her hair.

"Okay," he roared, holding up his red Solo cup. "Bex is here. Now the party can begin!"

There was a flood of raucous laughter and cheers, then Loretta Harris's serious voice breaking in. "…Monroe's body was found by employees at the beachfront restaurant where she worked. She had been dumped outside and when found—the sight was gruesome."

"Oh God." Bex crumpled into one of the empty desks, knowing she should run but unsure where. Her eyes were glued to the screen. There were a few more flashes, a few more pictures, then a computer screen.

A log-in.

IMHIM_HESME.

Bex's heart was in her throat.

The next picture showed the full log-in screen, Detective Schuster's avatar lined up under IMHIM_HESME's.

Bex clapped a hand over her mouth. IMHIM_HESME was Detective Schuster.

Someone you love is going to die.

"Bex!"

The hall was dark, but the silvery flashes from the screen illuminated the man in the doorway. Schuster.

He was dressed all in black, a bulletproof vest bulking his slim frame, a gun more terrifying than any Bex had ever seen strapped to his thigh.

Bex stood, surprised that her legs would even work. "Don't come near me," she said, her voice small but steady.

"Bex, we have to get out of here. You father is here. I need to get you somewhere safe."

"No." She shook her head, hot, angry tears flicking down her cheeks. "I know who you are. I know what you did. You're not going to get away with it. You're not!" Her fingers closed around the only thing she could find—an oblong vase full of pencils—and she launched it. It crashed at Schuster's feet. He quickly stepped around it, closing the distance between them. Bex mashed her finger on her cell phone's Send Call button.

"I'm calling my dad. I'm calling him, and he'll tell everyone that you killed all those women!"

"What are you talking about?"

"You're the Wife Collector! I know you are! You used me to frame my father! And now you're trying to kill Chelsea!"

"Bex—"

"I saw the charm you gave her, you sick freak. The earring? You took it when you killed Lauren's mother!"

Bex judged the distance to the door from where she was. In order to make it, she'd have to pass by Detective Schuster and his gun. She backed into a corner, barricaded herself behind a desk.

Schuster put out his hands. "No, I didn't. I didn't do any of that. I don't even know Chelsea or Lauren. Bex, who are they?"

"Shut up! You killed Dr. Gold too, didn't you? Didn't you?"

"Bex, you're wrong."

"Chelsea told me about you." Bex spit out the words, each one viler than the last. "She said she was dating a detective. Danny. Daniel Schuster."

"Bex, that's not me."

"Aren't you Daniel Schuster? Detective?"

"Yes, but—"

"You did it! He told me!" She pointed to the screen, frozen on IMHIM's log-in screen. "And *you* were the one on the site!"

"Bex, stop. Look." Detective Schuster unholstered his gun and laid it on the desk in front of him, then held his hands up. "I'm not armed. We can sit down and talk."

She wagged her head, pressing her phone to her ear. "My dad

will explain everything. You ruined my life, Schuster. You took away my dad, and now you're going to pay for it!"

"No, Bex, no." He held his hands in the air.

Bex could hear her father's phone ringing. It was loud, almost as if it was in stereo. She pulled the phone from her ear and the ring still sounded. She took a few steps toward the door, and the ring grew louder, reverberating through the hall. Schuster kept his hands up and took several steps back while Bex followed the sound. It was coming from a garbage can outside of the classroom—right by the entrance to D hall.

She peered into the mouth of the can, her breath hitching, each ring sucking that much more air out of the room as she saw her name flash across the screen. Bethy.

THIRTY-SEVEN

Bex snatched the phone from the can and whirled on Schuster. "What did you do to him?"

"Look at the phone, Bex." Schuster's voice was steady, even.

"How do you have his phone?" Her voice cracked.

"He tossed it. Your father. Your father is the Wife Collector." There was something soft, apologetic in his voice. "He was manipulating you the whole time."

Bex shook her head, disbelieving. Schuster was the Wife Collector.

He gently took the phone from her hand, flicking it on. He held it out to her, but Bex refused to look.

"Those are the calls he made to you. That's your number."

"No."

"He used you to get to her."

Bex shook her head again, a new round of tears pooling in front of her eyes. "No. He came back for me."

"He didn't, Bex."

She was about to respond when a primitive, pulse-stopping scream cut through the air.

Chelsea.

She took off running in the direction of her friend's screams, running until her thighs ached.

She would save Chelsea.

She wouldn't let another girl die.

"He's just a man."

Bex burst down the D hall just as her father was dragging Chelsea out of a classroom. She was screaming and kicking, striking out like a wet cat. Bex's father had his hands on Chelsea's neck as he slammed her up against one of the lockers, the thunking sound of her head against metal immediately stopping her shrieks. She went limp and he swiped his arms around her, sweeping her feet from under her.

"Leave her alone!"

Bex's father's head turned. "Oh, Bethy, this isn't what it looks like. You don't understand. It was Schuster. I had to get her away—"

Bex didn't hear what he had to say. Her eyes were locked on the keychain hanging from his pocket. A tiny, slick silver bird twirled at the end of a lanyard, its pink, jeweled eyes catching the dim light.

Tourmalines.

Dr. Gold's bracelet.

Chelsea whimpered. "Bex, please."

Bex was pummeled by a memory.

Another girl with white-blond hair. She swept Beth Anne up and Beth Anne laughed, loving the tinkling sound of the woman's laughter. Her mother's laughter.

Then he came in. A black cloud in their sunshiny kitchen, with heavy black boots that left ugly scrapes across the white linoleum floor.

Beth Anne was pulled against her mother's chest, where she was comforted by her mother's soft, steady heartbeat and her fresh milk smell before she was wrenched away, yanked by an arm and roughly shoved into a dining table chair. She heard the slap of palm against skin, and when she looked up, her father was cradling his cheek, the dumbfounded look on his face slowly simmering to white-hot anger.

"You're going to regret that."

Bex snapped back to reality, rage surging through her.

"Let her go."

A slow smile spread across Bex's father's face, his lips quirking up maniacally, making her blood run cold.

"Stay out of this, Bethy."

She took a step forward. "I remember now."

"Bex, stay back." Detective Schuster was a hairbreadth behind but Bex shrugged him off, knowing that he had a gun trained on her father. She didn't care.

"I was there that day in the kitchen."

The grin that had looked so evil and so full of confidence faltered for a split second.

"Get out of here," he spat.

"That's what she told you," Bex said.

She watched the hatred cut a red streak across her father's face. "You have no idea what you are talking about."

She could see Chelsea start to stiffen, could see her begin to blink her eyes, then squint. "Bex?"

"Let her go, Dad."

The word caught in her throat, her bravado replaced by fear for Chelsea. He was her dad, and he was a murderer. She had put him away once. She would do it again.

"Give up." In the floodlight around the school, Bex could see the police surrounding the building through the windows. Their guns were drawn. "It's not your time to be free; it's mine."

THIRTY-EIGHT

Everything happened in a blur. The police rushed in, and Chelsea and Bex were rushed out. They were each sitting on the tailgate of separate ambulances, Laney in front of Chelsea with Chelsea's parents fawning over her. Bex by herself, an itchy blanket slung over her shoulders.

When Detective Schuster walked up, she looked away, embarrassment burning to the tops of her ears.

"I-I'm sorry," she said.

"For what?"

Bex looked up incredulously. "Uh, for hiding a criminal. For accusing you of being a serial killer."

He jammed his hands into his pockets and shrugged. "Not the first time it's happened." He cleared his throat. "I want you to know that I meant what I said. We were looking out for you. You were never on your own."

"How did you—"

"Keystrokes. We were following your keystrokes."

Bex blinked, staring at her feet, at the tears that plopped onto the toes of her sneakers. When she looked up, Schuster was looking at her, hard.

"So you knew not to trust me. You knew that I would cave and try to save my father."

"No. I knew that… Bex, what you did, you risked everything not once, but twice. I can't even imagine how hard that must have been for you. I wanted to give you every kind of support that I could. Truth is, I never really got over what happened ten years ago."

"What are you talking about?"

Now Detective Schuster looked away, raked a hand through his hair. "I was young and stupid, a rookie gunslinger. I should never have involved you in your father's case. It killed me to do it again but I couldn't… I've spent the last ten years proud that I was able to protect you and guilt ridden knowing what making you talk must have done to you. I wanted the chance to make it right. I wanted to do it right this time, but your father…" He looked at Bex, his eyes glistening with moisture. "I was terrified that you'd be his next victim."

"In a way, I kind of was."

"Oh my God, Bex!" Denise came running, with Michael on her heels, followed by Trevor. They all swept her into a group hug. Bex didn't hug them back, dumbfounded, unsure of what to do. Detective Schuster stepped out of the way.

"Hi," Bex said softly.

"Hi?" Denise cradled Bex's chin. "She staves off a serial killer and all she says hi?" She plopped a series of loud kisses across Bex's cheeks and forehead. "I'm just so glad you're okay."

Trevor stood beside her, looking like he wanted to kiss her too, but he took her hand instead. "You're incredible."

"Oh, my girl. I feel like I need to make you seven hamburgers. And pancakes!" Michael pulled her into a rib-crushing bear hug.

"Don't you think she's suffered enough?"

"What do you mean you want to cook for me? I... You know that...he's my father. You don't have to keep me."

Denise looked taken aback. "You're not your father, Bexy. And we know we don't have to keep you. We care about you. We *want* to keep you."

Trevor laced his fingers through Bex's and pulled her to him. She inhaled his soap and cut-grass scent, for once thinking of only Trevor, of only that moment.

"And I *get* to keep you," he whispered in her ear.

For the first time in her life, Bex Andrews knew she was truly at home.

ACKNOWLEDGMENTS

As always, I have to acknowledge my incredible agent, Amberly Finarelli, who has always stuck by me, and Andrea Hurst, for being my cheerleader and my champion. Nothing gets by savvy editor Annette Pollert-Morgan, and for that, I am truly grateful!

I wouldn't be anywhere without my Wednesday writing gang, my awesome SVRWA chapter, and my gym fans who keep me on track (and off the couch!). Extra special thanks to one of my favorite authors and friends, April Henry, for duping me into a kidnapping and stun gunning, all in the name of better stories. Special thanks to all my amazing Wattpad readers and to my summer Teen Writer's Institute students for inspiring me, and the Hicklebee's bookstore Teen Authors Board who throw great Halloween parties and let me write on the walls!

Special thanks to Victim's Advocate Kasey Halcon for letting me pick her brain (your story is coming!), to Lee Lofland for providing me a steady stream of brains to pick, and to Jonathan Hayes for answering inappropriate questions about homicide.

You can't run from fear…

DON'T MISS HANNAH JAYNE'S
THE ESCAPE

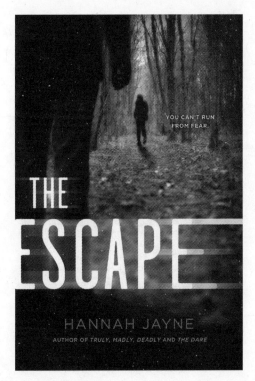

ONE

"Come on, loser!" Adam yelled over his shoulder.

Fletcher could hear Adam's laughter echoing back at him as he pumped his legs, intent on keeping the deep green of Adam's jacket in sight as he dodged through the forest.

There was no way Fletcher could catch Adam unless Adam stopped or dropped *dead*. Adam was the quarterback who brought Dan River Falls High School victory after victory, and Fletcher was the "weird kid" who sat at the back of the bleachers and drew in his notebook.

"Come on!"

A second wind broke through Fletcher's chest, and he felt the burn of adrenaline rush through his legs. He fisted his hands as the cool air dried the sweat on his forehead. A loopy smile cracked across his face. He could see Adam. He was gaining on him—not fast, but steadily. Adam was caught in the crosshairs of Fletcher's gaze.

"Who you calling 'loser'?" Fletcher called, still grinning.

Up ahead, Adam stopped, head bent, shoulders heaving as he struggled for breath. He was doubled over, staring at something on the ground. "My God, Fletch. Dude, you've got to see this."

• • •

It was just after six o'clock as Avery watched pink bleed into the sunny blue sky, casting a haze of twilight over the parking lot at the Dan River Falls Police Station. The cup of coffee that sat in front of her—more vanilla creamer than coffee—had long since gone cold.

A man strode into the room, his black uniform pressed so each crease was razor sharp. He was no-nonsense from head to toe: salt-and-pepper hair cut close to his skull, dark eyes focused, thin lips pressed together in a scowl. He walked past Avery and dropped a thick manila file folder on the giant desk.

"Dad," Avery moaned, pulling out the word. "Can we go yet?"

Chief Templeton looked at his daughter as if just noticing her—as if she hadn't been sitting there in that same spot for the last forty minutes.

"The line is going to be out the door. I'm going to starve to death while we wait."

"Not now, Avery."

"Fine. Then we're hitting the drive-through with the lights and siren on. I'm pretty sure my stomach is eating itself."

"Your stomach eating itself? Not happening, Avy."

"It happens! We talked about it in biology." It was a lie. Avery had no idea whether or not the stomach could or would eat itself. But it felt like it. She was going to launch into some other wild story to make the stern police chief crack a smile and bring him back to acting like her dad. But when he turned, Avery could see that there was no playfulness in his eyes. His lips weren't going to quirk up into a smile no matter how hard she tried. She swallowed, fear inching up the back of her neck.

"What's wrong, Dad?"

• • •

He couldn't remember the first blow, though his teeth were still rattling in his head. Had he been punched, shot, hit? His vision was a blur, and everything around him, every tree, every rock, seemed to blend together in one united mass of gray. He wasn't sure if the sky was above or below him, if the trees were standing or if he was.

Another blow.

The pain was dense at first, then exploded into a blinding burn. He blinked, dumbfounded, and tried to face his attacker. But his body was leaden. It was as if his feet were rooted in the soft blanket of pine needles on the damp forest ground. He knew he should roll his fingers into a fist and take a swing, but while his brain worked, his body didn't. Thoughts of action tossed around in his skull—run, yell, fight, punch—but everything moved in sickly slow motion except for the terror that overwhelmed him.

I'm going to die.

The thought came to him with a sickening dread.

I don't want to die.

Then came a gruesome thud followed by a sharp crack. The sound filled his ears before he registered that it was his bones breaking. *Snap, crack.* He knew another blow was coming and he tried to brace himself, balling up, wondering if the next hit would be the one that killed him.

TWO

"Adam Marshall and Fletcher Carroll," Chief Templeton replied.

Avery shrugged. "What about them?"

Adam Marshall was a jock at Dan River Falls High. He was a junior, a grade older than Avery, but she knew him—everyone did. Generally, Avery studiously avoided jocks and great-at-everythings, but Adam was different. Avery and Adam had been friends as kids, playing on the baseball diamond back when boys and girls and popularity didn't matter. Maybe that was why he was nice to her now. He smiled at her, calling her by name. He ushered along the mean girls when they were poised to pick apart whatever shred of confidence Avery had.

Adam was everything Fletcher Carroll wasn't. While Adam was a beacon of light with white-blond hair and a Crest-toothpaste smile, Fletcher was always hunched in his hoodie, hiding behind a mass of thick brown curls that were a half inch too long to be considered fashionably shaggy. Avery and Fletcher were neighbors. He was nice enough, but he kept to himself. He was the kind of kid who didn't really fit in but didn't really stick out either.

Chief Templeton drummed his fingers on his desktop, the sound like the rat-a-tat-tat of machine-gun fire. "They went hiking this morning and haven't come back yet."

Avery shrugged. "So?"

"So they were supposed to be back three hours ago. Fletcher's mother is here; she wants to file a report. Adam's parents are on their way as well."

"They've only been gone a few hours," Avery said. "They probably got drunk and passed out in a clearing."

Chief Templeton raised his eyebrows. "Is that what you kids do out there?"

Avery rolled her eyes. "Not 'us kids,' *some* kids. Some of us starve to death because our fathers promise cheeseburgers that never materialize."

But Avery's dad wasn't listening. He stared over her head at the graying sky. A little niggle of fear started at the base of Avery's spine, and she shifted in her seat to follow his gaze to the thick clutch of pine trees off in the distance. If it was gray here, it had to be near pitch-black out in the woods.

"It's too early to really be worried, isn't it, Dad?"

• • •

He was thirsty. His lips were burning, and his throat was raw from screaming. His head pounded so severely that his vision would darken and then snap back to clear before fading again.

He couldn't make out where he was.

He could feel the cold earth cradling him, a soft blanket of pine

305

needles haloing behind his head. A multitude of scents bombarded him as he struggled to gain awareness: the biting scent of pine, the mossy smell of dirt, and something else. Something metallic and cloying. He tried to turn his head, but it was immobile like his limbs. If he could see properly, he could figure out what was holding him down and pressing the breath from his chest. If he could move, even just an inch, maybe he could get away. But all he could do was take in a glimpse of the darkening sky each time his vision cleared.

Not far away, a few feet maybe, he could hear footsteps. At least he hoped they were footsteps, not some bear or whatever had walloped him into his current supine state. The crunch of dry leaves and popping twigs was getting closer. He was sure of it. A wave of primal fear coursed through him. As his adrenaline surged, he dug his fingertips into the dirt around him. *If I can push myself up*, he thought, *at least then I won't be a sitting duck.*

Though his spine felt as if it had been snapped in two, he pushed himself up with a slow groan that became a strangled, gurgling sound. Blood filled his mouth and trickled out his nose. Sweat bulleted his forehead and the thrum in his head grew more severe, like a talon in his skull, raking against the bone.

He tried to cradle his aching head, but one arm screamed in pain while the other fell at his side, useless, his elbow bending the wrong way. His stomach went to liquid at the sight of his own wounds, and he vomited, spit and blood and puke splattering the dirt next to him.

When he fell back again, the blue above had turned into the blackest night.

THREE

Avery could hear her father rustling around before the sun rose. She pushed herself out of bed and dressed quickly. She didn't need to ask what had happened—she already knew.

Her father had been the Dan River Falls chief of police since Avery was fifteen. That was the last year her family had been all together. One of her favorite memories was when they rode in the Founder's Day parade. The chief's black-and-white SUV had been wrapped with red, white, and blue crepe-paper streamers, and she and her mother had practiced waving delicately, her mother's lips upturned in a permanent smile.

Avery remembered the way her father had pulled her mother close, just before they turned onto the parade route. His fingers had tangled in her chestnut-brown hair as he kissed her. When they'd pulled away, her parents had both laughed. Her prim and pressed father had now sported bright red lips, a transfer of her mother's lipstick. Avery had groaned or gagged at her parents' unbelievably gross public display of affection, though secretly she'd liked that they were always touching, always smiling.

The next year, Avery and her father had ridden in the same car in the parade, but this time in silence. It was just the two of them driving slowly behind the marching band. Avery's mother's absence had been palpable, and Avery had gritted her teeth the whole time, trying to force a smile, knowing her father was doing the same thing.

After a few more blocks, the parade would be over, and Avery and her father would pretend they weren't watching for the clock to strike eight seventeen, the moment Caroline Templeton had been struck by a drunk driver on her way home from the Founder's Day barbeque, the moment she had been killed.

Avery's father had the coffee going and his travel mug out, so Avery started breakfast, pulling out a carton of eggs and the frying pan.

"No word on—"

Her father shook his head and filled both mugs, fixing hers with enough milk and sugar to turn it a pale brown while leaving his black. He screwed the lids on both, then took a sip and dropped two pieces of bread in the toaster as Avery cracked two eggs.

"No word. Green and Howard went in last night just before sunset but didn't see anything."

"Nothing?"

"Car was in the lot. Last one there. As far as we know, neither boy contacted anyone at home or any friends."

The toast popped up and Chief Templeton slathered each slice with butter, laying them on separate paper towels.

Avery flipped the eggs. "Well, if neither of them made contact, that could be a good sign, right? They're probably together."

The chief salted and peppered the eggs over Avery's shoulder.

She nudged him out of the way and slipped a fried egg onto each slab of toast. He handed her a bright-orange Windbreaker; she handed him one of the egg sandwiches.

"You know you're basically just keeping the kids out of the way, right?" The chief's tone was calm, but his eyes were wary.

Avery stiffened. She had been on more missing-person searches—unofficially, as she was underage—than most of the officers on her father's staff. But being sixteen kept her on "kid patrol," basically babysitting while the adult volunteers tromped through the forest, potentially ruining scads of evidence while pretending they were a bunch of television CSIs, no doubt.

"Yeah," she said through a mouthful of fried egg. "I know."

He chucked her shoulder. "Don't be like that. When you're of age, you can show off your detective skills. Until then, we do things by the book."

Avery looked away, thinking about her mother, about how she would zing the chief in the ribs and remind him not to be so serious. "By the book," she would mock in a terrible baritone. "I'm the big, bad chief."

Avery let out a tight sigh. "I know, Dad. By the book."

• • •

Is this what it feels like to die?

He wheezed, imagining his breath leaving his body around jags of broken bones and swollen flesh. He didn't really know what was broken and what was swollen, but judging by the pain, he guessed everything. He tried to swallow and winced when saliva laced with blood slid down his throat. His head hadn't stopped pounding and his stomach lurched.

He turned his head to the side, ignoring the twigs that dug into his cheek. Eyes closed, he vomited. He kept them closed—not at the pain, but in an effort to avoid seeing his innards, which he was sure he was spitting up. Then everything went black.

• • •

Avery was leaning over, tightening her hiking boots, when she heard the voice that set her teeth on edge. It was Kaylee Cooper, a girl who sported a wardrobe full of pink, fuzzy sweaters and cheerleading skirts that barely covered her butt. She was goddess-like and blond, with hair that nipped at her waist, and eyes that looked sweetly innocent until they narrowed and her gaze sliced you into ribbons. She was popular for being either a tease or a slut, Avery couldn't remember which, and she never moved without a swarm of girls orbiting her. They all looked the same, interchangeable, one popping into the Kaylee system as another fell away.

"Is this where we meet for the hike?" Kaylee asked Avery's arched back.

Avery straightened. "It's not a hike. It's a missing-person search. And yes." She handed Kaylee a clipboard. "Sign in here, please."

She watched as Kaylee produced a pink-and-white pen and signed her name with a flourish and hearts. *A flourish and hearts,* Avery thought, *while two kids are out in the woods, possibly injured, possibly dead.*

She shook her head at the annoyance that overwhelmed her and slipped on her bright-orange search-and-rescue jacket. It didn't take long for a group to form behind her, mainly kids from school, including Kaylee and her admirers. When Officer Vincent Blount came over to explain the details of the search, Avery hugged her arms across her chest, her feet tapping.

She was anxious to get into the woods. Though her conversations with Adam had dwindled as the years passed until they were virtual strangers in high school, he *had* asked her for geometry help. She'd been surprised and thrilled when they'd met in the library and he'd hung on her every word. They'd talked in hushed tones for hours—not about geometry but about everything, until the sun set and the librarian whisked them out. Outside on the sidewalk, he'd leaned in and she could smell the soap he used and his cologne and shampoo. Avery had thought Adam was going to kiss her then and there—but Kaylee had pulled up in her stupid new car and the moment had been ruined.

Now the teen search group filed into lines and started down the trail Adam and Fletcher would have walked. Avery took slow, deliberate steps, calling out the boys' names, the voices of the other volunteers nearby swallowed up by the foliage. Avery wasn't sure how long they walked, but they were deep enough into the forest that the overgrowth blocked out most of the sunlight and the temperature had dropped more than a couple of degrees.

She zipped her jacket and stepped away from the group—a cardinal sin, she knew—and headed toward a small bit of earth that looked to have been recently tromped through. She glanced over her shoulder at her group; they were taking a break. Most were drinking from water bottles or sitting in the dirt. No one seemed to miss her. She looked around and saw a path marked by more broken twigs, winding deeper into the forest, deeper into the shadows.

It was impossibly quiet where she was, as if the thick, leafy canopy snuffed out the outside world completely. The result was an eerie stillness that gave Avery goose bumps and sent a quiver through her stomach. A twig snapped behind her and she spun. Her body stiffened like an animal ready to pounce. Then came the rustle of pine needles.

• • •

It was back. It—he—whatever or whoever had done this to him was back, probably to finish him off. A tremor of terror rolled through him, each miniscule quiver making his bones crack all over again.

Just kill me. Just kill me and get this over with.

The only part of his head that didn't feel like it was stuffed with cotton pounded behind his eyes. The blood pulsing through his ears blocked out every other sound, but he thought he could hear the whisper of someone trying to get his attention.

Let him kill me.

He couldn't run, couldn't even stand, but something like hope pushed through him

No.

The footsteps grew more distinct. A crunch of leaves, weight on the hard-packed earth.

I don't want to die.

He could feel the tears warm his cheeks, and he gritted his teeth against the explosion of pain as he inched himself backward under a bush to hide.

Don't let it get me.

• • •

"Hello?" she called out. "This is Avery Templeton with Search Team Five. Hello?"

The silence was complete except for the steady thump of Avery's heart. She took a step forward and slid on the loose earth, tumbling forward onto her hands and knees. Rocks tore at her skin and the knees of her jeans as she slid. When she stopped—eight, ten feet at the most— she was breathing heavily, her mind reeling. She did a quick assessment for damage. Other than the sting on her palms, nothing hurt.

So why was there blood on her hands?

She brought her hands toward her face and grimaced at the streaks of rust-colored blood—congealed, mixed with dirt—that covered her palms.

She wasn't bleeding.

This wasn't her blood.

It was then that she heard the slow gurgle, the sparse intake of breath followed by a low, throaty whisper: "Avery, you have to help me."

Avery stared at the figure lying in front of her, allowing her eyes to adjust to the dim light.

"Please."

The word came out in a desperate hiss, and he clasped a muddy, blood-caked hand around her wrist, his grip limp, his fingers trembling.

She gasped. "Fletcher?"

ABOUT THE AUTHOR

Hannah Jayne decided to be an author in the second grade. She couldn't spell and had terrible ideas but kept at it and many (many) years and nearly twenty books later, she gets to live her dream and mainly does it in her pajamas.

She lives with her rock star husband and their three overweight cats in the San Francisco Bay Area, always on the lookout for a good mystery, a good story, or a great adventure.